T0090091

The Wages of Sin

Also by Nancy Allen

The Code of the Hills
A Killing at the Creek

The Wages of Sin

An Ozarks Mystery

NANCY ALLEN

WITNESS
IMPULSE

An Imprint of HarperCollins*Publishers*

EPub Edition APRIL 2016 ISBN: 9780062438751

Print Edition ISBN: 9780062438768
HB 10.19.2018

*To Patti Ross Salinas, my Bestie,
with thanks for three decades of friendship*

"For the wages of sin is death. . . ."

ROMANS 6:23

Chapter One

A STRING OF curses split the air under a bright blue September sky stretching over the Ozark hills. The unintelligible shout briefly muted the banjo picking that blared through the speakers of a battered black pickup truck.

A stone's throw from the truck, Chuck Harris huddled inside a blue nylon tent beside his girlfriend, Lisa Peters. She reached out and tapped him on the knee.

"Did you hear that?" she asked.

He pulled an earphone from one ear. "What? Say what?"

"Did you hear? They're screaming again. And it sounds like someone else is pulling out."

With a groan, Chuck rolled into a crouch and peeked out the mesh window. "They're leaving. The last sane campers."

"Are you sure?"

"I can see the taillights. And their gear is gone. It's just us and the psychos."

Lisa put her hands over her ears. "How many times can they play 'Folsom Prison Blues'?"

"And 'Dueling Banjos.' Gives me the chills."

"Huh?"

"Dueling Banjos. You know that old movie? *Deliverance?* With the murdering hillbilly retards. I think they're making the sequel right now."

"Don't say 'retard,' " she said under her breath; but he'd replaced his earphone.

They had arrived the day before, on a hot Friday evening, to spend Labor Day weekend at the scenic campground in Mark Twain National Forest, an unspoiled haven in the Ozark hill country. They had erected their tent under lush leaves, but their peaceful retreat was interrupted before nightfall by the arrival of a rusty pickup spewing noxious exhaust.

"It's just us and them now." Lisa unzipped the fabric door partway and stuck her head through the opening.

Chuck asked, "Are they still drinking?"

Dozens of beer cans littered the neighboring campsite, blinking silver in the late afternoon sunlight. Two men sat at a dying fire, passing a pipe.

"Smoking."

"God damn," Chuck said. "I'm a prosecutor, a county official in McCown County. I'm a prisoner in this blue nylon womb. I can't go outside."

"This isn't McCown County."

"Okay, but still. I'm technically law enforcement. What am I supposed to do, if I'm confronted with their criminal antics? Run up and say 'citizen's arrest'?"

Lisa reached into a duffel bag and pulled out a bottle of Fireball

Whisky. Taking a quick chug from the neck of the bottle, she said, "I didn't see the little girl out there. Or the woman."

"So they went home. Good for them."

"Chuck, they all drove here together in that piece of shit truck. How could a pregnant woman and a little kid get home from the middle of the woods?"

"Well, maybe they're on a nature hike." He slumped back on his sleeping bag. "This is not what I envisioned when you proposed this camping getaway."

Angry voices drowned out the banjo music once again. Lisa crawled back to the mesh window.

The two men, one tall, lank, and bearded, the other stocky, with a tangled ponytail, remained at the fireside. But a woman had joined the circle. She was young, in her midtwenties, with long hair tinted a deep henna hue, bordering on purple. A gray sweatshirt strained over her abdomen. The bearded man was shouting at her; he jumped to his feet and advanced on her, his fists cocked.

"She's got to be about nine months pregnant," Lisa said. "She could drop that baby right now."

As Lisa watched, the bearded man shoved the pregnant woman, barking an insult. The woman stumbled, knocking over the cooler that sat beside the campfire, spilling ice and beer cans into the dirt. Her companions roared. She lumbered to an upright position and struggled to right the cooler, scrambling to pick up cans and toss them back inside. She bent to stop the movement of a can rolling away from the others. The tall man grabbed a handful of her magenta hair, jerked her up and backhanded her, sending her onto the smoking campfire.

When the woman fell onto the fire, Lisa screamed. She jerked at the zippered door of the tent, fighting to open it. Chuck snatched her by the arm.

"What the hell are you doing?"

She turned on him, her eyes blazing. "That fucker. Beating up a pregnant girl. He threw her on the fire." She returned to the zipper, but it snagged in her shaking hands. "We've got to stop him."

Chuck grasped her around the waist and pulled her away from the nylon door. "Are you trying to get us killed?"

Lisa fought him, panting. "Do you think I'll stand by and watch that go down?"

He pinned her on the Coleman sleeping bag. "Jesus, Lisa, what do you think you're dealing with? Those crackers are crazy. They're criminals. A guy who'd beat up a pregnant woman—what do you think he'd do to you or me?"

They lay together in the tent for protracted, tortured moments as the screams rent the air outside.

"We have to call 911," Lisa said in a whisper.

"We can't get a signal out here. No access. We're in the middle of fucking nowhere."

They heard the man's voice again.

"I'm going to fuck you up, you fat whore."

Lisa moaned. "Oh Lord, Lord, Lord."

Chuck grabbed his backpack. "We'll make a run for the car. We can drive to Sparta, I think that's the nearest town, and contact the police there."

Chuck peeked through the mesh, then they scuttled out of the tent. As they ran for the car, Chuck tripped over the lawn chairs they'd set by their own campfire and fell on the hard-packed patch of dirt.

Lisa stood by the passenger door as he crawled to the car, saying in a hoarse whisper, "Hurry, for God's sake. Hurry."

Once inside the vehicle, the ignition roared, and Chuck hit the accelerator. The car swung by the neighboring campsite, where the tall man had the pregnant girl in a headlock, just outside the circle of the campfire. Her gray sweatshirt was smoking. The man with a ponytail sat in a chair, watching, and lit his pipe.

As Chuck and Lisa pulled away from the campsite and into the woods, they saw the child, a little girl, standing by the side of the road. She was a skinny waif with scruffy blond hair, regarding them with an unblinking stare behind broken eyeglasses.

Chapter Two

OH MY GOD. Let this be over, Elsie thought, doodling on the page of a legal pad. Assistant Prosecuting Attorney Elsie Arnold had been tied up in Judge Carter's court for nearly two hours that morning, representing the State of Missouri in a preliminary hearing. The criminal defendant was charged with robbery in the first degree. Only Judge Carter, Elsie thought, would be coldhearted enough to subject her to a robbery prelim on the Tuesday after Labor Day weekend.

Public Defender Josh Nixon was grilling the bank president, Donna Hudson, in cross-examination.

"So you were present at the time of the alleged robbery?"

"Yes—I said so. In my office."

"But isn't it true that, if you were shut up in your office, you did not have occasion to hear whether the defendant threatened any harm?"

"The buzzer sounded. I heard it." The woman sat stiff, with righteous indignation in every wrinkle of her face.

"The alarm, right? But you didn't hear any statements made by the defendant, did you? Because you remained safely in the back of the bank."

"I saw the bomb."

A comical grin grew on the defense attorney's face; Elsie closed her eyes so she wouldn't have to see it.

"The bomb?" he repeated.

"The box. The box with the tape."

The criminal complaint filed by the prosecution did not allege that the defendant had threatened the bank employee with a bomb. The criminal charge stated that the defendant threatened the use of what *appeared to be* a bomb.

"Describe this box, please."

"It was a box, about this size," she said, making a rectangle shape with her hands. "And it was covered with duct tape."

"Did the defendant detonate this deadly bomb? This dangerous instrument you described?"

The banker eyed the defense attorney with resentment. "You know what happened."

"Tell me. For the record."

"The bank teller gave him the money. Everything in her drawer. He ran out, left that box on the counter."

"Then what happened?"

"The bomb squad came and took over."

"What did they do? If you know."

"They exploded it." The lines deepened around the woman's mouth. "They blew it up. And the mess went everywhere."

"Mess? What kind of mess?"

Elsie wanted to cover her ears to block out the answer that was coming.

"The chocolate, the cherries."

Josh Nixon leaned on the empty jury box, nodding sagely. "So the bomb was not a bomb at all? It was—what did you say?"

"A box of candy. Chocolate-covered cherries. Wrapped in duct tape."

"And for the record, Ms. Hudson: was the money recovered? The money from the bank teller's drawer?"

"Yes, it was. But—"

Before she could complete her sentence, the defense attorney turned his back to her, cutting the witness off. "No further questions," he said, and walked back to the counsel table. Nixon slid into his seat, stretching his long legs out in front of him and tucking his longish sun-streaked hair behind his ear. He hadn't bothered to don a tie.

Judge Carter, a slim man in his forties with prematurely silver hair, peered at Elsie over his glasses. "Redirect?"

Elsie stood at the counsel table, looking at the bank president with an encouraging face. "But did it appear to be a bomb? When the defendant threatened the teller with it?"

"Objection," Nixon said, sitting up straight. "The witness wasn't present, has no way of knowing other than hearsay!"

Elsie barked back. "You're the one who opened the door on this line of questioning. In your cross-examination."

The bank president rose from her chair, the picture of aggrieved fury. "What I want to know," she said, "is who is going to pay? For that mess? The cleaning of the bank lobby?"

Judge Carter slammed the gavel. The bank president jumped, startled, and hopped back onto her seat on the witness stand.

"Ms. Arnold—further questions?"

"No."

"Any further witnesses on behalf of the defense?"

"No," said Nixon.

The judge turned to his clerk. "The court finds probable cause. Defendant is bound over to Circuit Court on the charge of robbery in the first degree. Arraignment to be held Friday at 9:00 A.M."

When the judge left the bench, Josh Nixon turned to whisper with his client, a long-haired young man with a bushy mustache. The president of Bank of the Hilltop, Donna Hudson, stormed off the witness stand and bore down on Elsie.

"How could I be treated this way in a court of law?"

"No one meant to mistreat you," Elsie said in a soothing voice. "It was just cross-examination—the defense attorney gets to ask questions. I explained that to you before."

"But I am the victim. My family owns the bank."

"That's right, Donna. But the defense has the right to confront the witnesses against him."

"Who gave that criminal the right to confront me? I am a tax-paying citizen."

Elsie backed up a step, angling to make a getaway. "The US Constitution. Sixth Amendment."

The banker's eyes narrowed; Elsie sensed that the woman didn't appreciate the finer points of the Bill of Rights.

"When will the court make him pay for the cleanup? The cleanup of the bank lobby?"

Edging closer to the door, Elsie shook her head. "Hard to say. You think this guy has any money?"

Mrs. Hudson's unhappy expression showed that the conversation wasn't over. But as she was about to speak again, Elsie's friend and coworker, Breeon Johnson, hurried into the courtroom and grabbed Elsie's arm.

"Downstairs," Breeon said.

"Now? Right now?" Elsie asked.

"Just one darned minute," Donna Hudson said. She opened a Louis Vuitton handbag and pulled out a Kleenex, rubbing furiously at her nose. Elsie eyed the bag with curiosity. It was probably the real article. Though as an employee of a rural county in the Ozarks, Elsie didn't have sufficient acquaintance with designer goods to distinguish the genuine product from a knockoff.

Elsie gave Breeon an inquiring look. "Can you wait a sec?"

Breeon tugged at her arm. "Can't wait. It's an emergency."

Elsie could see from Breeon's face that she was deadly serious. "Okay," she said. Looking back at the banker, Elsie spoke hastily. "The system is working, Mrs. Hudson. Your bank robber has been bound over; he'll be arraigned in Circuit Court, and his case will be set for jury trial. I appreciate your cooperation, and your testimony. But I have to get downstairs." She looked over to the door; Breeon had just vanished through it. "Something major is going on."

"But will he pay?"

The woman's voice rang in Elsie's ears, and she was tired of hearing it. Turning away, she said, "Yeah. Yes, Mrs. Hudson. He'll pay."

"How?"

"The old-fashioned way, I expect. With his liberty."

The banker protested, her voice shrill, but Elsie departed at a fast pace, and scrambled down the worn marble staircase of the McCown County Courthouse, catching up to Breeon at the back entrance to the Prosecutor's Office.

"What?" Elsie demanded, as Breeon punched the security buttons to access the private entrance. "What is it?"

Breeon shook her head in disgust. "Another murder. They found the body in a trailer home, right outside the city limits. Can you believe it?"

"Again?" Murder cases were rare in rural McCown County, a small community nestled deep in the Ozark hills of southwest Missouri. Elsie had handled a murder case over the summer, prosecuting a juvenile for the death of a bus driver. A second homicide, occurring within such a short period of time, would shake the entire community.

"Yeah, another woman," Breeon said, pushing the door open. "But a young one this time."

"Aw, shit," Elsie said.

Breeon gave her a look, righteous anger evident in her face. "She was eight months pregnant."

The news stopped Elsie in her tracks. "A double murder," she whispered.

Chapter Three

ELSIE FOLLOWED BREE down the hallway toward the office of their boss, Madeleine Thompson, the Prosecuting Attorney of McCown County, Missouri.

Dodging past a pair of uniformed deputies, Elsie asked, "Why does Madeleine want us in her office? Does she need help with the charge?"

"Don't know. I got an e-mail."

In front of Madeleine's closed office door, they met the other assistant prosecutors on the staff: Doug, the traffic attorney, and Dennis, who handled child support.

"Knock on the door," Bree said.

"We did," Doug said.

"Is she in there?"

"Yeah."

"With Chuck?" Bree asked.

"Don't know," Doug said.

Elsie pushed past them and put her ear to the door. "I can't hear anything."

The oak door flew open and she nearly lost her balance, tumbling into her boss, Madeleine Thompson.

"What are you doing?" Madeleine said, deflecting Elsie with a shove.

Elsie stepped back, covering her discomfiture with a laugh. "We're just reporting for duty. To meet with you about the homicide."

"I don't want you." Turning an indignant eye on Doug and Dennis, she said, "Why are you standing around my office? Why aren't you in court?"

Breeon intervened. "We got an e-mail, Madeleine. Stacie said you wanted to see us. All of us."

Shaking her head with a muttered slur against Stacie, the office receptionist, Madeleine grabbed a set of keys from her handbag and locked the door behind her. "I wanted to see you, Bree. And Chuck. The rest of you: back to work. This is a murder investigation, not a traffic ticket."

Chuck Harris was the chief assistant in the Prosecutor's Office, a Kansas City native who had been hired for the job, at least in part, due to his father's political connections with Madeleine. Breeon was the assistant with the most seniority; she had served as a prosecutor for five years, besting Elsie's term of service by nine months. A single mother from St. Louis, Breeon was a fierce advocate in court. Her grit served her well, as the only black attorney in a community that still ran on the good-old-boy system.

Elsie loved Bree, but she had a stellar trial record as well, and Madeleine's dismissal stung.

Doug and Dennis retreated, heading back to their duties in the courtrooms on the third floor of the courthouse. Elsie watched them as they hurried down the hall. But she remained, turning to Madeleine with a dogged look.

"I'd like to be in the loop," she said tersely.

Madeleine started down the hallway. "Oh please."

"Madeleine, I handled the last murder case in McCown County. Solo, you may recall."

"Yes—I recall what a mess that turned out to be."

Reflexively, Elsie's hand circled her neck, which bore the scar of the courthouse attack that landed her in the hospital during the trial of *State v. Tanner Monroe*.

Breeon jumped to her defense. "I think Elsie should be there with us. We're your felony trial lawyers. Me and Elsie and Chuck."

Madeleine stopped at Chuck's office and rapped on the door with her knuckles. She threw back her head, closing her eyes with an expression of weary resignation.

"Fine. Elsie can come along. If she doesn't say anything. I don't want to hear a single word."

Elsie knew she should keep her mouth shut, but she was unable to contain herself. "What if I have something important to contribute?"

Without responding, Madeleine fixed Elsie with a glare, her lipsticked mouth turning down in a deep frown. Though Elsie had served as assistant prosecutor under Madeleine for four years, they had never enjoyed a friendly relationship. Despite Elsie's outstanding trial performance—or possibly because of it—she and Madeleine butted heads on a regular basis. Elsie's friend Breeon summed the conflict up every time Elsie complained to her, with, "Elsie, you're not Madeleine's kind of cat. She'd much prefer a subordinate who'd follow her around with a dust broom."

Chuck Harris, the chief assistant prosecutor, emerged from his office, straightening his tie. "Ready?" he asked.

Madeleine nodded. "Let's go see Detective Ashlock."

Chapter Four

THE BARTON CITY Police Department was housed in a flat-topped two-story building on the town square, across the street from the courthouse. The McCown County Courthouse, an imposing stone structure, had graced the center of the town square for over a century. But the police department, erected in the 1960s, was a modest, utilitarian facility of yellow brick. Once the four attorneys were inside, they climbed the stairs to the second floor. Detective Ashlock led the way into a small conference room, the only space within the Barton City Police Department that could accommodate a group of five people.

Elsie watched him covertly, noting his red eyes and five-o'clock shadow, trying to read his expression. If she didn't know better, she'd have suspected he'd been crying, but she dismissed the idea. Elsie knew Ashlock well; they had been keeping company for the better part of a year. A former Marine and eighteen-year veteran of the Barton, Missouri, Police Department, Ashlock was not given to weeping.

He pulled a sheaf of papers from a folder, sorting through them with a drawn face.

"Did you just return from the crime scene?" Madeleine asked.

"The morgue. We were at the crime scene most of the night, but I headed to the morgue after I left the deceased's trailer." He started to say more, but fell silent, shaking his head.

"Pretty bad?" asked Chuck.

Ashlock blew out a long breath. "Oh yeah. Really bad."

Elsie leaned forward in her chair. "You okay, Ash?" Elsie asked in a quiet voice. He met her eye and sent her the ghost of a wink. Reassured, she sat back.

Madeleine pulled a pair of jeweled reading glasses from her handbag and balanced them on her nose. "Let's see what you've got, Bob."

He pulled a photo from the stack of papers, and placed it in front of Madeleine. Elsie had to scoot her chair closer to Madeleine to see what it depicted: a huddled body, facedown, purple hair matted in a pool of blood.

Elsie turned to Chuck. "Am I blocking you? Can you see?"

Chuck cast a bare glance at the photograph. Shuddering, he uncapped a pen. "Don't worry about me. I'm good." He picked up a copy of Ashlock's report and shuffled through the pages, making a notation in the margin.

Madeleine sucked in a breath as she studied the image on the table. "Weapon?"

Ashlock set another photo down on the table. "Baseball bat. Witness says he used his fists, at first. Then went at her with the bat."

"Cause of death?" Madeleine murmured.

"Coroner said skull fracture. There are probably abdominal injuries, too, from the looks of her." Ashlock coughed and rubbed his red eyes. "Just an initial finding, till the autopsy is completed."

"And the baby?"

"The coroner said the mother's death likely caused the baby to die in the womb. He speculates that the baby could've been saved if there'd been a 911 call in time. But by the time we found the mother, she and the baby were both dead."

With a careful hand, Ashlock set another photo on the table in front of Madeleine. From her position at the table, Elsie couldn't make out what it depicted; but after a brief glance, Madeleine pushed her seat back from the table and closed her eyes.

"Dear God," she whispered.

"Yep. Yeah." Ashlock cleared his throat. "It was a boy."

"Oh, Bob. I think this one's going to do me in. I'm getting too old for this."

Elsie looked at Madeleine with surprise. Her boss never revealed vulnerability; in Elsie's experience, Madeleine rarely gave any indication that she was a member of the human race. She had long suspected that ice water ran through Madeleine's veins. Of course, with Madeleine, it would be Evian ice water.

Chuck was jotting notes on a legal pad with a Mont Blanc fountain pen. To Ashlock, he said, "We have a suspect?"

"He's in custody. The deceased's boyfriend, a guy named Larry Paul. A local scumbag. Probably an addict, a meth head. I interrogated him. His statement was incriminating." He cleared his throat. "Larry Paul clearly indicated liability."

The name struck a chord with Elsie; she dimly recalled a court appearance against Larry Paul on a drug charge. She tried to remember the particulars, but couldn't. McCown County was a rural community in the heart of the Bible Belt, but like so many others, it was infected by the plague of methamphetamine production.

Chuck looked up from his legal pad with a solemn face. Compared to Ashlock's rumpled appearance, the chief assistant looked like a glossy ad ripped from *GQ Magazine*. He wore a charcoal gray suit with a crisp lavender shirt, and gold cuff links glinted on his French shirt cuffs. He said to Ashlock, "Madeleine told me you have an eyewitness."

"There were two witnesses. One is a guy named Bruce Stout— friend and associate of Larry Paul. We tried to locate him this morning, but he's either run off or hiding out."

Chuck said, "But you still have another witness to the crime."

Ashlock nodded once, with a humorless grin. In a rueful voice, he said, "We do." He shuffled through the papers a final time and pulled out a third photograph, a close-up depicting a child.

Elsie rose from her seat to look. Stepping over to stand behind Chuck's chair, she saw that it was a child of five or six, a girl with short blond hair that looked like it had been shorn with rusty scissors. Her face was hidden by a pair of broken eyeglasses held together with a safety pin on one side and a dirty Band-Aid on the other.

After seeing the photo, Chuck lurched back in his chair with such a violent retreat that he nearly knocked Elsie down. "What the hell," she snapped; but stopped when she saw that he was gasping for air.

"Chuck," Elsie said, slapping him on the back, "are you choking on something?"

In reply, he pointed at the photo of the child. All eyes were on him as he stumbled out of his chair and backed away from the table.

"I've seen her. The glasses," he said.

His face was pasty white, bordering on green.

"He's gonna throw up," Breeon said, and Elsie agreed. But Chuck surprised them all.

Elsie looked away as the dark circle spread on the fly on Chuck's charcoal gray Brooks Brothers suit pants.

IN THE HALLWAY of the police department, outside the conference room, Breeon grasped Elsie's shoulder and gave it a squeeze. "Elsie, you stop that. Stop mocking that boy."

Elsie raised a brow. "What are you deviling me about? I'm not making a sound."

"I can read your face. You're laughing on the inside."

Elsie rubbed her eyes with her hand. "Sorry, Bree. You're not a psychic, after all. Always thought you could read my mind."

"So you're not thinking about Chuck Harris peeing in his fancy pants."

Elsie shook her head. "Not right this minute. Nope." She was thinking of the photographs that Ashlock had shown them in the conference room; of the dead woman on the bloody floor of the trailer. And the little girl. The child's face was haunting. It recalled a photo series she'd studied in a history class at the University of Missouri, images of child laborers at the turn of the twentieth century. The girl with the broken glasses had the same expression, of a child who had seen too much, whose exposure to the ugliness of human nature had aged her beyond her years.

Restless, Elsie walked up to the door of the interrogation room and peeped though the narrow glass panel. "Wish I could hear what they're saying."

"Elsie, back away from that door. You'll embarrass him. He couldn't help himself."

"God—I know. It must've been a hell of a shock. Flips me out, and I wasn't the one who ran into the deceased and the suspect out in the woods, two days before he killed her."

"I know. This will haunt Chuck, it's bound to."

Elsie looked through the panel in the door again. "What's taking so much time in there?"

Breeon walked to a folding chair on the opposite side of the hallway and settled onto it. "Ashlock's taking Chuck's statement. It shouldn't go on too much longer."

Elsie leaned against the wall outside the conference room. "I thought Madeleine's head would explode when Chuck identified that little girl. It looked like her face-lift was going to come unglued." She started to laugh at her own joke, then caught herself. In a whisper, she said, "You don't think they can hear what we're saying, do you?"

Bree shook her head, but Elsie sidled up to the door again, to see for herself. Peering through the glass, she saw that Chuck's complexion had returned to a normal color, though his hands shook. Madeleine was sitting across from him with her arms folded, glaring over the top of her glasses.

Elsie said, "She looks like she bit on a sour pickle."

"Yeah, that's about right." Breeon checked her watch. "I've got to get back to court. You think we're supposed to hang around here much longer?"

"I'll ask."

Bree gave her a warning look. "Elsie," she said, holding out a restraining hand; but it was too late. Elsie tapped on the door and stuck her head inside.

"Madeleine, sorry to interrupt, but do you want us to wait out here? Or go on back to the courthouse?"

Madeleine's head jerked up at the interruption. She opened her mouth to speak, but clamped it shut, as if reconsidering her words. Looking away from Elsie, she said in a frosty tone, "I want Breeon to wait. Shut the door."

"Okay."

As Elsie was pulling the door closed, Madeleine raised her voice. "And please—have the courtesy to let us complete this without further interruption."

Once the door latched shut, Elsie turned to see Breeon regarding her with weary resignation.

"You've got some nerve, hon," Bree said.

Elsie shrugged as she walked over to join Breeon on the metal chairs. "It's cool. My buddy's in there with her. She tries not to beat me up too much when Ashlock's around."

Elsie's relationship with Detective Ashlock provided a valuable buttress against Madeleine's dislike of her.

She slumped down in the metal seat, stretching her legs in front of her on the tile floor. "Madeleine says you're supposed to stick around. But not me."

Breeon sighed, with a weary exhale of breath. "What's she want with me?"

Their conversation was cut off when Madeleine appeared in the doorway. Though she started to slam the door behind her, she seemed to abort the impulse, catching the door at the last minute and pulling it gently shut. She turned and focused on Breeon, her face frozen with displeasure.

"Breeon, do you have a jacket at the office? A blazer?"

Breeon shook her head. She was wearing black slacks and a

white blouse, standard office attire. Jackets were not considered a necessity for standard courtroom duty, but when the women appeared for jury trials, they wore suits.

Irritation flashed across Madeleine's face; she pulled off her glasses with a jerk.

"I have an extra in my office; it's black, it should do. You can wear it." Looking Breeon up and down, she added, "Though it will be a tight fit. Just don't try to button it. I don't want you pulling out the seams."

"Thanks," Breeon muttered.

Standing behind Madeleine, Elsie pulled a comic face and tried to catch Breeon's eye, but her friend wouldn't take the bait.

"We're calling a press conference," Madeleine said, her voice brisk.

"You want me to appear in the press conference?" Breeon asked.

"Yes, I want you to appear; why else would I put my clothes on your back? You need to look presentable."

Elsie asked, "So what's the conference about? The murder?"

"What else would it be?" Madeleine started down the stairs, gripping the bannister so tightly, the tendons stood out in her thin hands. Breeon and Elsie followed close behind. "I'm going to let the public know I'll be seeking the death penalty."

Breeon stopped in the middle of the stairway. Elsie bumped into her, nearly losing her footing.

"Madeleine," Breeon said, "I can't assist you on this case. I can't serve as second chair."

Madeleine wheeled on her with a face like Medusa. "Don't mess with me. I cannot endure any more madness today. Of course you'll assist me. Chuck is out of the picture, and he's my chief assistant. I can't do it alone."

"Madeleine. I don't believe in the death penalty." Breeon's voice was resolute and unapologetic, her posture erect as she towered over Madeleine, who stood two steps below her.

Madeleine's eyes blazed. She clutched the manila file folder in her right hand and swung it at the cinder-block wall. The file connected with a crack that make Elsie take a step back in retreat. "Well, shit," Madeleine said. "Shit shit shit."

Elsie's quick intake of breath caught in her throat. *Madeleine said shit,* she thought, with wonder.

It was a red letter day.

Chapter Five

THE WOMEN LEFT the police department in strained silence. While waiting on the sidewalk for a car to pass, Madeleine said, "You are a prosecutor, Breeon."

"I certainly am."

"And it's your job and responsibility to uphold and enforce the law in Missouri."

"Yes, it is."

The car moved slowly by, an ancient white Oldsmobile, driven by a silver-haired man.

Crossing to the middle of the town square, Madeleine said, "Missouri has only two possible punishments for first degree murder. The death penalty or life without parole. You knew that when you signed on for this job. The prosecution decides when it's appropriate to ask a jury to impose death, and I believe that the facts of this case justify it."

Elsie watched Breeon's face. It was shuttered and resentful, her jaw locked.

Looking over her shoulder at Breeon, Madeleine said, "You are a member of law enforcement in this community."

"That doesn't mean I can't draw a line," Breeon said.

They reached the courthouse steps. Elsie remained at Breeon's side, ready to offer support if necessary.

Madeleine wheeled around to face Breeon. "Why am I just hearing this? You've been on my staff for four years."

"Five. Five years."

"Fine—five years. Whatever. Why on earth did you withhold your opinion on this issue?"

"It never came up."

Madeleine turned on her heel and climbed the courthouse steps, the high heels of her shoes clicking an angry staccato beat. Elsie watched as she bypassed security and disappeared through the rotunda.

She sidled up to Breeon and gave her arm a friendly squeeze. "Geez, Bree, I didn't know you felt so strongly about the death penalty."

"Well, I do."

"Where's this coming from?"

With a weary sigh, Breeon leaned her back against a marble pillar on the courthouse exterior. "Where's it coming from? What do you think? I'm a black woman from St. Louis. Grew up not far from Ferguson."

"Oh," Elsie said. The shooting of an unarmed black teenager in Ferguson, Missouri, had led to national riots. "So that's why? Because of what happened in Ferguson?"

"No, it's because of the way the death penalty is applied. Have you ever looked at the numbers? The stats? The percentage of black people who are executed, versus white people? The death penalty isn't fairly implemented. It's another legal tool that fosters inequality in the justice system."

Breeon pushed away from the pillar and headed into the courthouse. Elsie followed, digesting Bree's objections as a deputy waved them through the security entrance, and the women bypassed the metal detector.

Elsie caught up to Bree. "I get what you're saying. And I know that the penalty tends to be misapplied on a socioeconomic basis: poor people get the death penalty, rich people don't. But still, Bree—in a case like this." Elsie's voice dropped to a whisper. "A pregnant woman clubbed and beaten to death. It gives me a gut reaction: son of a bitch that killed her ought to fry."

Breeon shook her head. "See? Your terminology shows how out of date that point of view is. Nobody fries. The electric chair is obsolete. We don't burn people or boil them in oil. Just take care of it with a couple of injections. But that doesn't make it better."

"I didn't literally mean 'fry.'"

"No, you meant it in a figurative sense. Which implies that you want the defendant to suffer a hideous death. And that proves my point. It's a bloodthirsty penalty, founded on vengeance rather than justice."

"Geez, you sound like I'm Count Dracula. This is a philosophical question. Don't make it personal."

"It's not just philosophy to me. Two guys I went to high school with are on death row."

Bree's revelation shocked Elsie into silence, and they walked up the stairs without further comment, making their way to the second floor of the courthouse. Outside the main entrance of the

Prosecutor's Office, Stacie, the office receptionist, was waiting for them.

"Elsie," she said, waving a frantic arm. "Madeleine wants to see you."

Breeon turned to Elsie with a knowing look. "You're up."

"You think?"

Elsie hurried around the rotunda and dodged into the office, fairly running down the interior hallway. Madeleine's office door was wide open.

Elsie stuck her head inside. "Hey," she said.

Madeleine sat slumped at her desk. Her scarlet lipstick was freshly applied, but without precision, like a clown's mouth.

"Before you come in: do you have any philosophical opposition to the death penalty?"

Elsie paused for a moment, turning the question over in her head. In this particular case, the defendant was a white man, so she would not be contributing to Breeon's view of unequal application by race. And there was no question in her mind that the crime was heinous enough to merit the maximum penalty. "Not in this case, no."

"Are you a witness? Did you encounter the defendant or the deceased on a camping trip last weekend? Or, I don't know—does the suspect hang out at any seedy bars you like to frequent?"

The last comment stung. Elsie crossed her arms at her chest in a reflexive gesture and leaned against the door frame. "Well, I can't say for certain. Because I go to a lot of dives."

"More's the pity." Madeleine rested her elbows on her desk and buried her face in her hands. "Get on in here," she said.

Chapter Six

IVY WALKED UP the steps to the first grade classroom. She paused at the door before entering, to scent out danger. It was a habit of hers, borne of experience.

The teacher, Mrs. Fulton, stood in the corner with a parent, taking instructions about her son's peanut allergy. A few students were already seated and talking, others were still putting their rain jackets and backpacks away at the back of the classroom.

Ivy walked up to the coatrack. She didn't have a jacket; her foster mother said they'd wait till next month, when the check came. But she didn't mind, the weather wasn't even cold yet. She pulled her blue backpack off her shoulder and hung it on a hook. She liked how the foster mom had written IVY on it in black marker. It really belonged to her.

A classmate had a SpongeBob lunch box hanging next to his Batman backpack. Ivy experienced a flash of envy. The kids who brought lunches in lunch boxes were an elite group. Not required to wait in lunch line for cafeteria workers, they grabbed a lunch table by the open window, unzipping their hordes of riches: real sandwiches made at home, tubes of pink and green yogurt, cookies, Goldfish crackers.

Spongebob's face smiled at Ivy on the vinyl lunch box; she gazed at it with longing, wondering what treasures were stored inside. Without meaning to, she reached out and stroked the yellow box with her index finger.

"Hey!" Jacob stood at her shoulder. "That's mine!"

Ivy snatched her hand away and hid it behind her back. Jacob pulled the lunch box off the hook and clutched it to his chest. "Don't touch my stuff."

Ivy's face burned. A second boy, taller than Jacob, ran over and stood by his side. "Ivy germs," he whispered.

Jacob hung the yellow box on another hook, at a safe distance from Ivy's blue backpack. "You can't touch anything of mine. I don't want Ivy germs."

Rigid, Ivy stood in the spot by the coatrack hooks, focusing on the happy face of the princess on her blue backpack. The teacher, Mrs. Fulton, called over to them in a stern voice.

"Jacob? Ivy?"

When the children didn't answer, she walked toward them, though Jacob's mother placed a restraining hand on the teacher's arm.

"What's this all about?" asked Mrs. Fulton.

Jacob's face was flushed. "She was touching my lunch box."

Mrs. Fulton's voice was calm, but firm. "We talked about this, Jacob. You know our class rules. How do we treat each other?"

Jacob's mother tapped the teacher's shoulder. Ivy stole a glance at the mom. She was pretty, with shiny dark hair. The skin on her arms was smooth. She didn't have sores and spots like Ivy's mom had.

Ivy mentally corrected herself: like the mom she used to live with. Before she was killed dead.

Jacob's mom said to the teacher, "He's sensitive about the peanut allergy. We've taught him to be. He has to be so careful."

Mrs. Fulton ignored Jacob's mom. Through her glasses, she fixed the two boys with a knowing look. "What were you saying?"

The taller boy hung his head, but Jacob wasn't cowed. "We don't want her germs," he said stoutly.

"Now, Jacob," his mother began, but Mrs. Fulton cut her off. "We talked about this yesterday, but I guess you weren't listening. At recess, you'll walk the playground three times before you can play with your friends."

Jacob's eyes shone with tears when the teacher pronounced his sentence; but still, he whispered, "She has germs."

"Four times," Mrs. Fulton said. "You'll walk it four times."

Jacob's mother tugged at the teacher's elbow. In a hushed voice, she said, "Really, Mrs. Fulton, everyone's concerned. It was all over the news this week. There's some really disturbing talk about those people. How do we know the children aren't in danger?"

The teacher quelled her with a look, but Ivy didn't see it. She just stared at the princess's smiling face on the blue backpack and clutched her hands into fists. *Don't touch anything,* she told herself.

The princess's face blurred. Ivy missed her mom.

The dead one.

Chapter Seven

SEATED IN A purple vinyl booth at the Sycamore Diner on the west side of the town square, Elsie watched Madeleine tear into her third packet of Equal sweetener. Madeleine stirred the white powder into her steaming coffee with a vengeance, clinking the spoon against the sides of the crockery cup.

"So you talked to Lisa Peters today? That juvenile officer who witnessed the abuse at the campground?" Madeleine asked.

Elsie nodded. "I went by to see her this afternoon, talked to her over at her office at Juvenile Hall. She's pretty freaked out about it, kept saying that if she and Chuck had just done things differently, Jessie Dent might still be alive. If Larry Paul had been arrested for the abuse at the campground, he wouldn't have been free to kill her in their trailer Monday night." She shook her head, recalling Lisa's distress. The young woman had wept when she talked to Elsie, her face swollen with grief, repeating time and again that they'd called 911 when they finally got a signal, but it wasn't enough. They should have followed up. They hadn't done enough. "I think she's going to take some time off this week."

"Oh fine. Another government employee who will be unavailable. My chief assistant. His friend, the juvenile officer. And Breeon."

Elsie cleared her throat before she spoke. "I think Bree explained it pretty well. The historical application of the death penalty in this country—"

"I know all about the history of the death penalty," Madeleine said. The corner of her mouth twitched. "We'll just have to deal. You and I. Working together."

Elsie leaned forward, her elbow on the laminate tabletop, trying to ignore Madeleine's clear reluctance to join forces. "Sure. We'll be fine." She focused on Madeleine's spoon, still clattering in the cup.

"You're good with children."

Elsie looked up, surprised by the admission. "Well, thanks."

"The little girl, the witness. She'll be your job. I need you to—"

Madeleine's instruction was interrupted by the arrival of the waitress, a portly girl in jeans and a worn Route 66 T-shirt, wearing a plastic nametag which read *Jeanie*. She set a green salad in front of Madeleine.

"You forgot the dressing. I ordered my dressing on the side."

"I'll get it," the waitress said as she placed a steaming plate before Elsie. "Elsie, for your vegetable, did you say you wanted the macaroni and cheese, or the cottage cheese?"

"Mac and cheese, please."

"I'll bring it right out, Elsie." With a glance at Madeleine, the waitress added, "And that salad dressing."

Elsie caught Madeleine looking at her dinner with disapproval. "Smothered chicken," Elsie said, a shade defensive. "Can't get it just anywhere."

Madeleine pursed her lips and looked away. "Macaroni is not a vegetable."

Elsie reached for the saltshaker. "Do you think you'll want the little girl on the witness stand at the preliminary hearing?"

Madeleine picked at a tomato wedge with her fork. "What do you think?"

Elsie nearly dropped the saltshaker into her gravy. Setting it down beside her plate, she stopped to think, staring at the mound of mashed potatoes without seeing it. She began, "We'll need her at trial for sure. She'll be instrumental when we face a jury. Not only to talk about what she saw, but to generate sympathy. And to make the case for death."

Madeleine nodded, sipping her coffee. "In a murder case, people forget the victim."

"I know. I felt that in the Tanner Monroe case, no one was thinking about the poor dead bus driver; the whole focus in court was on the fifteen-year-old defendant."

"It happens."

A grudging seed of respect germinated in Elsie's head. Maybe Madeleine knew more than Elsie realized.

Madeleine twisted around on her side of the booth, eyes darting up the aisle.

"What?" Elsie said.

"I need more coffee."

Their waitress appeared through the swinging kitchen door, and Madeleine called to her, her voice a bark.

"Coffee! Please!"

The coffeepot arrived. The waitress wouldn't look at Madeleine as she poured. To Elsie she said, "How's everything tasting today?"

"Oh my God, Jeanie, it's great."

"I had it for lunch. It hit the spot." Jeanie's sullen look brightened.

As the waitress walked away, Elsie turned her attention back to Madeleine. "The witness is really young—just six years old, right? She'll need work. First off, we'll have to demonstrate that she understands the oath."

Madeleine nodded her agreement. Child witnesses had to establish to the court that they understood the difference between telling the truth and telling a lie; the judge had to be satisfied that the child's oath was meaningful.

"The summary of her statements in the police report was horrific." Madeleine nibbled the corner of a saltine cracker. "I can't sleep. It's keeping me up nights."

Elsie sawed at the chicken patty with her knife. Staring at Elsie's plate, Madeleine said, "I don't know how you can eat that."

"I gotta keep up my strength." Elsie looked down at the platter; the Sycamore served generous portions, and she'd devoured a fair amount. Maybe she should leave a bite or two on her plate, just to look dainty.

But her resolution was destroyed when Jeanie swept by and slid the side dish of macaroni onto the table, saying, "Sorry. Almost forgot."

With a sigh, Elsie dug her fork into the golden dish of starch. She looked up at Madeleine and said, "Gotta eat my vegetables."

A brass bell hanging from the front door of the diner jingled, and a young man in white shirtsleeves, with longish sandy-streaked hair, walked to the cash register.

"It's Josh Nixon," Elsie whispered.

Madeleine twisted around in the booth to take a look. "Don't say anything. He might hear you. Your voice carries."

"I called in an order to go, Octavine," Nixon told the cashier.

Octavine, a woman past sixty whose curly perm was an alarming shade of pink, whispered something to Nixon that made him laugh. Madeleine watched them with suspicious eyes, then leaned in across the booth, speaking close. "Judge Carter appointed the Public Defender to represent Larry Paul. I suppose that means Josh Nixon will be his attorney."

Elsie watched Nixon flirt with the redheaded cashier. "Could be worse. Nixon's not a liar, not unethical."

"Is that the best you can say about him?"

The women scooted back in their seats as Nixon turned to them and approached. With a cordial expression, he walked up and grasped a metal coatrack attached to Elsie's side of the booth.

"Looks like you ladies are working overtime," he said.

Madeleine sat very erect and spoke in her chilliest tone. "Mr. Nixon, we're consulting on a case. So if you don't mind—"

Nixon plucked a dinner roll from Elsie's platter. Pulling off a chunk of bread, he said, "Bet I know the case you're talking about." He popped the bread into his mouth and chewed.

"Don't put your dirty hands on my food. Damn it, Nixon, you probably just came from the county jail." Elsie pushed her plate out of his reach.

"As a matter of fact, you're right, I did." He focused on Madeleine. "Just had a chat with a new client I've been appointed to represent. Guy named Larry Paul. He tells me your detective at the Barton PD interrogated him before he had a chance to obtain counsel."

Elsie spoke up. "You can be absolutely certain that Detective Ashlock advised him of his rights before questioning. One hundred percent certain."

"Well, that's a comfort. I'll sleep better." He wiped a bread crumb from the corner of his mouth. "Of course, I'll attack it. Move to suppress the statement. It wasn't voluntary. My client was under the influence of narcotics."

Research the effect of inebriation on the validity of a suspect's waiver of rights, Elsie thought; her hand itched for a pen, so she could write a note-to-self. But she retained her game face. Her expression was serene as she said, "Good godamighty, Nixon. If Larry Paul was all turnt up, that's no fault of Ashlock's."

"How'd the autopsy turn out? On the deceased?"

Elsie glanced at Madeleine; she was sure they had not received the autopsy yet. The procedure took time, and they would have to await a written report of the pathologist's findings. It would be an even longer wait for the toxicology reports.

Madeleine stiffened. Piercing Nixon with a look, she said, "You're not entitled to discovery yet. We won't be sharing any particulars with you at this time."

"Hey, Josh! Honey, I got your order." At the cash register, Octavine held a white paper bag aloft.

Josh didn't move away. He tossed the filched dinner roll onto the tabletop, then said, "Better have your doctor test the tissue for AIDS. Your deceased gave it to my client. Poor old Larry."

Nixon walked off with a leisurely stride, stopping to pick up the bag from Octavine.

As the bell at the diner door jangled to signal his exit, Elsie remembered what she liked least about Josh Nixon. He was always full of surprises.

Terrible surprises.

Chapter Eight

ELSIE SHIFTED IN an ancient folding chair in Judge Carter's chambers, wincing as she heard the metal seat creak. She hoped the old relic wouldn't crumple beneath her. Madeleine would probably attribute the collapse to the macaroni and cheese at the Sycamore Diner.

Madeleine and Josh Nixon sat in comfy leather club chairs facing the judge's walnut desk. All three of the attorneys were silent, watching the judge toy with the sheet of paper in front of him. He lifted one hand and ran it through his silver hair.

Judge Carter looked up. "This will be his first court appearance."

Nixon's tie was askew on his chest. He adjusted it and said, "We'll waive the reading of the criminal complaint. No need to give the press more ammunition."

A shade of displeasure crossed Madeleine's face. Elsie read the meaning behind it; Madeleine wanted to maximize press exposure on the murder case. She was a political animal, and a case of this magnitude could generate positive spin for the Prosecutor's Office.

Judge Carter said, "If the defendant isn't going to hear the charge, why do we need to bring him over? It's a security burden. *State v. Larry Paul* has already tied up thirty minutes of my morning."

"The public has a right—" Madeleine began, before Nixon cut her off.

"The hell with the public. Are they on trial? Judge, I don't want a circus; that won't help my cause. But I'm making a motion regarding bond and I want it on the record. And Larry Paul needs to be in court when I make it."

Judge Carter sighed, a weary sound. "Why?"

Nixon tugged at his tie again, as if he was unfamiliar with neckties. "Oh, you know. So he can see what a great job I'm doing."

Madeleine scoffed out loud.

Unperturbed, Josh continued. "And we need to talk about a change of venue, at some point."

Elsie glanced at Madeleine. Her legs were so tightly crossed that Elsie could see the white outline of her kneecaps.

Madeleine said, "The citizens of McCown County have the right to see justice done in their own jurisdiction. There has been tremendous public outcry concerning this crime."

"That's exactly my point," said Nixon.

Judge Carter shut down the debate with a wave of his hand. "Venue won't be my call. Save it for the judge in Circuit Court."

A tap sounded on the door connecting the judge's chambers to the courtroom. Eldon, Judge Carter's bailiff, poked his head through the door. "We got him, Judge."

"Okay, then." Judge Carter rose and zipped up his black robe. "Let's go."

Elsie folded her battered chair and set it against the wall. She wasn't used to the role of the silent partner; it didn't suit her. But she was trying her best to defer to Madeleine and keep her mouth shut.

As the attorneys followed the judge through the side door and into the courtroom, the bailiff said, "All rise."

The recently refurbished courtroom had room for only a single counsel table with four chairs, where opposing attorneys and their clients sat elbow to elbow facing the judge's bench.

Nixon headed to the far end of the counsel table, beside his client. Madeleine placed her hand on the chair at the other end, marking her territory. That left Elsie in the only remaining spot: a middle seat, directly beside the defendant.

"Be seated," the judge said, as he settled in his high seat and opened a paper file.

Elsie watched the defendant from the corner of her eye as he struggled to take his seat. His hands and feet were cuffed, trussed together with a metal chain. The orange jumpsuit was a poor fit for a tall man; the suit strained over his shoulders and his ankles jutted out in the style of an adolescent wearing high-water pants.

Madeleine hissed in her ear. "Be prepared to make suggestions on the bond issue."

Confidence restored, Elsie flashed her a smile. "No problem, Madeleine; I'll handle it."

Madeleine took a quick intake of breath. "Excuse me? I'll handle it. If you have any burning thoughts, write them down and pass them to me." Madeleine shoved a legal pad in front of her; Elsie turned to a fresh page and uncapped a pen. *I'm Helen Keller,* she thought. *Mute. Talking only to Anne Sullivan, with my fingers.*

The defendant shifted in his chair, brushing Elsie's elbow. She jerked away from the contact like she had been touched with a live wire. Their eyes met; his were pale blue, without a hint of gray.

Frozen, she stared at Larry Paul. His face was expressionless, but she fancied she could sense the darkness, the quality about him that was off, somehow. The defendant wasn't like other people; he was a man who would bludgeon a woman and kill his unborn child.

"I was high," he said to her, in a whisper.

Elsie gasped as the courtroom began to buzz. Nixon grabbed the defendant by the shoulder and jerked his client away from Elsie.

"Don't. Say. Anything," Nixon said in a tense voice.

Judge Carter banged the gavel. "Order," he said, and the spectators in the gallery hushed. The benches were full of reporters, drawn to cover the story from all of southern Missouri and northwest Arkansas. "We have a first appearance in the case of *State of Missouri v. Larry Edward Paul.* The State appears by Madeleine Thompson and Elsie Arnold; Defendant appears in person and with his attorney, Josh Nixon." The judge picked up a sheet of paper. "Defendant has been charged with two counts of Murder in the First Degree."

Nixon stood. "Your honor, the defense waives the reading of the charges and enters a plea of Not Guilty."

A woman at the end of the front row whispered, "Did you hear him say he was stoned on drugs?"

Elsie expected the judge to slam the gavel again, but he turned to his computer screen. "I have a morning clear on my calendar; I can give you three hours on September twelve. We can set the preliminary hearing at nine o'clock on that date. Or I can give you two hours in the afternoon on the fifteenth."

"Let me check, your honor," Nixon said; and Madeleine echoed the same answer.

"Defendant is being held without bond," Carter said, and Nixon stepped away from his chair.

"Your honor, I'd like to speak to that. Defendant moves for a set bond amount, one that he can meet."

"The State objects," said Madeleine. "State stands by its recommendation against bond."

Josh Nixon took his cue to recite the Sixth Amendment prohibition against excessive bonds. "This man has not been convicted of any crime, your honor; the criminal complaint filed by the State is a bare accusation."

Elsie scrawled *Flight risk* on her legal pad, and shoved it where Madeleine could see it.

"He's a flight risk," Madeleine said. "Because of the charge."

Because of the PENALTY, Elsie wrote. *He's looking at the Death Penalty!*

Madeleine glanced down. "This is a death penalty case, your honor. We are asking for the maximum penalty under law."

With a flourish, Elsie wrote, *No greater reason to flee exists.*

Madeleine raised her chin, and said with gravity, "Your honor, no greater reason to flee exists."

Elsie could see the local newspaper reporter nodding as she wrote the words on the pad. A nugget of resentment lodged under Elsie's chest.

She turned to face Nixon, waiting to hear his response. He had the look of someone who was about to light a rocket fuse.

"Well, your honor, there's also the security issue. At the jail."

Here it comes, Elsie thought.

"My client is infected with AIDS."

A woman in a mustard yellow jacket jumped from her chair, stepping over her seatmates to flee from the room. Startled, Elsie wondered whether she was frightened by the revelation; but a glance at the pad of paper she stuffed into her bag indicated otherwise. More likely, she was a reporter trying to scoop the other news stations.

"Judge, that can't color your decision on bond. The defendant is not in any danger," Madeleine said.

"The other inmates may worry that they're in peril," the judge said in an undertone.

Nixon placed a supportive hand on the defendant's shoulder. "He requires medical attention from a doctor who has experience treating his condition."

"There is medical assistance at the county jail," Madeleine said smoothly.

"Oh come on."

"There is," she insisted. "Dr. Gray visits the jail weekly."

"Get serious, Madeleine. Dr. Gray isn't even an MD; he's a DO. So is that the best arrangement McCown County is willing to make? We can fight the issue in federal court, if that's how you want to do it."

Judge Carter slapped the palm of his hand on the bench. "Mr. Nixon, there's no need to threaten me with federal court."

As the debate wrangled on, the defendant lifted his cuffed hands to his face and stuck his index finger into his mouth, plunging it all the way down to his knuckle.

Elsie watched, wary; was he trying to make himself gag? Vomit?

The icy blue eyes rested on her, unblinking. Then he pulled the finger out of his mouth with a popping sound. He reached over and wiped it on the back of Elsie's right hand.

She jumped out of her chair, tipping it over. "Jesus Christ!"

The judge stopped in midsentence; both Madeleine and Nixon swung around to look at her. Madeleine's face was a mask of angry disbelief.

But Elsie was backing away from the counsel table. "He rubbed his spit on me," she said, scrubbing her hand against the fabric of her skirt.

In the effort to distance herself from the defendant, she didn't see her overturned chair. Elsie stumbled against it and fell, hitting her head on the wooden railing that separated the public gallery from the parties in court. As she collapsed, she clutched her head with a shriek.

Only the defendant laughed.

Chapter Nine

GROGGY, ELSIE SQUINTED her eyes and tried to focus. A face was inches away from her own, blowing stale coffee breath up her nostrils.

The bailiff, Eldon, snapped his fingers at her, nearly tweaking her nose. "Elsie! Wake up!"

She tried to sit up, but the movement sent a vicious twinge through her head. "What the hell?" she whispered, massaging a knot on her skull with a tentative hand.

Judge Carter called from the bench, "Should I clear the courtroom?"

Bracing herself with her elbows, Elsie turned to respond the judge, and saw Larry Paul smirking at her. A wave of anger coursed through her veins, blurring her vision again.

Madeleine stood at her side and gave her a smart rap on the shoulder. "Are you all right? Can you stand?"

Elsie tried to rise from the tile floor, grasping at the wooden railing for balance. "I'm kind of dizzy."

Judge Carter said, "Do we need an ambulance?"

Resolutely, Elsie shook her head, and immediately regretted the movement. With an effort, she grasped the wooden spindles to pull to a stand. "No, Judge, thanks. Maybe I could just sit out in the hall for a minute and let my head clear."

The bailiff looked doubtful. "Shouldn't she stay where she is at? Could be she has a back injury."

Impatience made stars dance before Elsie's eyes. "I hit my head, Eldon. Not my back." With an involuntary groan she took a step to prove her point, and toppled sideways, landing at the feet of a television reporter from *Good Morning Four States*.

"Sorry," Elsie muttered, as he scooted out of danger.

A deputy approached her; with his arms crossed against his chest, he looked at Elsie on the floor, assessing her. Deputy Joe Franks was a slight man in his forties.

Franks said, "Reckon you ought to carry her out of here, Eldon?"

The bailiff gave a slow whistle. "Don't know that I can. Too heavy."

Elsie grimaced with chagrin. Even a blow to the head couldn't mask the sting of the bailiff's implication.

"We'll both tote her. You get her around the chest and I'll grab her feet," Franks said.

Though Elsie squawked in protest, the men executed the plan, bearing Elsie out into the rotunda like a supersized bag of potatoes. When they deposited her on the wooden bench outside the courtroom door, Eldon groaned with relief.

"Glad I don't have to do that all day long, I tell you what."

"Oh, Jesus Christ," Elsie muttered.

Deputy Franks appeared incapable of speech; he wheezed until his face turned violet.

"Maybe you need to cut back on the smokes, Joe," Elsie said, miffed.

Deputy Franks nodded as he walked off, still gasping. Madeleine darted through the doorway and stood over Elsie, regarding her with her lips pressed together in a thin line.

The bailiff gave Madeleine a subservient nod. "Mrs. Thompson, I'd best get back in court see what Judge Carter wants me to do next."

Madeleine waved a hand in dismissal, still focusing on Elsie. When Eldon walked away, Madeleine took a deep intake of breath before she spoke.

"I need help."

Elsie raised her head from the bench; she wasn't sure she'd heard Madeleine correctly. "What?"

Madeleine broke eye contact and looked off with a pensive air. She paced the hall of the top floor of the courthouse, studying the ceiling. After several moments of silence, she said, "The stained glass is filthy."

Trying to gauge the focal point of Madeleine's attention, Elsie also looked up and stared at the green and blue stained glass windows decorating the third floor of the old courthouse. The old structure was a local jewel, one the community refused to desert for newer quarters. Built on classical lines, with a low dome over a rotunda, the white stone courthouse had changed little since its construction in 1905; and the stained glass panes of the dome had been set in place a century ago. They did in fact look grimy.

"Is that a problem? Those windows are a hundred years old." She didn't follow Madeleine's train of thought. Perhaps, she thought, her head was still too muddy.

"It's going to be the death of me," Madeleine whispered.

"What?" Elsie sat up on the bench. "You're not talking about the windows?"

"Heavens no," Madeleine snapped, glancing at Elsie. "The case. I'm too old for this. I simply must have someone help me."

"Madeleine, you've got me." Elsie's voice held an apologetic note.

Madeleine responded with a pointed look. After a pregnant pause, she gave a decisive nod. "I'm calling in the general."

Elsie was working on a fitting reply when the courtroom door opened and a hum of voices distracted her. Eldon and Deputy Franks, joined by two other deputies, walked through the door with Larry Paul, flanking him on both sides. Josh Nixon followed a pace behind.

"Mr. Nixon," Madeleine said, her voice sharp.

Nixon turned and gave her an inquiring glance. When she waved him over, he walked toward the women. Once he was within earshot, Madeleine said with a hiss, "We are calling in the Missouri Attorney General. I just wanted you to know."

"Why? Can't you handle your own case? With your ace assistant?"

Nixon gave Elsie a wink. She ignored it.

"I can certainly handle my case. But you apparently can't control your client." Madeleine's voice grew shrill. "Maybe the Attorney General can bring you both under control."

The exchange was drawing a crowd. Three reporters stood nearby, looking on with growing interest. One of them adjusted a microphone on his navy jacket.

The reporter with the microphone edged closer to Madeleine. "Can we ask some questions, when you have a minute?"

"The prosecution can't comment," Madeleine said. Nixon backed away from her, laughing with scorn. The Public Defender often accused the McCown County Prosecutor's Office of pandering to the press, to the detriment of the defendants. They had once filed an ethics complaint against Elsie for speaking out in front of reporters. Though the charge was later withdrawn, the recollection still irked her. She wanted to wipe the snotty grin off Josh Nixon's face.

Madeleine turned her back on the group and headed toward the worn marble stairway. Rising from the bench, Elsie followed Madeleine down the stairs, trying to keep pace, though she was still wobbly.

"Madeleine," she said, pleading, "don't bring in a stranger. It's not necessary. We can do this."

At the bottom of the steps, Madeleine spun to confront her. "Have you taken the child's statement yet? The eyewitness?"

Elsie grasped the brass handrail, adding her fingerprints to scores of others tarnishing the metal. "No. Not yet."

"Why not?"

"You didn't tell me—" When Elsie saw Madeleine's complexion take on a scarlet hue, she backpedaled. "I didn't think there was a rush. We haven't even been set for preliminary hearing yet."

"We have now. While you wallowed on the bench in the hallway, Judge Carter set it for preliminary hearing. Next week."

Elsie whistled. "That's pretty soon."

"Get that social worker, Tina what's-her-name, and go take that child's statement. I need her ready." With a warning glance, she said: "You better be able to get her on the stand a week from Friday."

Madeleine stormed off in the direction of the women's restroom. Elsie really needed to relieve herself, too. She watched Madeleine open the bathroom door with a bang.

I can hold it, she thought, and headed to her own office.

Chapter Ten

AT FOUR O'CLOCK in the afternoon, Elsie sat in the passenger seat of Tina Peroni's Volkswagen.

"So you got a good foster care placement for her?"

"Yeah, pretty good, actually. A young couple with a baby, Holly and Dale Hickman. I think they're taking in a foster child so the mom can afford to stay home with the infant. But she's nice; he has steady employment; and they have a stable home life. And it keeps Ivy in her same grade school."

Tina fell silent, drumming her fingers on the steering wheel as she drove down a residential street. Elsie was reassured by Tina's words. She had a high opinion of Tina Peroni and considered her a friend. Tina was dedicated and savvy; and despite twenty years in social work, had not succumbed to burnout. They had worked as a team on many cases involving child victims, most recently the Kris Taney case—a father who'd abused his daughters, and was currently serving a life sentence for rape as a result of their efforts.

Elsie glanced over at Tina. "So that's good, right? Ivy doesn't have to adjust to a new school, with all the other upheaval in her life."

Tina nodded. Pulling up beside a small ranch style house covered in yellow aluminum siding, she adjusted her glasses. "There she is. Sitting right out front."

Elsie rolled down the window to get a good look. A bespectacled child wearing a purple T-shirt sat on the concrete steps of the yellow house.

Tina tapped Elsie's arm. "You want to talk to the foster mother first?"

"No. I want to see the kid. Get a feel for her, see what I'm dealing with."

As Elsie and Tina walked up the asphalt-covered driveway, the child peered at them through her glasses, her face a blank. When they approached the steps, Tina said, "Hi, Ivy. I'm Tina, back to see you and your foster mom again. How's it going?"

Ivy blinked. "Okay." She pushed up her glasses. They sat at a crooked angle on her face.

"This is Elsie. She works at the courthouse, and she's a friend of mine. Can she sit out here while I go inside and talk?"

"I guess," Ivy said.

Tina gave Elsie an encouraging wink and stepped up to the doorbell. As Tina entered the house, Elsie settled down beside Ivy.

The girl dipped into a can of blue Play-Doh resting at her side and pulled out a fist-sized lump. With a deft hand, she rolled it on the step.

"I got new shoes. And a new backpack," Ivy said.

Elsie brightened. The topic of new property was a fine place to commence an acquaintance. "A new backpack is totally cool," Elsie said. "What color?"

"Blue. I like blue. It got a princess on it."

Elsie flashed a confident smile; she might be on the dark side of thirty, but she knew the Disney girls backwards and forward. "I bet you picked Cinderella."

Ivy shrugged, concentrating on rolling the blue dough into a snake. But Elsie persisted.

"Because if the dress is blue, it's Cinderella. Blue dress? Blond hair? Ribbon at her neck?"

Ivy didn't answer. She scratched her nose. An angry rash circled both sides of her nostrils.

It seemed to Elsie that she wasn't gaining ground with the Disney princess angle. She shifted to a direct approach.

"Ivy. I'm so sorry about your mama."

Ivy's face closed. Thrusting her hand into the Play-Doh can, she dug out a blue lump and popped it into her mouth.

Elsie gasped. "Don't," she said, more sharply than she intended.

Ivy looked up through the smudged eyeglasses set askew on her nose. "What?"

"Oh, Ivy, sweetheart. You don't eat it. Spit it out."

Ivy chewed, with a rebellious expression. "It's good."

Elsie watched the girl's chin move as the ball of dough made a wad in her cheek. She looked like a man dipping snuff, enjoying a chew from a can of Skoal.

"It's bad for you, Ivy," Elsie said, keeping her voice gentle.

"Don't taste bad. Tastes like salt." The girl had a direct quality that was unsettling.

"Well, it's really not something you want to eat. It has artificial colors. Chemicals." With an involuntary gesture, Elsie reached out and pushed Ivy's cat-framed eyeglasses onto her head, adjusting them so they sat straight under her brow.

Lodging the lump of dough in her cheek, Ivy hung her head and toyed with the blue snake. "I don't eat it all the way. I just like how it tastes."

"Would you please spit it out? Pretty please?"

Ivy complied. She rose from the step and spit the blue lump into the spiky bushes that lined the front of the house.

Returning to the front step, Ivy coiled the snake in a circle on the concrete. Turning her back to Elsie, Ivy switched her attention to a battered cigar box that held broken crayons. She lifted the box from its position on the concrete step and held it in her lap. Ivy fished through the box, picking up and discarding the colored stubs.

"Where'd you get your color box?" Elsie asked.

"They're mine. From my old house." In a defensive voice, Ivy repeated, "They're mine."

"What are your crayons doing out here? Are you going to make a picture?"

"I brung them," Ivy said, pulling out a brown crayon from the box. With care, she peeled the paper away and set the bare crayon on the step, under the bright afternoon sun. Propping her chin on her hand, Ivy sat, watching it.

Elsie was hesitant to broach the topic of Ivy's mother again. She decided to cover other important territory. Reaching into Ivy's cigar box, Elsie picked up a red crayon.

"I bet you know your colors, don't you, Ivy?"

Ivy nodded, glancing at the crayon Elsie held.

"Do you know this one?"

"Red."

"That's right! It's red."

"We learned colors in kindergarten."

"That's why you're so smart. You've been to school." Elsie rolled the crayon between her finger and thumb, keeping it before Ivy's face. "Hey, Ivy. What if I said, 'This crayon is green.'"

"It's not," Ivy said, a look of disapproval crossing her face.

"You're right. So if I said it was green—when we know it's really red—would that be telling the truth?"

Ivy shook her head.

"Or would it be telling a lie?"

Ivy nodded. "Lying."

"Right! That's right! It would be lying." Elsie dropped the crayon back into the box. "Ivy," she said in a conversational tone, "is it wrong to tell a lie?"

Ivy didn't answer for a long moment. She picked up a twig and used it to poke the naked brown crayon she'd set on the step. With the twig, she rolled the crayon, turning it over on the concrete.

The silence made Elsie nervous. She would need to demonstrate to the court that the girl understood the meaning of the oath to tell the truth. Ivy would have to articulate to the judge's satisfaction that she knew the difference between the truth and a lie.

She tried again. Gently nudging Ivy's leg with her knee Elsie asked again. "Is it wrong to tell a lie? Ivy?"

Ivy nodded, poking the naked brown crayon with the stick.

Elsie let out a breath. "That's right." Though she was hesitant to push her luck, Elsie followed up. "Why is it wrong to tell a lie?"

"Jesus says."

Elsie blinked. Though she had not formed a precise expectation as to the child's response to her question, the reference to Jesus took her by surprise. Apparently Ivy's deceased mother had attended to the child's religious education.

"How'd you know that?"

"Church." With a jab, Ivy poked at the crayon. "Look," she said, smiling down at it.

The brown crayon was glistening in the sun, and had taken on a liquid glitter. Elsie pointed at it, saying to Ivy in a cautious tone, "You're not going to eat that."

Ivy gave her a confiding look, revealing a row of baby teeth that bore signs of serious neglect. "It looks like a Tootsie Roll."

"It looks like one. Kind of," Elsie hedged. "But it isn't."

Ivy nodded with a philosophical shrug. Elsie said, in a worried tone, "Really and truly, don't put that in your mouth. It's not a Tootsie Roll."

"Naw," Ivy said. "I ate one yesterday, and it wasn't no good."

BACK IN THE front seat of Tina's Volkswagen, Elsie scribbled notes on a legal pad, summarizing Ivy's statements.

She tapped the pen on the paper, pondering, and then looked over at Tina. "So who's taken Ivy to church? How does that fit into the late Jessie Dent's lifestyle?"

Tina shook her head.

"I think it's a recent development. It's the foster family. And the counselor."

"The counselor?"

"Yep."

"Okay, enlighten me. Why is a child psychologist reciting the New Testament in the treatment?"

"The counselor is not a psychologist."

Elsie frowned. "I thought you were getting her in to see one of the people at The Victim Center in Springfield."

Tina shot her an apologetic look. "The Victim Center agreed to see her. It was all set." At an intersection, Tina hit the brake with more force than necessary, sending Elsie's upper body against the shoulder harness. "It's a logistics problem. The foster mother doesn't want to transport her all the way to Springfield every week."

Elsie made a sound that was a cross between a snort and a raspberry. "She's a stay-at-home mom. What else does she have to do?"

Tina frowned, serving up a look of reproach. "Holly Hickman is a woman with an infant—a new baby. Who has taken in a traumatized foster child. Don't minimize her burden, please."

Abashed, Elsie backpedaled. "I didn't mean to disrespect her."

"You know, that's the kind of rhetoric that keeps women from supporting each other."

"Yeah. I know, it was stupid."

"We'll never unite as a gender—"

"Jesus! I take it back, okay? She's busy, I get it."

"Yeah, there's the baby. And her car's a junker, barely gets her to the grocery store. So we looked for a local option."

"For counseling?"

"Yep."

"But we don't have a child psychologist in Barton," Elsie said. In fact, the small county seat in McCown County had no practicing psychologist at all. "How about the new pediatrician?"

"I tried him. He says he's swamped. No time. Not qualified. No education or background in this kind of thing." Tina gave Elsie a knowing look. "I think I let it slip. The word 'Medicaid.'"

"Yeah, dirty word. Fucking greedy bastard."

Tina sighed. "So we can't make arrangements out of town, because of the foster mother's limitations. And the doctor in town isn't interested. I had to take what I could get."

"Which is?"

"The senior pastor at Riverside Baptist. He does counseling."

"Shit," Elsie said in a whisper.

"Hey. Beggars can't be choosers."

"Why didn't you try the Disciples of Christ? The pastor there is great."

"You gotta be licensed, go through training. The Baptist dude is licensed."

"Wait—Riverside Baptist? It's gotta be Albertson."

Tina nodded, keeping her eyes on the road. "Reverend Luke Albertson."

Elsie groaned. "Good Lord, Tina—you are one of the few stalwarts with the courage to be openly gay in our backwards little community. How can you tolerate it, turning that girl over to Albertson?"

Tina shook her head and said again, "Beggars can't be choosers. Got to make do with what's available." She gave Elsie a curious side glance. "How are you up to speed on the Right Reverend Albertson? You don't go to Riverside Baptist."

"No. But Ashlock does." Elsie closed her eyes and dropped her weary head onto the headrest of Tina's car before she remembered the lump on her skull. With a hiss, she sat up straight.

Chapter Eleven

IN THE LIVING room of his mother's brick bungalow, Bruce Stout sat in near-darkness. The plastic blinds were drawn, hanging askew; and the window facing the street was covered from the outside. Aside from one bulb in the overhead fixture, the only source of light in the room came from a television set, sitting on a plywood stand in the corner. Bruce looked away from the television screen when his mother, Nell, entered the room.

"What're you going to do?" she asked, walking over to his recliner with a can of Natural Light beer.

He popped the top and the beer gave a hiss. He took a long swallow and set it on the table beside half a dozen empty cans.

"Nothing," he replied, without looking at her.

With a dour face, Nell crossed her arms against her chest and glowered as he pointed the remote control at the ancient television set.

"There ain't nothing on. How come you ain't got cable no more?"

"I cut it off," Nell said. "I didn't like them shows. A hundred channels of nothing."

He pushed the button again and the screen went blank. "Three fucking channels. No point in having a TV at all."

With a grim smile, she said, "You can watch the news. See how your buddy is getting on at the jail."

"Shut the fuck up." He tossed the remote onto the scarred side table beside his chair, knocking two beer cans to the floor.

With a weary grunt, the woman bent over to pick up the cans. "You need to be thinking on this."

"I don't need to do nothing. He's in jail. They're going after him, not me."

"They're going to give him the death penalty. You think he's going down alone?"

Nell stood in front of his recliner, hugging the beer cans to her chest. When Bruce pushed the chair into a reclining position and stared at the ceiling in silence, she said, "Son, don't be stupid."

He lifted an empty can and threw it at her head. "Don't you call me that, Ma."

With her bare foot, she shoved the footrest of the recliner to the floor, returning him to a sitting position.

"I think I done raised a fool," she said, emphasizing the last word. "Any man who's going down is gonna take someone with him. It's the way folks are. And he's got plenty of shit on you. On all of us."

"I didn't touch that bat."

"But you was there."

"Who says?"

"The child. She'll tell. She'll flap her jaw and say who knows what-all. And that girl has seen plenty over there at the trailer."

Bruce tipped the can and chugged the beer, wiping his mouth when he was done. "Get me another Natty Light."

"You done drunk them all."

"Shit," he whispered, tossing the can onto the floor, where it rolled under the couch. A black ringtailed cat emerged from its spot beneath the couch and began angrily scratching the worn upholstery with its claws.

Staring at the cat he said, "That cat done tore up everything in this house. I don't know why you don't get rid of it."

"He acts better than you." She reached down and stroked the cat's fur. It stopped its assault on the couch and arched its back with pleasure.

"I'm hungry. I need something to eat."

She scratched the cat's head. "I can make you a bologna sandwich."

"I want me some barbeque. Didn't you bring nothing home from Smokey's? You was there all day."

"Smokey Dean's not running no soup kitchen over there. Him and his daddy didn't get where they got, giving it away for free. You want a sandwich or not?"

"Fuck," he said with a groan. "You feed the cat better than your own son."

As she stood, leaning over him, the overhead light cast a silver glow on her gray hair and left her face in shadow. "I'll make that sandwich. And you start thinking about what you're going to do."

"About what?"

"About the girl."

She walked away, her bare feet slapping on the tiled floor. Closing his eyes, Bruce pushed the recliner back again.

Once his mother left the room, he started to cry.

Chapter Twelve

AT SEVEN O'CLOCK on a Sunday evening, Elsie should have been stretched out on the couch in her apartment, shouting at the television screen during an episode of *Sister Wives* while sipping a cold bottle of Corona.

Instead, she was rattling the church bulletin at Riverside Baptist, waiting for the Sunday night service to begin.

Ashlock nudged her with his elbow. "Relax. Ease up. You're fidgety as a kid."

"Yeah. Nervous as a whore in church," Elsie responded, crossing and uncrossing her legs.

Ashlock flinched, turning to see whether his teenage son had overheard. Ashlock's son, Burton, had moved in with him a few months prior, after protracted negotiations with Ashlock's ex-wife. Elsie stole a glance at Burton, to see whether her comment had shocked him; but the young man exhibited no particular interest in Elsie, or in his father, for that matter. He sat at the end of the pew, his short-cropped head bent over his phone. Most likely he was playing *Clash of Clans*.

"Burton. Put that away," Ashlock said in a whisper. Burton looked up, his expression neither resentful nor surprised. With good-natured resignation, he slipped the phone into the pocket of his khaki pants.

He was a good-looking kid, Elsie thought, in the scrubbed, all-American-boy style. At fourteen, he was slight in size, the arms extending from the sleeves of his orange polo shirt slim as a girl's. *Too bad he didn't inherit his father's build,* she thought, then chided herself for comparing a boy of fourteen to a man of forty. The kid was still a lump of clay. No telling how he might turn out.

A drumroll and the clash of cymbals announced the start of the service as musicians took to the stage. A guitarist fiddled with the dials on his amplifier, sending an earsplitting whine into the sanctuary.

Elsie grimaced. "My favorite. A praise band."

Ashlock elbowed her and she hushed. An overhead screen flashed the lyrics to a praise hymn and the congregation rose to sing.

Elsie was no stranger to hymn singing; she had been herded to the Walnut Avenue Disciples of Christ church every Sunday morning from infancy through high school graduation. But the thrumming beat of drums and bass guitar made her uncomfortable. As the congregation raised their voices and lifted their arms into the air, she found herself longing for the wheezy pipe organ of her childhood church.

The song was interminable. The few lines displayed on the screen weren't difficult to interpret; but the instructions "Repeat 5 times" grated on her. *I'm not feeling this,* she thought.

Once they were invited to sit, she let her mind wander. During preliminary matters of church business, the Old Testament read-

ing and the Minute for Mission, she made a mental list of tasks she
needed to accomplish on Monday. The list was daunting.

Beginning to fret, she pulled out a pen and started scratching
notes on the church bulletin. Underneath the prayer chain list,
she scrawled:

#1 Check computer file—autopsy report received?
#2 Need additional testing, Jessie D & baby—AIDS???
#3 Discuss: security for L Paul, in court; in jail; (transfer?)
#4 Contact Tina; set up new meeting with Ivy (AIDS test???)
#5 Other witness? Bruce (last name?) need to locate!

She looked up from the notes. Ashlock caught her eye and
furrowed a brow in disapproval. Elsie looked away, unrepentant,
and scanned the crowd. The congregation enjoyed a broad demo-
graphic sample from the community; silver heads were seated in
rows alongside young families. A cluster of high school teens sat
together, occupying the far aisles. Elsie wondered why Burton
wasn't among them.

Sweeping her eyes to the opposite side of the sanctuary, she
suddenly spotted Holly Hickman, Ivy's foster mother, seated near
the front, with her baby on her shoulder and Ivy at her side. Ivy's
head was bent; Elsie leaned forward to see what the child was
doing. She appeared to be scribbling on a sheet of paper with a
crayon.

Elsie was so focused on Ivy that she didn't hear the pastor
call the children up for the kids' sermon. Toddlers and grade-
schoolers made their way down the aisle of the nave, some at a
run. The foster mother nudged Ivy; Ivy shook her head. Holly
sighed; handing the infant off to a dark-haired man on her left—

must be her husband, Elsie thought—she took Ivy by the hand and led her to the carpeted steps leading to the altar.

As children gathered on the steps, the pastor, Reverend Luke Albertson, stepped around speaker cords and band equipment to join them. With a beatific expression, he said to the congregation:

"Let the little children come to be, and forbid them not."

So, Elsie thought. *You think you're Jesus Christ.* She snorted.

A woman seated in the pew ahead of Elsie peered over her shoulder with a reproving look. Ashlock pinched her thigh. It was not a friendly squeeze.

Reverend Albertson addressed the assembled children. "Kids, I have a big announcement, and I wanted you up here when I make it. You know we had a dream, a vision, that we would build a new addition to house a gymnasium for our kids to enjoy. Well, that vision is going to become a reality, a lot sooner than we ever hoped."

He grinned at the congregation. "A member of the community has stepped up and made a commitment to fund it. Not even a member of our congregation—though I hope that will change soon. Brothers and sisters, Riverside Baptist is getting that new addition!"

The women and men in the pews whooped and cheered. Ashlock applauded. Elsie fanned herself with the bulletin.

"This man wants to remain anonymous, and I respect that. But let me just say: he makes the best pulled pork in southwest Missouri."

Elsie stopped waving the bulletin. *No way,* she thought. *Not Smokey Dean Mitchell.*

The pastor looked down at the children. "Alrighty now; let's get down to business here. How many of you are on a team?"

The hands which shot up belonged mostly to boys. The pastor called on them: three tall boys played in the Mighty Man Pee-Wee football league; half a dozen were in Little League baseball; and a handful of boys and girls claimed soccer. A number of toddlers sat among them, one girl sucking her thumb. One of the tots spoke up in a piping voice, but Albertson ignored it. Only a few of the school-age children remained silent, hands in their laps. Those not claiming a sport were three girls in ill-fitting clothes, a fat boy, and Ivy.

The preacher pointed a finger at the chunky kid. "How about you? You like to play games?" The boy nodded. "What kind?"

The boy hesitated. His hair was shorn into a buzz cut; Elsie could see a flush coloring his features. "Computer games, mostly."

"Lord deliver us," the pastor said with a groan. "Computer games!" Playing to the audience, he said, "I see the devil's hand at work. Sounds like fuel for next week's sermon."

The congregation burst into merry laughter as the boy's neck flushed scarlet. Elsie glared at the preacher with a scowl she didn't try to hide. *Getting a laugh at the kid's expense. What a jerk.*

"Ivy," he said. Elsie didn't expect to hear the preacher call the girl by name. "Do you like games?"

Ivy shrugged. He pressed on. "Candyland? Checkers? Chutes and Ladders?"

Damn, Elsie thought; *I should pick up Candyland for her at Walmart.* It nettled her that the preacher originated the idea.

"Yeah," Ivy whispered.

"You like those games?"

Ivy nodded.

"Ivy, do those games have rules?"

She fiddled with her glasses. He apparently took the movement as a yes.

"Sure they do! You can't just take your game piece up to the gingerbread house unless you follow the rules! Kevin," he said, turning to a snub-nosed boy, "if you strike out when you're at bat, can you just head out and start running the bases?" Reverend Albertson jumped up and began to run in place. The crowd burst into another round of gleeful hilarity.

"No? Because you gotta follow the rules, right? Well, all of life is like that, you know?"

He squatted on his haunches, reached behind the nearest amplifier, and picked up a maroon bound Bible.

"What's this?"

"The Bible," several children chorused.

"Well, that's right. But it's also a rule book. A rule book for all Christians to follow. Hey, kids: do you think you get to pick and choose what rules to follow in this book?" There was no immediate response from the children, and he continued: "Or are you supposed to follow all of them? Every single one?"

One of the football boys spoke up. "All of them," he said stoutly.

Reverend Albertson stood, nodding his approval. "That's right. From the mouths of babes, huh? This book," and he held it aloft, addressing the congregation, "is the inspired word of God. We aren't cafeteria Christians at Riverside Baptist. We don't pick and choose." He looked down at the children, still sitting at his feet. "Okay, kids; you can go on back to your seats."

As the children wandered back to their places in the pews, the preacher continued. "This great country was founded on the rules in our sacred text, hundreds of years ago. But things have changed in the country we love. Nine people in Washington, DC, who wear black robes, have forgotten that. They've lost their way."

Oh shit, Elsie thought. *Here it comes.*

"Because the Bible is clear. Homosexuality is sin. The Old Testament says so: In the Book of Leviticus, Chapter 20, verse 13, the Lord said to Moses that if a man lies with a man, as he'd lie with a woman, that's detestable! He shall be put to death! Do you think God was joking around when he said that to Moses? Does the Supreme Court of the United States think they know better than the Lord God?"

He flipped the Bible open to a place marked with a gold ribbon. "There's more to be found on the same topic, in the New Testament. The Apostle Paul had some things to say on the subject."

Elsie leaned over to Ashlock. "The Apostle Paul was a total asshole," she said. Ashlock didn't respond to Elsie's observation. The woman sitting in front of her gasped, but didn't turn around.

"Paul condemned the sin of homosexuality in First Corinthians! He said that homosexuals will not inherit the kingdom of heaven. Will! Not! Inherit!"

He raised his voice to a higher pitch. "In the Book of Romans, Paul condemned women and men who commit indecent acts of homosexuality. That's women and men, friends. An equal opportunity condemnation!"

One man cheered, a few tittered and chuckled. But in large part, the congregation waited for the big finish.

"Oh, but the Supreme Court—those black-robed know-it-alls, who think they can rewrite the morals of our nation, say that homosexuals have the right. The right to marry. The right to sin with impunity. Well, friends, you know what my friend Mike Huckabee says about that. 'The Supreme Court is not the Supreme Being!' "

That was the punch line, and the churchgoers knew it. Those who were able to stand jumped to their feet, applauding. The elderly and infirm lifted their hands into the air.

Elsie kept her seat, crossing her arms across her chest. Ashlock's son, Burton, stood with the others. Ashlock turned to look at Elsie. With an apologetic shrug, he said, "My ex."

By the end of the service, she was fuming, conducting extensive, heated arguments in her head in which she took the Reverend Albertson down. When they filed out of the sanctuary, Ashlock tried to herd her toward the side exit, but Elsie was too fired up to make an easy escape.

She waited in line with those who wanted to shake hands with Albertson and touch the hem of his garment. When her turn came, she ignored his outstretched hand.

"Just want you to know," she said, "I am in total agreement with the court's decision in *Obergefell v. Hodges*."

Reverend Albertson gave her a blank look and didn't respond. She thought she must have confused him by making reference to the case name.

"The Supreme Court case, declaring that same-sex marriage is a Constitutional right. When the decision was announced, I said, 'God Bless America!' "

Albertson let his hand drop to his side. "You can't pick and choose, ma'am. You believe or you don't."

"You want to know what I believe? I believe in individual freedom. And I believe that there are five people out of the nine on the court who are looking out for us."

Sadly, the preacher shook his head. "That's the Lord's job." He reached out and took her hand, giving a gentle squeeze. "I hope you'll be back. I think you have a lot to learn."

Elsie pulled free and walked out into the warm evening air, facing a scarlet sunset without seeing it. She was chastising herself for not getting the last word. When they reached Ashlock's car,

Burton got in while Ashlock held her back and spoke into her ear in a low voice. "I know you're upset about the service. But I don't want to go into it in front of Burton. This is the church his mother wants him to attend."

"How can you tolerate having Burton under the influence of that preacher?"

"It's part of the deal. And I'll do whatever I have to do to keep my boy with me."

"But Albertson's a homophobe. And an idiot. And I'll bet whatever you want to put up—he's a misogynist." Elsie pulled her purse onto her shoulder with a jerk. "I don't give a damn what your ex-wife wants. I am never darkening the door of this pit of snakes again. Never."

They got into the vehicle and Ashlock drove away from the church, his silent disapproval palpable.

Chapter Thirteen

DODGING THE TRAFFIC on the town square on Monday afternoon, Elsie made her way across the street to the Barton City Police Department. She'd received an urgent text: the assistant attorney general had arrived, and they were meeting with Ashlock in his office.

She dashed up the stairs, anxious to know whether she'd missed anything important. Bob Ashlock's office door was closed. She paused a moment to tuck her hair behind her ears and make sure that her shirt was buttoned and her pants zipped.

Then she opened the door. "Good afternoon!"

Madeleine jerked in her chair. "Can't you knock?"

Rising from his seat, Ashlock greeted Elsie with a warm smile. "Elsie and I don't stand on ceremony, Madeleine. Come on in; take my seat."

"Ash, no. Thank you. I can stand."

"I insist."

She sat behind his desk, because she knew it would make him uncomfortable if she stood while he sat. He was courtly in some old-fashioned ways. She was a twenty-first-century woman, but couldn't deny that it was nice to sit down after standing in court all morning.

Elsie shifted her attention to the newcomer in the room. Flashing a smile, she reached across the desk and offered her hand. "Nice to meet you at last, Mr. Parsons. I'm Elsie Arnold, assistant prosecutor."

"My pleasure. Call me Sam." He took her hand and gave it a brisk shake, squeezing her fingers a shade too tightly. Elsie knew that message: he thought he'd show her who was boss.

Guess we'll both get to see what we're made of by the time this case is done.

Samuel Parsons leaned back in his chair. "Maybe now we can get down to business. The detective here says he's got his forensic reports back. But he's a little coy about what they reveal. You ready to show us what you got, Ashcroft?"

Though it wasn't a crime to recall a name incorrectly, Elsie glanced to Ashlock, to see his reaction.

He smiled, just a little. "The name's Ashlock."

"Ashlock? Yeah. What'd I say?"

"Ashcroft," Elsie said. "You called him Ashcroft. Like the former attorney general."

Parsons laughed, showing his full set of teeth. Elise took a moment to size him up. Parsons cut an impressive figure, with a luxurious head of salt-and-pepper hair, brushed straight back into a mane. He wore a pair of eyeglasses with black rectangular frames, perched on a broad nose. The vest of his gray suit had a gold chain from which a fob dangled, catching the sunlight that shone in through the window. Staring at the twinkle, Elsie pondered whether the vest covered a paunch.

Glancing at Ashlock's figure as he leaned against the door frame, Elsie reflected that he never wore a vest. Didn't need to, she thought, looking at his flat stomach. Nothing to hide.

Ashlock walked over to a gray metal file cabinet in the corner of his office and pulled out a manila file folder. "I made a copy for each of you," he said, handing off sheets of paper.

"Did you e-mail this?" asked Madeleine. "I don't think I saw it."

"Didn't send it yet. It's sensitive. I wanted to discuss it in person first."

"What you got here, Detective?" Parsons asked, adjusting his eyeglasses.

"Forensic report on the deceased, Jessie Rose Dent."

"The murder victim—the mother? Madeleine, did you tell me she had AIDS? That what this is about?" Parsons asked.

Madeleine leaned in toward the Attorney General, confirming their earlier conversation. Elsie scanned the report that Ashlock handed to her. The words on the pages gave her a sinking feeling in her gut. She looked up at Ashlock; their eyes met.

"Oh shit," she said, and he nodded in response.

"Elsie!" Madeleine said, but Parsons broke in. Glancing from Elsie to Madeleine, he said, "We got a problem, Elsie? Tell me it's not a worse PR wrinkle than the pregnant woman with AIDS." He pulled a tragic face.

Ashlock said, "Forensic tests showed some surprising facts."

"Like what? Let's cut to the chase." Parsons folded the report in half and focused on Ashlock, looking over the top of his eyeglasses.

"Blood tests show the victim had controlled substances in her system at the time of death."

"Shit," Parsons said. Madeleine didn't seem to notice.

"What kind of drugs?" Madeleine asked. Setting the forensic report on Ashlock's desktop, she said, "I didn't bring my reading glasses."

"Hell getting old, huh, Madeleine," Parsons said with a jovial nudge.

Madeleine cleared her throat, crossed her legs tightly and focused on Ashlock. "Was it some kind of pharmaceutical substance? She could have a medical condition that would explain it."

Elsie spoke up. Eyes scanning the report, she said, "Madeleine, it's here on page two. Methamphetamine. Marijuana. Alcohol."

"Sheeeit." Parsons dragged the word out into three long syllables. "So we have a murder victim, eight months pregnant, mother of a young child. But she's drunk and high on meth at the time of her death."

Ashlock nodded. "Yep." He scratched his neck. "We seized a pretty sizeable bag of meth from the trailer when we were processing the murder scene."

Elsie made a face. "Do you think they were cooking it there, Ash?"

"No. No equipment, no smell. I'd sure like to know where they got it from."

Parsons said, "Excuse me, folks, but you can work out your drug cases on your own time. I'm here to lend a hand in this murder case. And set me straight again: this woman had AIDS?"

Madeleine said, "We're requesting additional testing," but Elsie broke in.

"If the defendant gave that poor woman AIDS, it's hardly a mark against her."

Both Madeleine and Parsons began to speak; his voice boomed over hers and Madeleine broke off as Parsons said to Elsie, "Are you stupid? Or just wet behind the ears? Don't you realize they will attack the victim as their defense to the crime?"

"Mr. Parsons," Ashlock said.

"What?"

"Don't call Ms. Arnold stupid."

"Huh?"

"Ms. Arnold is the smartest woman of my acquaintance. It's offensive to me, hearing you talk to her that way."

Madeleine told him in a whisper, "Detective Ashlock and Ms. Arnold are good friends." After a moment's pause, she repeated, "Very good friends."

Parsons looked at Elsie with a knowing eye. "I see. I see I see I see." He leaned back in his chair, tipping it so that the wooden back rested against the wall. "Ladies and gentleman, you have pulled me into a can of worms."

"I'm so sorry," Madeleine said.

"A hornets' nest," he said. "A nest of vipers. I can already feel the sting, the bite."

"Samuel, please understand I didn't withhold this information from you; when I asked for your assistance I didn't know."

He reached out a large hand and squeezed Madeleine's knee. "No need to apologize. I like a challenge. And by God, this case is a challenge." He gave Madeleine's knee one last squeeze, and then rubbed his hands together. With a nod in Elsie's direction, he said, "So—Ms. Arnold, is it? Elsie? The smartest woman this detective has ever known?" He stopped to grin at Ashlock. "Tell you what we're gonna do. We are going to suck the poison on this snakebite."

Elsie nodded slowly. "Okay."

Parsons leaned forward, his elbows on his knees. "Want to know how? We are throwing her to the sharks."

So many animal metaphors, Elsie thought. "What exactly do you mean?"

"We won't give the defense the chance to slice and dice this gal. We'll gut her first. Throw her to the dogs."

Dogs, sharks, Elsie thought, but his intention was clear. "Are you going to attack the victim in a murder case? Our murder case?"

"I'm going to call her every name in the book. We don't need her."

Elsie blinked. Shaking her head, she said, "You've lost me. Of course we need her. The case is about the crime committed against her. She was beaten to death."

"She's a pimple on society's ass. Pregnant woman doing drugs—not fit to breathe the same air as the rest of us. But fortunately, we can raise up another victim: a blameless victim, who didn't do anything to deserve his fate. The baby."

Madeleine stared at him in awe. "The unborn child. Sam, that's brilliant."

"And I can pull in the troops to give us a hand in that regard." Parsons looked over his eyeglass frames at Madeleine. Elsie thought perhaps he was trying to look shrewd; but he came off as popeyed. "I have connections with the Missouri Right to Life."

"Sam, that's wonderful." Madeleine beamed at him.

"We'll have people storming the courthouse to demand justice for that unborn child."

As Parsons laid out his plan, Elsie's jaw locked. She exchanged a glance with Ashlock, then she said, "No one deserves to be bludgeoned to death. This woman was beaten to death with a baseball bat. And now you're going to bludgeon her in court?"

"Watch the master at work. Listen and learn." Turning to Ashlock, he said, "Well, Detective, is there any other good news you have to share with us today?"

"The lab found the presence of semen in the deceased. She'd had sexual intercourse shortly before death."

Parsons groaned. "Beg pardon, ladies, but who would want to screw a big old pregnant lady with AIDS?"

Elsie looked to Madeleine, hoping that her boss would raise an objection on behalf of their deceased victim, but she remained mum. With a sigh of frustration, Elsie flipped through the pages of the report, scanning them for the information Ashlock described. "Ashlock, I didn't catch that, about the semen, but it's good: good for the prosecution. Because it shows that their relationship was intact. What kind of monster has sex with a woman and then beats her to death?"

"Well, that's a problem. The semen doesn't match the defendant."

Samuel Parsons snorted. "What a whore."

Elsie gasped, an involuntary breath catching in her throat.

"Good thing we've got that unborn baby. Get any good pictures of it? Make it look sweet? We need it in one piece."

Bile rose in Elsie's throat as Parsons spoke; she swallowed it back.

Parsons rubbed a finger under his nose. He said, "What about the little girl, that daughter of the victim? Is the defendant her daddy?"

"No," Madeleine said. "Different father."

"Good. No divided loyalty. I flipped through your file, looking for the child's statement, but I didn't see it in there."

"That's Elsie's responsibility. The child witness will be hers."

Parsons pulled a stick of gum from the pocket of his jacket. He wadded the gum wrapper and tossed it at Elsie. "How about it, Elsie? Where's that statement?"

"I haven't taken it yet."

He looked at her with amazement. "Just what are you waiting for?"

Elsie said, "I'm still establishing a relationship," but he cut her off.

"Are you waiting for her memory to improve? Maybe you think the passage of time will sharpen her recall of past events. You think that's how it works?"

"Generally, no. But with a child—"

"With a child, you better nail it down immediately. Because who knows what the hell they'll say later." He hefted himself out of the chair, saying, "Okay then, let's go."

Madeleine jumped out of her chair, saying, "Where are we going?"

"We're going to see that little girl and lock her testimony down. Right now. What did you say her name is?"

"Ivy," Madeleine said. "Ivy Dent," she repeated, as she and Parsons exited the office and strode down the hallway. With a dark look aimed at Parsons's back, Elsie followed.

Chapter Fourteen

ELSIE WAS STILL grousing when Ashlock pulled up to Ivy's foster home. "What a total fuckwad."

As Ashlock put his car in Park, his eyes met hers. "You got that right."

"How am I going to work with him?" She picked a small CVS bag off the dash and stuffed it in her purse.

"Remember the goal, that's all. This case isn't a party. And it's not a sprint. It's a marathon. And you're trying to see justice done."

Privately, Elsie wondered how many more metaphors she would hear by the day's end. But she nodded in agreement. "That's right, Ash. I've got to keep my head wrapped around that, and ignore the personality shit."

"That's my girl." He opened the car door and gave her a wink. "Let's get in there before they scare the kid to death."

Elsie and Ashlock made their way to the front door. Through the screen, Elsie could see Madeleine and Samuel Parsons sitting on the sofa in the living room. When she pushed the door bell, Madeleine came to open it. "What took you all so long?"

Her voice was less waspish than the tone Elsie was accustomed to hearing; she attributed it to Ashlock's presence.

He spoke up. "We made a quick pit stop." As Ashlock and Elsie walked into the room, he nodded in Parsons's direction, giving a silent acknowledgment. The foster mother, Holly Hickman, bustled into the room, bearing a wicker tray with four plastic tumblers. "I made tea," she announced.

When she set the tray on the coffee table, Parsons picked up a tumbler, and said in a voice of gratitude, "You are an excellent hostess, Mrs. Hickman. I'm parched." He took a big swig from the ice-filled glass.

"Oh," Holly said modestly. "No trouble. It's just instant."

Madeleine rattled the ice cubes in her glass. "We should get started."

"Where's Ivy?" Elsie asked.

"Oh gosh," Holly answered, her face contrite, "she won't come out. She's acting shy. I thought we'd give her a minute."

"You are a sweetheart, Mrs. Hickman, that's a fact. But why don't you run on back and try again," Parsons urged.

As soon as the woman left the room, he pointed at the glass of tea in his hand and made a face, sticking out his tongue and shaking his head. Madeleine giggled like a girl in middle school.

Ash's features were stony as he averted his face from the pantomime. Elsie raised her glass and took a sip. Admittedly, the beverage was vile: sickly sweet, with a harsh lemony tang. She swallowed it, refusing to meet Parsons's eye. *Dick,* she thought.

Mrs. Hickman returned, pulling a reluctant Ivy in her wake. Parsons rose, and said in a pleasant voice, "Well, hello there, young lady."

Dinosaur, Elsie thought, *nobody calls a kid "young lady"*; but she smiled so hard she feared her cheek muscles would spasm.

Ivy pulled her hand free of the foster mother's grasp. From the look in her eyes, Elsie thought she might flee; but the girl backed into the corner where a small TV sat on a particleboard stand and dropped cross-legged onto the green carpet.

Parsons and Madeleine exchanged a glance. Sotto voce he said, "Tell the cop to start recording."

Madeleine nodded, and turned to Ashlock; without comment, he pulled a recorder from his briefcase. A small end table was close by Ivy's position on the floor. Ashlock set the recording device on the table and flipped it on. Parsons picked up a wooden dining room chair and placed it near Ivy. He turned the chair backwards and straddled it, resting his arms on the chair back.

"Hey there," he said. "I'm Mr. Parsons."

Ivy studied him, scratching at a rashy spot beside her nose.

"I bet your name's Ivy," he said.

There was a long pause before she replied. "Maybe," she said.

He cocked his head to one side, aping disbelief. "Maybe? Maybe? I bet a hundred dollars it's Ivy."

She stared through the broken glasses. "I ain't got a hundred dollars," she said.

At that, Parsons whooped. The sudden noise made Elsie jolt backwards in her seat.

"You're a little feist," he said. "Gonna have to watch what I say." Suddenly, his jolly demeanor disappeared, replaced by a grave and solemn countenance.

"Ivy, I hear you lost your mother."

She turned her head toward the picture window.

"Now, don't look away. I know it's a sad, sad thing to lose your mother. But I'm a lawyer all the way from the State Capitol. You know where that is?"

Idiot, Elsie thought. How the hell would this first grader know the State Capitol?

When Ivy shook her head, Parsons said, "It's in Jefferson City, Missouri. Can you say Jefferson City?"

"I don't want to."

Elsie yelped with involuntary laughter. She tried to cover it with a cough when Madeleine turned a scorching eye on her.

Parsons sighed. "Well, that's fine. But I came from the State Capitol because I'm going to help put the man who hurt your mom in jail. And you are going to help me."

Ivy's glasses had slipped down her nose. She pushed them back.

"So you need to tell me what you remember about that night. The night your mother went to heaven."

Ivy scooted away from Parsons until her back was up against the TV stand. "I don't know you."

Parsons smiled. "Sure; we just met. But I told you, I'm a lawyer from Jefferson City. I'm here to help you."

Ivy looked away and remained mute.

"Ivy, did you see what Larry Paul did to your mama?"

When Ivy maintained a dogged silence, Ashlock bent and spoke to Parsons in a low voice. "Let Elsie try."

Parsons swung around to Madeleine. "You called in the General for assistance. Do you want to turn it over to the private? It's your call."

Madeleine's eyes shifted. She gave an apologetic sigh, a dainty huff of regret. "Well, she's worked with her before."

Parsons stood, an ironic half grin wrinkling his meaty face. "By all means. Don't want to interfere."

Without waiting for more encouragement, Elsie seized her plastic CVS bag and dropped onto the carpet beside Ivy, emulating the girl's cross-legged position on the floor.

"Ivy, you know me. I'm Elsie."

The child nodded and slid her eyes to Parsons, who stood nearby with his arms crossed. "Him I don't know."

"He's okay," Elsie said in a cajoling voice. With a smile, she said, "What do you think is in here?" She held up the bag.

Ivy shrugged, petulant. "Dunno."

"Look and see."

The girl opened the bag and peered inside. Her suspicious expression disappeared and she pressed her lips together to hide a smile.

"What do you think?" Elsie asked.

Ivy thrust a small hand into the bag, pulling out a multi-pack of Play-Doh in bright colors; and reaching in a second time, uncovered a box of forty-eight Crayola crayons.

"You like it?"

Ivy nodded. She opened the box of crayons. Lifting them to her nose, she inhaled deeply.

Elsie reached out a hand. "Can I take a turn?" Ivy handed her the box, and Elsie breathed in, rolling her eyes in ecstasy. "Oh man. Does anything smell better than a new box of crayons?"

Ivy hid a smile with her hand. Her fingernails were stubby, her cuticles chewed and scabby.

Elsie heard Parsons whisper to Madeleine. "Bad idea to bribe the kid. Defense will say it affects her veracity."

Elsie ignored him. Keeping her spot on the floor, she reached over to the coffee table and retrieved the legal pad she'd left there.

"Those colors totally need to get out of the box. You want to draw?"

Ivy nodded.

"Can you draw a picture of your house? We don't need a picture of your new house, this house; we know what it looks like. Can you draw your old house? The trailer where you lived with your mother."

"Okay." Ivy sorted through the colors, then picked a black crayon. On the legal pad, she sketched a rough rectangle. "It's a trap house," she said, in an offhand tone.

The statement made Elsie gasp; she tried to mask the reaction with a feigned cough. *Oh shit,* she thought. Glancing sidelong at Madeleine and Parsons, she saw no visible response to Ivy's statement. Clearly, they weren't tuned into rap music; hardly a surprise. But Elsie knew that "trap house" was a drug-related term.

"Where are you? Put yourself in the picture."

Obligingly, Ivy chose a blue crayon and drew a stick figure beside the rectangle, then scribbled the hair yellow. "That's me."

"You're outside."

"Uh-huh."

"Ivy," and Elsie spoke in a calm voice, "the night your mom got hurt so bad by Larry Paul, where were you then?"

Ivy clutched the crayon so tightly, Elsie thought it might break in two. "Which time?" she asked.

The question was a reasonable one. Elsie and Ashlock had reviewed the history of domestic disturbance calls to the trailer; disputes between Jessie Dent and Larry Paul had a history of turning violent. Chuck Harris and Lisa Peters had witnessed a violent interlude less than forty-eight hours before Jessie Dent's murder. Elsie needed to narrow the scope of her inquiry.

"The last time. The night your mom died."

Ivy didn't look at her. Focusing on the legal pad, she pointed at the stick figure she'd drawn.

"Right, that's you; I can tell. It's a good drawing. But where were you that night?"

With a resolute face, Ivy jabbed the figure again.

"Please tell me. Tell me what you mean."

Ivy poked the picture for a third time.

"I like it when you talk to me, Ivy. I like to hear you talk."

Ivy lifted her finger from the paper and used it to scratch vigorously at her hairline. Briefly, Elsie wondered whether the foster mother should check her head for lice.

"That's where I was at."

Elsie felt a sinking sensation in her chest. "You were outside? Outside the trailer?"

Ivy nodded.

"Well, there goes the eyewitness," Parsons said, turning on the couch to Madeleine. He pulled off his eyeglasses and ran his hand over his face.

Elsie smoothed the sheet of paper. It bore wrinkles from Ivy's index finger.

"Okay, Ivy, let's back up. Before you went outside: who all was in the trailer?"

"Me."

"Right. Who else?"

"Mama. And Larry. And Bruce."

"And who is Larry?"

"Mom's boyfriend."

"And who is Bruce?"

"Mama's number two boyfriend."

Elsie kept her face pleasant, though Parsons was groaning audibly. "Your mama had two boyfriends?"

"Mama was a trap queen. She said so."

Shit, shit, shit, Elsie thought. "What were they doing?"

"Drinking. Partying. Bruce brung it over from his mom's house."

"What were you doing?"

"I was watching the TV. But they told me to get out."

"Why?"

"They was getting high. But it made me mad, because there ain't nothing to do outside, and it was dark out there."

Ivy took the black crayon and scribbled over the paper. "It was black dark."

Elsie watched her turn the paper black. Gently, she said, "Ivy, you told a policeman that Larry hit your mama with a bat."

The child's jaw clenched. She nodded.

"But Ivy—if you were outside, how do you know that?"

Ivy picked up the yellow crayon she'd used to color the hair on the stick figure. With angry strokes, she colored a spot in the middle of the rectangle. She looked at Elsie with eyes so fierce that for a moment, her face was not remotely childlike. "I peeped. I peeped in the window."

Elsie nodded. "And what did you see?"

"I seen Larry go after Mama. He punched her first, and she hit him back. Then he hit her in the head with the bat."

"Did he hit her anywhere else?"

The child's voice was a strangled whisper. "The belly."

Elsie knew the child was ready to shut down. "And what about Bruce?"

"He just smoked the pipe. On the couch. He didn't do nothing."

Ivy's face contorted. "He was her number two boyfriend. And he didn't do nothing." She flung herself onto the carpet, burying her head in her arms. Her shoulders heaved. Elsie watched in silence as one of Ivy's arms snaked out, groping for the crayons and the package of Play-Doh. She scooped them under her chest, clutching them with a protective arm.

Chapter Fifteen

Ivy slumped in the chair across from the pastor's desk. She pointed her toes, trying to touch the floor; but her legs were too short, the chair too high. She swung her legs, taking a peek at her new pink tennis shoes from Walmart.

The pastor smiled at her, his teeth shining like a wolf in the cartoon she saw on TV. Her foster mother let her watch cartoons every day, on Saturday and after school. The TV had cable. Before moving to the foster home, Ivy had never heard of cable.

"How's everything at home, Ivy?"

She scratched her nose; the itchy patch was getting better. "Good."

"You like your new house?"

"Sure."

"Bet your mom makes good food for you. Good, nutritious meals."

No answer.

"What'd you have for breakfast today?"

Ivy thought, took a moment to recall. "Cheerios."

"With bananas?"

She frowned. "No."

"I had cornflakes today. With slices of bananas and skim milk." He held up his arms like a bodybuilder. "Breakfast of champions."

Ivy flinched. She didn't like to hear about cornflakes and bananas. It was Larry Paul's favorite, too.

Last summer, on a rainy Sunday morning, they ate cornflakes and bananas in the trailer. By nine in the morning, Ivy's mama already looked tired and worn; she was still working at Smokey Dean's then, had been working all night. And Bruce Stout had brought his dog to the trailer the night before, and it peed on the rug again. Mama said she didn't have the energy to clean it up. Ivy's nose wrinkled from the stink of the dog's urine. But she didn't complain about it.

When Mama spoke up over breakfast, Ivy tensed in her chair. Because Mama brought up the baby again.

"Larry," she said, shaking her head wearily, "you got to help me out."

Larry hadn't answered; just stared at Jessie over the rim of his water glass.

She pulled the tattered bathrobe around her swollen belly. "This baby has flat wore me out. Smokey says I can't stay on at the plant much longer, I'm so big. You got to think about money. Maybe you can do more for Smokey. And shit, honey—you got to give me a hand around here. It smells like piss in here."

Ivy stole a look at Larry. His hand was beginning to shake; it was a bad sign. A bad, bad sign.

The cereal flew so suddenly that Ivy thought she dreamed it, but the empty bowl rested in Larry's shaking hands. And her mother's face, frozen in dismay, dripped with milk. Cornflakes fell from her cheeks, and a slice of banana stuck to her chin until she wiped it off. Then Jessie told Larry she was sorry.

"Ivy?" the preacher said. "Ivy, what are thinking about?"

She tried to focus on the preacher, but it took a moment. Because in her mind, she could only see flying milk and cereal, with bananas spinning in midair.

"Are you happy with your new mom and daddy?" He leaned back in his chair, looking at her with benevolent interest.

Something about his voice didn't ring true. Ivy wasn't used to people who didn't say what they meant. It confused her.

"You know they ain't real. Real mom and daddy."

The preacher shook his head with disbelief. "Why do you say that?"

"They ain't my people."

"Your what?"

Ivy tried to retreat into the chair, pushing back into the cushion. "My people. Family."

The preacher picked up a pencil and tapped it on the pad of paper in front of him. "Who are your people, Ivy?"

The question made her stomach twist. Because to answer it, she had to acknowledge her loss.

"Nobody," she whispered.

He leaned forward. "What's that? I can't hear you."

She stared at him, reluctant to speak of it again. Finally, she said, "Nobody. I got nobody."

The pastor spoke with a gentle tone. "Ivy, that's not true. You're blessed. You've been blessed with a foster mom and foster daddy. And a beautiful baby brother."

She looked away, unable to look him in the face as he spoke the lie. Her foster mom was nice to her. Bought her shiny new things at the Walmart, possessions Ivy had never dreamed to own. But she knew the difference between the way Holly Hickman looked at her baby, and the way she regarded Ivy. Kin was kin. Everybody knew that.

"And you have a big family. A big, big family." The preacher stretched his arms wide. "Everybody in this church."

Ivy cocked her head. She felt no particular kinship with all those people sitting in the congregation on Sundays, and on Wednesday nights.

"Do you know that?" Reverend Albertson asked.

She shook her head.

"Well, it's true. Do you know why it is? It's because you, Ivy, are a child of God."

Ivy digested the statement. It had a certain appeal.

"Why, Ivy, there's lots and lots of people in this town who care about you. I was just talking to a man the other day, and he made me promise to keep an eye on you. You know who that was?"

Ivy shook her head. How could she know?

"It was your mother's boss, before she passed away. Dean Mitchell, Jr. What do you think about that?"

Ivy sucked her lips over her teeth and pressed down so hard she bit herself. Smokey. Smokey was watching. Smokey was everywhere. Smokey wanted to know what she'd told the preacher. Wanted to know if she talked about the meth they kept at the trailer, to sell for Smokey. But she said nothing. Kept her mouth shut.

"How do you feel about your mother? The one who died?"

A jolting pain hit in Ivy's chest; she gritted her teeth. "I sure do miss her."

"Do you want to see her again?" His voice sounded like he was offering a candy bar. A Twix, or a Hershey's.

"She's dead," Ivy said, her voice flat.

"But we can be reunited. At the throne. Ivy, you can see your mother again, and the sweet baby who never opened his eyes. But there's one thing you must do."

"What?" Because she'd do anything. Anything, to see her mother. She wasn't so much interested in the baby. She never knew him.

"You must be born again."

The overhead light reflected on his thinning hair. He was older than Larry, mom's no-good boyfriend who had killed her with the bat. But Larry was hairy all over: his head and face and chest and back.

This preacher had a pink hairless face; and the thin golden hair on his pink scalp, parted and combed over, shone like a halo under the fluorescent light.

"You can be saved. Then you'll see your baby brother and your mother. You'll be reunited with them, and with our savior Jesus Christ. All you have to do," and he leaned forward like Larry handing somebody meth, "is come up on Sunday morning and be baptized."

Ivy didn't know that the preacher could be trusted. And she didn't like the idea of being up in front of the whole church. Too many eyes on her. It wasn't safe. But the offer was too tempting to pass up.

"Okay. I'll think on it." She lowered her voice to a whisper. "Maybe I'll do that."

Chapter Sixteen

It was midafternoon when Elsie opened the screen door into the courthouse coffee shop, delighted to see that it was nearly deserted. The morning coffee crowd and noon lunch diners had departed, leaving the cluster of gray Formica tables empty, save one in the corner.

The longtime proprietor Silas, a trim man in a stained apron, emerged from the cooler clutching a five-pound package of hamburger. "What can I get you, Elsie? Grill is still hot."

"Oh, thank goodness, Silas," she said. "I need a cheeseburger."

"Onion?"

"Yes, please. No lettuce or tomato."

"It'll be just a minute. You need a Diet Coke?"

"Oh yeah."

While Silas poured a soda from the fountain, Elsie unclipped a bag of Lay's potato chips from the dispenser and opened it. Leaning against the counter, she eyeballed the couple at the sole occupied table: it was Josh Nixon and a middle-aged woman with strawberry-blond hair fashioned into an elaborate pouf.

"Elsie," Nixon called. He waved her over. She picked up her Diet Coke and made her way reluctantly.

"Hey there," she said.

Nixon pulled out the chair next to his. "Sit," he said with false enthusiasm.

She slid onto the plastic seat. Pulling the paper from her straw with a tug, she gave him a no-nonsense look. "What's up?"

"Do you know Claire? She's from Springfield."

Elsie nodded, giving the woman a tight smile. "We've met. In court."

Claire O'Hara was a criminal defense attorney with a strong trial record and a tough reputation. She had worked as a defense attorney for twenty years, and was able to command some of the highest fees in southwest Missouri. Legend had it that Claire was a tiger, and she knew how to get the fee up front.

Claire extended a puffy hand. "Nice to see you again."

Elsie gave the hand a brief squeeze, noting that a half-dozen gold bracelets circled the woman's wrist.

Claire turned to Josh with a feral grin. "I was the defense attorney for one of Elsie's very first jury trials. A stealing case, I think."

"Embezzlement," Elsie said.

Claire ignored her. "The jury was only out for twenty minutes. That's a record for me—almost. Isn't that right? Wasn't it about twenty minutes before they found him not guilty?"

Elsie sucked on her straw. "Something like that," she said. Elsie recalled the twenty-minute verdict like it was yesterday; she'd wept in the stall of the woman's bathroom afterwards, battling self-doubt.

Claire nestled closer to Josh Nixon. "She was so wet behind the ears. I felt sorry for her, I really did." Claire laughed heartily, then stopped abruptly. "Can I have a chip?"

"Sure," Elsie said, offering the bag.

Claire took three. "My blood sugar. I'm getting woozy." She turned to Josh and gave him a girlish grin.

"Elsie!" Silas called from the counter. "Got your burger."

She picked up her Coke. "I should probably take it to go. Got stuff to do upstairs."

Josh reached out and gripped her arm. "Eat it here. We need to talk."

When he didn't release her, she looked down at his hand on her arm, and gave him an inquiring look. "We do?"

"Yes," he said in a decided voice.

Somebody wants to ditch old Claire, she thought with a mean fizzle of satisfaction. "Okay," she said, setting her Coke back down. Josh freed her arm. "I'll be right back."

She winked at Claire, who looked like she'd sucked a sour lemon. Elsie picked up the burger, pausing to snatch up packets of mustard and ketchup, and settled back in her chair.

Claire had taken over the bag of Lay's.

"What's cooking with you two," Claire asked in a deliberately casual tone. "Big bad case? Or big bad romance?" She turned on Josh with an insinuating smile.

He didn't look at Claire when he answered. "Elsie is part of the prosecution team in the *State v. Larry Paul* case."

Claire adjusted the sunglasses atop her head. "The murder case with the pregnant victim?"

Elsie and Josh both nodded, and Claire flashed a grin at them. "I don't envy you all being on either side of that old mess."

Elsie doctored her burger with the mustard and ketchup. "Murder cases are never uncomplicated," she said loftily.

"Is that right?" Claire said. "How many murder cases have you handled?"

Blood rose in Elsie's face. "One."

Claire chuckled. Jingling her bracelets, she said, "Josh, if you need any advice from the soul of experience, just give me a call. I'll be glad to lend a hand."

He nodded. "Thanks, Claire. I will."

She rose, hauling the leather strap of a cherry red Coach briefcase onto her shoulder. "I'll let you kiddos get to work."

Elsie was chewing on a bite of burger. "Nice to see you," she said with her mouth full.

"Oh sure, yeah. You know, Elsie, we have a friend in common."

Elsie raised her eyebrows, unsure who the friend might be.

"Dean Mitchell. Dean Junior," said Claire. She gave Elsie a knowing wink, turned her back, and headed out the door.

Elsie nearly choked on the mouthful of hamburger. She sucked down Diet Coke to help her swallow.

"Who's Dean Mitchell?" Josh asked.

"Dean Mitchell—Junior—is Smokey Dean. Son of Dean Mitchell, Senior, the original Smokey Dean. Dean Senior started the meatpacking and barbeque empire that Junior has inherited." Staring at the doorway Claire had departed through, Elsie said, "Yeah, that was a shot. Dean Junior was my blood enemy, back in school. To this day, I do my best to avoid him. Why on earth would she want to be pals with Smokey? He's mean as a snake. Good Lord, Josh, Claire O'Hara is insufferable." Elsie turned back to Nixon and gave him a raised brow. "But she seems to like you."

He expelled his breath with a long puff. "Thank God you showed up. I didn't think she'd ever leave."

"Faker. I knew you didn't have any business to discuss." Elsie stared inside her empty Lay's bag. "Bitch ate up all my chips."

Nixon reached into a folder and pulled out several pages. "Oh, there's always business."

While he sorted through the papers, Elsie said, "Did I mention that the tests came back on substances the police seized at the trailer the morning they took Larry Paul into custody? And the substance which looked suspiciously like meth turned out to be meth. Ashlock's wondering whether your client would like to answer some questions about that. Want to set that up?"

Nixon barked a humorless laugh. "Oh, I think Ashlock has done all the talking he's going to get to do with my client. Do you want to accept this copy of my new motion?"

"Yeah, sure. What is it?" Elsie pushed her plate to the side, so she wouldn't run the papers through hamburger grease.

"Request for leave to take a deposition. And here's something for you." He tore off the spare carbon of a bright pink subpoena form. "I figured you'll have to produce her."

As she scanned the pink subpoena, Elsie's brows made an angry furrow in her forehead. "What the fuck?"

"I'm going to depose her. The kid."

The subpoena Nixon had served upon Elsie ordered Ivy Dent to appear and be deposed in the case of *State v. Larry Paul.*

"This is unprecedented."

"Well, it's a murder case. And she's the only witness to the crime who's still available. Stout fled."

"She's six years old."

"Makes it even more crucial that the defense have the opportunity to fully examine her story."

Elsie jumped to her feet. "We haven't even held the preliminary hearing yet. You have no right, no right to do this now. I will oppose this."

Nixon leaned toward her, speaking in a conciliatory voice. "Sit down, Elsie; let's talk this through. This is a death penalty case."

"Goddamn it, Nixon, I can't let you take advantage of a child witness. I'm going to scream and shout to the judge on this. Why should you get to depose her when you'll have the opportunity to cross-examine her at preliminary hearing? You're double dipping. You just want to trip the kid up."

"I'll make a deal with you." He reached out and put a hand around her wrist but she shook him off.

"Fuck you. What can you offer that I'd want to hear?"

"Maybe I'll waive preliminary hearing."

The suggestion took her by surprise. She stepped back to the table. He pushed the chair toward her again. "Sit down."

She sat. "Is this a trick?"

"No trick. I'll waive preliminary hearing if you'll produce the kid for a deposition."

Elsie looked away, debating the merits of the proposition. Aloud, she said, "In a deposition, the judge won't be on hand to rein you in."

"True," he said. "But the defendant won't be there either."

Depositions could be long and messy, and a witness could be asked questions that a judge wouldn't permit in court. But the environment was far less intimidating than a courtroom, particularly for a child witness.

Elsie gave him a hard stare. "I want that waiver in writing."

"No problem. Do we have a deal?"

Elsie started to agree before she stopped in midphrase. "I'll have to run it by Madeleine."

Chapter Seventeen

NELL STOUT DROVE her dirty white Buick sedan slowly down Delmar Street. On the passenger side of the front seat, her son Bruce sat beside her, wearing sunglasses and a fishing hat studded with lures.

"They're going to know you're up to something, driving like that," he said. With his molars he bit off a length of beef jerky and chewed.

"You're scarfing down jerky and soda pop when we're trying to do a job here." Nell hissed in disgust. "No wonder you can't hold down a job. Even Smokey don't want much to do with you."

"Quit riding me."

"Well then, you keep your eyes open for the child. If we know when she comes and goes, you'll be able to snag her and see what's she's up to."

Bruce swallowed. "Why don't we just go on to her house?"

"Why don't you just choke on that jerky? We got to figure out what's going on."

"I know what's going on. Larry done got pissed off at Jessie and he gone after her with a bat. And she died. End of story."

His mother cut her eyes at him. "You don't know shit," she said.

When they neared Ivy's foster home, Nell drove past it and parked in front of a house two doors down. "Give me a piece of jerky."

Bruce took the bag from his lap and handed it over. Nell pulled a strip from the bag and nibbled the tough smoked hide with her front teeth, like a rabbit.

"Too bad your back teeth is gone. That ain't no way to eat jerky. You gotta tear it." And he demonstrated, gripping the hide between his back molars and pulling.

Nell swallowed, giving him a sour look. "When you get to be as old as me, you'll be glad to have a tooth in your head," she began, but paused as the school bus turned the corner and chugged down the street.

"Scoot down," she mumbled around the wad of meat in her mouth. "Make sure she don't see you."

"Don't tell me what to do," he said, but he slumped in his seat and tugged the hat lower onto his face.

The bus stopped at an intersection several houses down the street. Children exited the vehicle: two big boys, followed by a cluster of girls. After several moments passed, Ivy emerged, pausing to pull her blue backpack high onto her shoulders.

They watched her amble down the sidewalk, a sheet of manila paper in her hand. A girl in a yellow jacket was half a block ahead of Ivy, but she stopped and turned her way.

"Ivy," she called.

Ivy stopped on the sidewalk. She reached up and adjusted her glasses, but didn't move to join the girl on the sidewalk.

"Oh, Ivy," the girl in the yellow jacket called again, in a singsong voice.

In the Buick, Bruce whispered, "What's she doing?" but his mother shushed him.

The girl in yellow began to backtrack, advancing toward Ivy on the sidewalk. Ducking her head, Ivy stood her ground.

"Some friend of hers, you think? Maybe we ought to head out of here," Bruce said in an uneasy whisper; but Nell shook her head.

"Ain't no friend," she said.

The girl sauntered up, closing the distance between them on the sidewalk. "Whatcha got, Ivy?" she said, with a nasty smile.

Ivy narrowed her eyes. She didn't reply.

When she was within arm's length of Ivy, she shouted: "I know what you got! Ivy germs!" She reached out and knocked the paper from Ivy's hand.

But as the paper fluttered to the sidewalk, Ivy reached out and snaked her fingers around the other girl's wrist, then gave it a vicious twist.

The girl backed away, fighting to free herself. "Stop it! Let me go!" But Ivy doubled her hold, using both hands to hang on.

"You're hurting me!" She finally released herself from Ivy's grasp. "I'm gonna tell!" She turned on her heel and ran away.

Ivy knelt down onto the sidewalk and picked up the paper. With her hand, she dusted it off, then blew on it, and wiped it a second time. She let out a long breath, and tugging at the blue backpack with her free hand, Ivy resumed her path down the sidewalk.

In the Buick, Bruce cleared his throat, and pushed his fishing hat back into place. One of the lures snagged his finger, and he pulled it away with a jerk. "I don't know about this, Ma. Seems like a lot of people around here. Kids and everything."

Watching Ivy enter the front door of the yellow house, Nell shook her head.

"Nah. This'll be easy. Easy as pie."

Chapter Eighteen

ON THE DOUBLE-SIZED mattress in Elsie's one-bedroom apartment, she rolled onto her side and studied Ashlock. He lay on his back with his eyes closed, his chest rising and falling. The hair on his chest, she noted, was starting to turn gray.

They had just finished an evening romp, which though it was uncharacteristically speedy, had nonetheless gotten Elsie where she wanted to go. Staring at Ashlock's five-o'clock shadow, she thought that her orgasm was more the product of her own concentration than any particular attention on Ashlock's part.

He exhaled out with a deep sigh. It didn't sound like a sigh of ecstasy. She nudged him with a bare knee. "What are you thinking about?"

His eyes opened, and he looked at her with surprise, as though he'd forgotten she was there. "Huh?"

"What is going through your head? Is it Burton?"

Ashlock's teenage son was still a sensitive topic. Elsie had no intention of stepping in as a substitute for the boy's mother, and Ashlock had never indicated that it was a role he wanted her to fill.

When he didn't answer immediately, she said in a threatening tone, "Don't tell me you're thinking about your ex." Now that Ashlock was the primary custodian of his son, his communication with his ex-wife, a born-again Christian who was the mother of his son and two grade-school daughters, had become much more frequent. And contentious.

"Lord, no. Not her. Or Burton." He closed his eyes. "I've got to locate Bruce Stout."

Elsie kicked the tangled sheet out of the way and sat, leaning against the headboard. "That's really flattering. You're thinking about some dirtbag while you're screwing me."

Ashlock gave a halfhearted laugh. "Not during. After."

"Oh. That's different. Totally cool, then."

He rubbed his face with his hands. "Sorry, Elsie. I'm frustrated, that's all."

Scooting back onto the mattress beside him, she stroked his arm. "You don't need Bruce Stout to make our case. We have a ton of forensic evidence. We have the murder weapon. We have the little girl. And fuuuck, Ash," and she leaned in to whisper in his ear. "Larry Paul? He confessed."

He scratched the ear she'd whispered into. "Yeah. He did."

She propped herself on an elbow again. "You made him sing like a bird, Ash." And she was no longer worried about the Motion to Suppress that Josh Nixon had threatened, early on. Elsie had done her homework on the inebriation issue, and was confident that the law was on their side.

"But he said he wasn't alone that night. Bruce Stout was with him and Jessie Dent in her trailer."

"So? Are Bruce Stout's prints on the murder weapon?"

"No." He didn't sound convinced.

"Did Larry Paul try to attribute the murder to the other guy?"

"Not when I questioned him. But he was zoned out, stoned out of his mind. He'll change his story; he's bound to. And if I can't locate Stout, well—it leaves a hole."

Elsie sat up in bed. "It doesn't endanger the verdict. The case is airtight. Open and shut." She looked down at her bare thighs with a critical eye. It would be nice to have muscle tone in her legs. But it wasn't like she had all day to exercise. She covered them with the sheet and sat up straight.

Ashlock reached out and cupped her breast. "You're a pretty sight."

Elsie smiled. Sometimes he said exactly the right thing.

He gave a gentle squeeze and dropped his hand. "But there's no such thing as an airtight case. You know that as well as I do. The defense can always spy a pinhole."

She nodded, thinking. "You've already done a search for the other guy—Bruce."

"I've been to his house twice, once with a search warrant. Looked high and low. If his mother's hiding him out, she's not giving it up."

"He lives with his mother?" She reached to the bedside table, where a glass of Diet Coke sat. The ice had nearly melted, diluting it to a light tan color. She drank it anyway. "I thought you said he was in the drug trade."

"Small time. He's a no-account. Not smart enough to sell much."

"What does his mama think?" Elsie pressed the wet glass against her neck. The September evening was warm.

He scratched the stubble on his jaw. "Not sure what to make of old Nell Stout. She's worked in the kitchen at Smokey Dean's Barbeque as long as I can remember. Worked for old man Dean, before his boy took over the franchise. They may have her at the meatpacking plant now, outside the city limits."

"Oh shit. Smokey Dean, Junior. I can't stand him."

The mention of Dean Mitchell conjured up ugly visions of Elsie's adolescence. Dean had been a year ahead of Elsie at middle school in Barton. He was the biggest kid in school, the product of early puberty onset and unlimited access to his family's barbeque pit.

Whether he became a bully because of his size, his upbring-ing, or his nature, Elsie didn't know; but he had terrorized the middle school, taunting bespectacled girls like Elsie and flinging the bookish boys down the stairways. When the principal tried to penalize the boy, Smokey Senior—one of the most successful men in the county, with friends in local government and on the school board—hired a lawyer and threatened the school district with a lawsuit for harassment of his son. After that, no one even tried to restrain Dean Mitchell Junior's reign of terror.

"Smokey Dean is a dick. And his old man was a dick, until he died. Do you know what Junior used to do? He would hold my head under the water at the city swimming pool in the summer. I almost quit going." She took a gulp of watery Coke. "And it was hot as hell at my house."

"Son of a bitch." Ashlock caressed her arm. "I bet you put up a fight."

"I was no match for him. But my mother was." At the recollec-tion, she laughed aloud: when Marge Arnold learned the reason Elsie was avoiding the city swim park, she drove straight to the pool, hunted young Dean Mitchell down in the snack bar, and confronted him.

"She grabbed him by the ear. It was positively Victorian." Elsie threw back her head and crowed.

"Did it work?" Ashlock asked, grinning at the story.

"Yeah—for me, anyway. He looked for other victims, but he didn't fuck with me anymore. My mother was one woman who didn't put up with his shit." She pulled the hair off her neck, found a hair tie, and tied it back. "His dad went to the middle school that summer, and said if his son was assigned to Mom's English class, he'd sue."

"That boy would've benefited from a year under Marge's thumb." He threw the sheet back. "I better get going. Burton will be waiting."

"Can't he walk home?"

"It's getting dark; I'm not comfortable with him walking all that distance. We're across the highway. And he'll want to eat. Fourteen-year-old boy."

She wrapped her hand around his penis. "If you were fourteen, we could go for a second round."

He stroked her cheek. "If I was fourteen, you'd be in jail." He patted her hand and shifted to get off the bed. She released him.

"Guess I'm eating alone," she said. She'd been eating alone more often than not, since Burton moved to town.

"You can eat with us, if you want." His voice was noncommittal rather than persuasive; she knew he was only asking out of politeness.

"If you were fourteen, I'd be in kindergarten."

Zipping his pants, he said, "I bet you were a smart-mouthed kindergartner. But I wouldn't have messed with you on a bet, your mama is too scary. Hey, tomorrow's Saturday. Burton has a practice for the debate team. Want to get some lunch? Hang out, just the two of us."

Elsie shook her head. "Can't do it tomorrow. It's Mom's birthday, and I'm running around with her." She gave a weary sigh. "We got too damn many relatives, Ash. The only time I see you anymore is at the courthouse."

He didn't reply; just pulled her to him for a kiss, then walked away, buttoning his shirt as he left.

Chapter Nineteen

ELSIE PULLED HER Ford Escort off I–44 and drove down the highway loop of Mount Vernon, the county seat of Lawrence County, Missouri. When she reached the Red Barn restaurant, she took a right onto the gravel drive and pulled into the only empty spot on the lot.

"They're already busy. Hope we don't have to wait for a table," Elsie said.

Elsie's mother Marge unbuckled her seat belt. "It'll be worth it."

Inside the restaurant, a woman in black jeans with blond hair pulled back from her face with a rubber band greeted them. "There's a booth in the corner," she said, indicating the table with a nod of her head.

Beaming, Marge Arnold scooted into the booth as the waitress pulled plastic menus from their spot behind the napkin dispenser and set them on the table.

"You want the breakfast buffet today?" the waitress asked.

"No, ma'am," Marge said firmly. "Ordering from the menu."

"Can I get you all something to drink?"

After they asked for coffee and Diet Coke, Marge reached across the red-checkered table and squeezed Elsie's hand.

"This is so fun."

Elsie smiled. "Happy birthday, Mom."

Marge let out a happy sigh. Studying the menu, she said, "Daddy is so jealous. Breakfast at the Red Barn."

"He could've come along."

"He wanted to. But when he heard you were taking me to the flea markets in Carthage, he backed out. Daddy says he doesn't care a thing about other people's junk." She rolled her eyes. "He's working in the yard today."

The blonde waitress walked up, balancing two cups of coffee in her right hand, and set down the Diet Coke in front of Elsie. "What are you hunting for today, Mom?"

"Oh, you never know. Postcards of the Ozarks, maybe. Or lady head vases. They might have some pretty earrings like my grandmother wore. It's a treasure hunt."

"Mom, you could find that stuff on eBay."

"Now what would be the fun in that?"

The blonde waitress returned. "What can I get you all today?"

Marge smiled, handing back the plastic menu. "I'll have the chicken fried steak breakfast."

"How do you want your eggs?"

"Over easy."

Elsie ordered scrambled eggs and bacon. As the waitress walked away, she whispered, "Mom. That comes with three eggs."

"I know it does. It's my birthday."

"And you're not supposed to order eggs over easy in a restaurant." She trained a look of daughterly disapproval toward her parent.

"Says who?"

"There's a warning on the menu." Elsie pulled the menu back out to demonstrate, but Marge waved it away with a flip of her hand.

"That's just something they have to do. Silly business."

"Well, it's a regulation."

"Elsie, for goodness' sake. I have been eating eggs for fifty-nine years. If they were going to kill me, I'd be dead." She shook her head and exhaled in disgust. "These silly new rules. Did you know that they're petitioning the school board in Barton to regulate what parents can bring to the elementary school parties? No candies or cookies or cakes. Silliest thing I ever heard."

Elsie yawned. "I guess they're concerned about childhood obesity."

Marge scoffed. "As if that was the most terrible misfortune that could befall a child. Why Elsie, you were chubby in grade school."

It was a sore spot. "Thanks for reminding me."

"You were so pretty! Just a little plump. And when you got to be a teenager, you slimmed right down."

Their breakfast arrived. Elsie's bacon and eggs couldn't compete with Marge's sizzling feast of fried meat with gravy, eggs, potatoes, and biscuits spread across two crockery platters.

"I'll share," Marge said, but Elsie lifted a hand in dismissal.

"No, Mom; I want you to have at it."

Marge poked the fork into the yolk of one of her eggs. "There's more trouble heating up with the school board, you know."

Elsie was only half listening. Her attention was on her breakfast. "What's that?"

"That child. The little girl, your witness." Marge pressed her lips together. "Some parents are petitioning the school board to have her removed."

Putting her fork down with a clatter, Elsie said, "What the fuck?"

"Hush." Marge glanced around the busy restaurant to see whether they had been overheard.

"That little girl—her name is Ivy—has just experienced the most brutal loss of her mother. Witnessed it with her own eyes. The community should be lifting her up." Involuntarily, Elsie pictured the child's face, the broken glasses, and righteous indignation rose in her chest.

"They say she has AIDS." Marge whispered the word.

"Shit. Shit. Shit. Shit. Mother. She does not have AIDS."

Two heads at the adjoining booth turned to listen. Elsie ignored them. "Who's spreading that around? It's defamation."

Marge said, "I told the teachers that it's ridiculous, treating that little girl like Typhoid Mary. Because she won't spread AIDS. It's a sexual disease."

"Blood transmission spreads it. But it doesn't matter a damn, in this case. She doesn't have it."

Concern shone out of Marge's eyes. "Are you certain? Because I'd like to spread the word, see if I can stop the tempest before it goes too far."

"Quote me." Elsie took a savage bite of bacon, chewing fast and swallowing. "That kid can't seem to get a break."

Daintily, Marge sliced through the fried meat with a steak knife. "Honey, you have to get that child a new pair of glasses. Every time I see her picture in the paper, I just want to cry. She looks like something out of Tennessee Williams."

A mental picture of the child passed though Elsie's head. "She seems Dickensian to me." Like Oliver Twist, if he was a girl, she thought. Or Artful Dodger. Or some combination of both. "Mom,

I'm not an optometrist. But I'll mention it to her social worker—it's Tina, she'll get on it. You're right, we have to get her into some new glasses."

As Marge returned her attention to her eggs, Elsie thought: *Don't want the kid to creep out the jury.* She instantly regretted the thought, wondering how she could be so callous.

Marge was gazing around the restaurant, checking out the other patrons. As Elsie toyed with a slice of toast, she heard Marge gasp.

"There's Vera Brown. Oh my goodness gracious sakes."

"Who?"

"Vera Brown." Marge was speaking in a stage whisper, her face animated with delight behind her spectacles. "We went to school together, back at Barton High. Vera was the most darling girl in class. Pretty enough to be in the movies. First runner-up for the McCown Peach Queen."

Elsie followed her mother's eye and identified the target of her attention, an attractive woman with a luxurious head of waving hair that almost brushed her shoulders. "She still looks good. But if she was the beauty of McCown County, how come she came in second?"

The McCown County Peach Queen Pageant, a highlight of the annual county fair in August, was still a local tradition. In Elsie's youth, she refused to compete, and had attempted a grassroots campaign to eliminate the contest from the fair activities. The idea hadn't taken off.

Irritation flashed across Marge's face. "That Madeleine Thompson. Her daddy wanted her to wear that crown, and by God, he saw to it that she did."

Elsie perked up. "Madeleine's father stuffed the ballot box?"

Marge leaned across the table to whisper in Elsie's ear. "He influenced the judges. Namely, that awful old Dean Mitchell. I refuse to eat a bite of Smokey Dean Barbeque, as you well know. Because I don't respect them." Settling back in her seat, she frowned again, reliving the injustice. "Madeleine wasn't even a senior; she was three years behind us in school. She should've waited her turn. Looked like a beanpole in a swimsuit. Vera won the swimsuit competition."

Laughing, Elsie wanted to press her mother for details about Madeleine, but Marge jumped up. "I'm going to go over there and say hello."

As Marge headed across the restaurant, Elsie reached across the table with her fork, stabbed a large bite of chicken fried steak and ran it through the liquid egg yolk, smiling inwardly at the thought of Madeleine as Peach Queen. Had to cheat to wear the crown. In McCown County, some things never changed.

Chapter Twenty

Ivy sat at a long table in a book-lined room. Through a single window, the sun shone directly in, hurting her eyes. She adjusted her glasses, but it didn't help.

She sat so low in the wooden chair that her chin nearly rested on the table. She crossed her arms on the polished surface of the table, and used them as a cushion to bury her head, providing momentary relief for her sun-blinded eyes.

A sharp tap at the door startled her. She looked up: the door had a panel of glass with chicken wire embedded in it. Black letters were painted on the glass. She knew the letters, but couldn't make out the word: ETAVIRP. The man with the fancy suit, with a golden necklace dangling at his belly, poked his head through the door.

"Good morning," he greeted her.

He entered the room, baring a toothy smile in her direction. Ivy's foster mother followed behind him, the baby at her shoulder, wrapped in a blue flannel blanket.

"Do you all need me?" Holly Hickman asked in a tentative voice.

"What? What's that?" The suit man, settling into the chair at the head of the table, right beside Ivy's seat, turned his attention to her foster mom.

Holly said, "It's time to feed the baby. He'll fuss if I don't keep him on a schedule. I just thought I'd go find a quiet spot." Apologetically, she added, "If it's all right with you, Mr. Parsons."

Mr. Parsons showed all his teeth, uppers and lowers. Ivy was amazed to note that not a single tooth was missing. "You go right ahead. Take care of that big guy." Placing a hand on Ivy's shoulder he said, "Ivy and I will be just fine."

Ivy steeled herself to sit still, not to jerk away from the man's hand on her shoulder. She didn't like him, could sense that his smile was false. But she knew that this man was in charge.

As the foster mother hurried out of the door, Elsie slipped in.

"Where's Madeleine?" asked the man.

"Running kind of late. She'll join us as soon as she can." Elsie smiled at Ivy. "Hey, Ivy. How you doing today?"

Ivy nodded in response. She peeked at Elsie's bag, hoping it might hold presents for her. Probably not.

As Elsie settled in a chair across the table from them, Mr. Parsons pointed at Ivy and demanded: "When are you going to get her some glasses?" Ivy stared at his hand. He wore a big gold ring with a red stone in it. *He's rich,* she concluded. That would explain all those teeth.

A cross look crossed Elsie's face. "You're the third person this week who has asked me that question. You do understand: it's not the job of the Prosecutor's Office—"

He cut her off. "Then you light a fire under that foster mother. Or the social worker or whoever you need to deal with."

"Fine. I'll try."

Ivy struggled to straighten the glasses on her nose. The Band-Aid that held the arm together was clean. Her foster mother had put a new one on before they left the house this morning.

He lowered his voice. "What about the hair. Can you do something about her hair?"

Elsie shot a look at Ivy then turned back to Mr. Parsons and whispered, "Let's not discuss this right now, Sam."

"There won't be a later. I'm running back to Jefferson City this morning. And when I come back for preliminary hearing," and he stopped to wave in Ivy's direction from his seat at the table, "I want her to look presentable."

"Hush," Elsie said.

He looked at Elsie with disbelief. "Don't you tell me to hush."

"We shouldn't have to worry about a prelim, anyway. That's why we're here today."

Mr. Parsons raised his voice, but Ivy wasn't listening. She watched the sunlight sparkle on his ring.

"You think you can shush me like a subordinate? Like a child? I'm in charge here."

Again, Elsie whispered. "Don't hurt her feelings."

"I have come all the way down here to provide assistance to your office, in this godforsaken part of the state. I will not be shushed by a young upstart."

Elsie's face reddened and she opened her mouth to reply, but stopped when Ivy spoke up from the end of the table.

"I like them."

Both adults turned their eyes toward her. "What's that, young lady?" the man asked, baring his false smile.

"My glasses. I like them. They work good."

She swung her feet, hoping to mask her shame.

Elsie stood, picked up her bag, and came to sit at Ivy's left. In a quiet voice, she said, "They work, because they can help you see better. Right, Ivy?"

Ivy nodded, grateful for the understanding.

Elsie gave a smile, like she was about to tell a secret. "Did you know I wear glasses, too?"

When Ivy inspected Elsie's face, there were none to be seen. She shook her head.

Elsie widened her eyes. "Contact lenses. But I take them out at night, and put my glasses on."

Ivy didn't respond. She digested the information.

"I got my glasses in—let me think—the third grade, I guess. So I was a little older than you. Getting that first pair of glasses was exciting."

Ivy didn't recall any particular excitement. Her mom had been mad that they had to go to the clinic, two times, to get the job done. It was a lot of trouble, she recalled.

"Do you know what happened? I stepped on them in my bedroom and broke off the arm. My mom thought it was pretty careless, but what you gonna do? So we got new ones. When your glasses break, you replace them with a new pair."

Ivy looked from Elsie to Mr. Parsons in confusion, uncertain what they wanted from her. "I don't got no money. Glasses cost. I know that much."

"Oh, Ivy, honey," Elsie said, placing a warm hand on her arm. "It's not your job to get it done. I'll talk to your friend, Tina Peroni."

At the end of the table, Mr. Parsons opened a big pile of papers. "Now," he said in a loud voice, "let's get ready to roll, girls."

"Ivy," Elsie said in a soothing voice, "today a man will come and ask you questions."

Ivy stared through her glasses at the man seated at her right hand. "Him."

"No, not him; Mr. Parsons is here for the prosecution, for the State."

Ivy sighed. "A policeman."

"No," Mr. Parsons said, waving the palm of his hand in dismissal. "Not a nice policeman. It's the defense attorney."

Turning on Mr. Parsons with her lips pressed in a grim line, Elsie gave her head a little shake, but he ignored it.

"This is a deposition. Can you say deposition?" he asked.

Ivy gave him a flat stare. "I don't want to."

"What? Say the word?"

She didn't respond.

"Repeat after me. "Dep-o-zi-shun.""

The girl made no attempt to parrot the attorney's long word. She dropped her head onto her folded arms. Her voice muffled, she said, "Answer questions. I don't want to do that. Not today." She peeked out to see their reaction.

Elsie gave the man another look. Pulling a pink piece of paper from her file, she nudged it under Ivy's arm. "Do you like pink?"

After a moment, Ivy nodded.

"See this paper? Is it pink, would you say? Or purple?"

Ivy peeked at it. "Pink," she whispered.

"Look here," Elsie said. She placed her index finger on the line that bore Ivy's name. "Can you read that?"

"Ivy."

Elsie smiled, beaming encouragement. "That's right. That's your name. So this pink paper says that you, Ivy," and she pointed at the typewritten print again, "are coming here today— here's the date—to answer questions." In a confiding tone, she said, "This is official. That means you are important."

Mr. Parsons pointed his finger at Ivy. She didn't like to be pointed at. He'd done it three times so far, that very day. "Don't volunteer anything. Just answer the questions. Don't provide additional information."

Elsie's eyes closed for a moment, and her jaw hardened. When she opened her eyes to look at Ivy, her face was serene. "Whenever you are asked a question, just tell the truth. That's all you need to do. Easy-peasy."

The man opened his mouth to speak, but snapped his jaw shut when the door opened behind him. Another man entered, a good-looking guy. He didn't look scary at all. Ivy figured he was the kind of dude that Larry Paul could smack down with ease. But Larry was in jail. Ivy liked to think of Larry locked up in a jailhouse. It made it easier to sleep at night. Most of the time, anyway.

Josh Nixon entered, wearing creased khakis and a rumpled dress shirt, with sleeves rolled up to the elbows. His long hair, brown with streaks of blond, flipped over his forehead, and he tucked it behind his ear.

"Morning, all," he said, setting a Styrofoam coffee cup on the table. He had a fabric briefcase hanging from his shoulder. He pulled some printed pages from the bag before he sat down. "Beautiful day, huh?"

Samuel Parsons just nodded in reply. Ivy regarded Nixon with a blank stare.

Now that the deposition was about to proceed, Elsie was tensing up, though she took pains to hide it. She said, "When is your court reporter going to get here?"

"She's already here. It'll be Candy Miller; I saw her in the parking lot. Probably dodged into the coffee shop. Or the bathroom."

Elsie started to pull a disgruntled face, until she saw Ivy watching. Samuel Parsons swiveled in his chair. Folding his arms behind his head, he pushed away from the table and stretched his legs across the floor. The court reporter, a woman in her thirties in a figure-hugging red dress, arrived a moment later and almost tripped over his feet as she entered.

Parsons jumped up. "So sorry, ma'am. Hope you're not hurt," he said. His focus flickered from her bust to her face and back again.

"I'm fine," she said, turning to Josh Nixon with a lipsticked megawatt smile. "Josh, sorry to hold you all up."

Josh winked in reply, and her smile widened. Turning to Elsie, he said, "Elsie, you know Candy Miller, right? And Candy, this is Sam Parsons, acting as Special Prosecutor, from the Missouri Attorney General's Office."

"In Jeff City," Parsons added.

"I'll set up right here by you," Candy said, giving Josh a cozy nudge, "and we can start right up."

While she set up her court reporting device, Elsie placed her hand on Ivy's shoulder. "They will ask you whether you will tell the truth to the questions. Remember when we talked about telling the truth? That's all you need to do."

Josh Nixon shot Elsie a puckish glance, but she ignored it. "Okay, Ivy?" she said.

Ivy scooted back in the chair as far as her small body could go, and pressed her head against the chair back as if she wanted

THE WAGES OF SIN 119

to brace herself for the onslaught. She nodded, looking straight ahead.

Parsons said to Nixon, "We reserve all objections except as to the form of the question."

"Sure," Josh said, without looking in his direction. He studied Ivy.

The court reporter turned to Ivy and said, "Raise your right hand."

Ivy raised the left one.

To Candy Miller, Elsie said, "It doesn't really matter," but the court reporter repeated, in an insistent voice: "Right."

Elsie pushed Ivy's left hand down and tapped the right with her finger. Obliging, Ivy raised it.

Candy Miller said: "Do you swear to tell the truth, the whole truth, and nothing but the truth?"

Ivy didn't answer immediately. Finally, she said, "I don't know you."

Candy Miller looked startled, as if Ivy had spoken in an unknown tongue. At Sam Parsons's end of the table, a loud snort sounded.

Elsie did quick damage control. "Ivy, this is Ms. Miller. She's a court reporter. That means she'll write down every word we say today. It's her job. And it's her job to ask you the question about telling the truth. She's not trying to be nosy. She has to ask."

Ivy's face was still suspicious. "Okay."

Candy repeated the oath, and Ivy said "Yes" in a murmur.

"You'll have to speak up, Ivy," boomed Parsons's voice. "Can't hear you."

"Be a loudmouth," Elsie said to Ivy. "Like him." She gave the girl a conspiratorial grin, and Ivy's mouth twitched in response.

Elsie looked at Josh and nodded. He leaned on the table, tapping a pencil on the scarred wooden surface.

"Ivy, this is a deposition. I'll ask you questions, and you'll answer them. We'll start with an easy one. How old are you?"

"Six."

Elsie had expected another whisper, but the girl's voice was clear.

"Do you go to school?"

"First grade."

"What's your teacher's name?"

"Mrs. Fulton."

"Do you know what day it is?"

The girl screwed up her face, as if thinking hard. "We have a board at school with the day on it. But I didn't go to school today."

"Can you read and write?"

"Not good." She pushed the bridge of her glasses onto her nose. "Not too good."

In a quiet voice, Josh said, "Your mother died, isn't that right?"

Ivy dropped her head on the table; it made an audible thump when her forehead connected with the wooden surface.

"Does she need a minute?" he asked, unapologetic.

Elsie spoke, close to her ear. "Just answer his questions. Then you'll be done, you can go on back to school. You can be there by lunchtime. Recess, maybe."

The room was silent for several tense moments while all eyes were fixed on the child's scruffy head. When she finally lifted it, her face was stony.

"Larry killed my momma. With the bat."

"Who is Larry?"

"Mama's boyfriend."

"What's Larry's last name?"

"Paul. He's Larry Paul."

"Did he live with you and your mother?"

"Mostly."

"Where did you live?"

"In the trailer." She chewed her index finger. "Now I live in town. In a house."

"Did your mother work?"

Ivy shrugged. "Some. She worked at Smokey Dean's and she'd bring me barbeque home. But she got too big and her feet swoll up."

Parsons leaned back in his chair and motioned to Elsie, speaking in a loud whisper. "How could a woman with AIDS work in food service?"

Elsie answered impatiently. "ADA protection, I guess. AIDS is a disability protected under the Americans with Disabilities Act."

She turned away from Parsons, hoping to end the commentary. She heard him say, "But—food?" She ignored it.

Nixon asked Ivy, "Did Larry work?"

"Larry? At a job?"

"Well, yes. Work."

"No way."

Nixon leaned back in his chair. "Never?"

"Nah. He couldn't hold no regular job. He was always broke."

Nixon fell silent for a moment, scribbling a notation in pen. While he checked his notes, Ivy said, "If it cost a quarter to shit, he'd have to throw up."

Parsons let out a squawk. Nixon tried to catch Elsie's eye, but she wouldn't look his way. She scooted closer to Ivy, hoping to provide support through physical proximity.

Nixon asked, "Where'd you hear that?"

Ivy's face took on a hunted look. "I don't know. Everybody says it." After a pause, she added, "Not to his face," as if imparting a rule of etiquette.

"What's it supposed to mean?"

"Huh?"

"What you said. About if it cost a quarter—you know."

Ivy blinked at him behind the glasses. "It means he don't got no money."

"But who said it?"

Ivy stuck her middle finger in her mouth and chewed on it. Elsie could see blood seeping from the torn cuticle of the girl's hand.

She spoke up. "I object. This has been asked and answered."

Nixon waved Elsie off, looking irritated by the interruption. "This is a deposition."

"I know it is."

"Judge Callaway isn't here to rule." Nixon focused on Ivy again. In a voice that was deliberately casual, he said, "What do you know about Larry Paul's employment history? His earning capacity?"

"Don't answer, hon," Elsie instructed Ivy. Turning to the court reporter, she said, "I want to make a record of my objection, for the court to rule upon at a later time."

Nixon threw up his hands. "Why are you doing this?"

"Did you think this was going to be some macabre digging expedition? At the expense of a first grader? If so, you shouldn't have invited me."

Sam Parsons whistled between his front teeth; an admiring sound.

"Okay, all right; let's chill out. I'll move on. No problem." Nixon sounded deliberately cool. Elsie opened her mouth to frame a retort, then shut it. She had won this round.

Nixon leaned back, regarding the child. Elsie could see the

wheels turning in his head. She didn't like that look; she didn't know where the inquiry was headed next.

"Ivy. You told the police that you weren't in the trailer the night when your mother was hit."

"I told her." Ivy pointed her finger at Elsie. The cuticle oozed blood.

"Okay. But if you were outside, how did you see what happened inside the trailer?"

"I looked. In the window."

Nixon regarded her with solemn eyes. "What did you see?"

Elsie's heart did a thump in her chest; involuntarily, her hand reached out to cover Ivy's, but she pulled back and folded her hands tightly in her lap.

"He hit her. With the bat." The eyes blinked fast behind the glasses, but her voice didn't break.

"Where?"

Ivy didn't answer immediately. She cocked her head. "Everywhere."

"No, I mean—where were they in the trailer? Tell me what you saw."

"They was all partying. And Mama was on the couch, looking at TV. They wanted Mama off the couch, so they could see their show. She said her feet hurt." After a pause, she said, "Her feet was swoll up. Because of the baby."

"Did you hear this? With your own ears?"

Ivy nodded. "Yep."

"How, if you were outside?"

"Window was open. It was hot."

"Were there curtains? Or blinds?"

Ivy shook her head. "Got no curtains in the trailer, except

Mama put a tarp over the window in the bedroom. So people can't see us naked."

"When did he hit your mother with the bat?"

"I told you. She didn't get up right away when he said to. Because she was going to have the baby. Said she was wore out and swoll up."

"And he hit her with the bat because she wouldn't get up."

"She would've got up if he'd waited a minute. He was mean." Under her breath, she repeated, "He was mean."

Elsie was pawing through her notes with a frantic hand, trying to see whether the facts Ivy had just revealed in her deposition were consistent with her prior statement. Was the swollen feet/television scenario a new revelation? That was the problem with repeated opportunities to question a witness, particularly a child. Inconsistencies invariably cropped up.

Nixon paused, leaning back in his chair and scratching his head. Ivy leaned back and scooted her lower body down in the chair, touching her toes to the floor.

"Where did he get the bat?"

Ivy struggled to regain her position in the chair. "By the door."

"What door?"

The child blinked. "Trailer only got one door."

"Who did the bat belong to? Was the bat yours? To play ball?"

Ivy laughed. The sound made Elsie jerk in surprise. She studied the girl's face, amazed to see genuine mirth.

"I don't know nothing about playing ball."

"Who was playing with the bat, then?"

Her face darkened. "Nobody playing with the bat."

"So it was for protection, then."

"Huh?"

Patiently, Josh set his pen down. "Was it there in case a burglar came? An intruder?"

Ivy stared at him through the glasses, her face inscrutable. "It was for if somebody come that wasn't suppose to."

"All right, then." Casually, with an encouraging look, Nixon asked, "Did your mama and Bruce do some work on the side? To make extra money?"

An alarm went off in Elsie's head; rising to a half stand, she exchanged a look with Parsons, at the end of the table.

He jerked to attention. "Objection. Irrelevant."

Nixon smiled and nodded. "Your objection is noted. Ivy, you can answer."

"Oh no I can't."

The court reporter stopped tapping the keys on her device, and gave Josh Nixon a questioning look. He drummed his fingers on the table. "Don't worry about the objection, Ivy; this is a deposition. Answer the question."

"No."

The single word filled the room with tension that was palpable. Elsie scooted her chair closer to Ivy's. Nixon shot Elsie a pleading look, but she turned a blind eye, looking to Parsons for direction.

He shrugged. "Your witness," he said.

Elsie sighed. Tucking her hair behind her ears, she turned and leaned her head down, trying to make Ivy look at her, but Ivy wouldn't meet her eye. "Ivy, you can go ahead and answer. In court, we'd have a judge to say whether Mr. Nixon is asking questions that go outside of what was done to your mom. But in this room, there's no judge here, so you just answer now and we can try to fix it later."

Nixon was tapping the pen on his pad with a rapid beat. "Who used to come to the trailer, Ivy? To see your mother and Larry?"

She lowered her head and peered at him over the top of her glasses, a mulish expression on her face.

Long seconds ticked by. Elsie's hands started to sweat; she left a moist print on the wooden table before she wiped her hands on her skirt.

"Ivy," Nixon said, in a voice of command. "Tell me."

The child met his stare. "I don't never tell who come to the trailer."

"Why?" Josh asked. "Why not?"

The girl swallowed before she said, "Because I don't want to die and burn in hell."

Chapter Twenty-One

NELL APPROACHED THE front door of her house on foot, walking across the high weeds of her yard. Under dirty aluminum awnings, two large signs, hand-printed on cardboard, covered both of the windows facing the street. They read: NO TRESPASSING.

A big yellow dog was chained to the lone tree in the front yard, a large ginkgo tree. It littered the lawn with foul fruit in autumn, pods that emitted an animal stench when they were trodden upon. Nell walked through them, not bothering to tiptoe through the ginkgo berries. There were too many to avoid, and she had grown accustomed to them over the years. At her approach, the dog jumped up and barked ferociously, straining at its chain.

"Oh, hush your mouth," Nell said. "Shut the fuck up," and poised to aim a kick at the dog's ribs. The dog slunk back under the tree, its tail between its legs.

She opened the screen door, two panels of net sagging in a wooden frame. A boot-sized hole gaped in the bottom half of the screen.

"Bruce!" she said. When she heard no response, she raised her voice to a shout. "Bruce!"

"What?"

From the kitchen, Bruce ambled into the front room carrying a pizza box. "Jesus, Ma. Your shoes smell like shit."

She pointed a finger at the pizza. "Where'd you get that?"

"From Pizza Inn. What you think?"

Through the hole in the screen, the black ringtail cat entered the house with a dainty leap. It sidled up to Nell, rubbing against her ankles.

"When you gonna fix that hole," Bruce asked, dropping onto the couch in the front room and balancing the pizza box on his belly.

Nell reached down and slid her hand down the cat's sleek back. It walked between her legs and nudged her with its head.

"Funny you say that," Nell said, walking to the screen door and poking the hole with a dirty white athletic shoe. The sole of the shoe was gummy from the fruit of the ginkgo tree. "You done it."

"Go get me a piece of screen and I'll patch it."

"Nah."

"Why the hell not?"

"Cat likes it." Nell kicked the cat away from her feet and walked up to the couch. She stood over her son, watching him sink his teeth into the remaining crust of his pizza slice.

He chewed and said, "I can't fix it anyhow, cause you won't give me no money. Go get me a piece of screen and I can fix it right up."

Taking care not to upset the balance of the box, he picked up another slice and opened his mouth to receive the pointed end. Before he could bite into it, Nell slapped it out of his hand.

The pizza fell onto the tile floor, top down. Bruce looked at it with a woebegone face and then jerked to a sitting position, keeping a tight hold onto the remainder of his pie.

"What the fuck you do that for?"

Nell pointed at the soggy Pizza Inn box and asked, "How you done pay for that pizza?"

"Huh?"

"What'd you use for money? You're so broke, if it cost a quarter to shit you'd have to throw up."

Gingerly, Bruce picked the slice of pizza off the floor. Plucking a tuft of cat hair with his thumb and forefinger, he pulled the fur off of the slice and tossed the hair back onto the floor.

He took a bite. "From you," he said.

A battered handbag of faux brown leather hung from her shoulder. "I took my purse with me. So where'd you get that pizza money?"

He finished eating, swallowed, and cleared his throat. "From the stash."

Her eyes flashed; with a vicious swing, she flung the handbag into his face. "You goddamn fool. You don't touch that money." She pulled the bag back to strike again, and he covered his head with his arms, letting the pizza box tumble to the floor.

"Goddamn it, Mama. Stop it!"

She was poised to strike again when a ringtone sounded inside her bag. She dropped the purse on the top of the sofa cushions and dug inside, pulling out the phone and inspecting the caller identification.

"It's him," she said.

She glared at Bruce as she answered. She adopted a respectful tone as she said, "Hey, big boy."

As she listened to the voice on the other end of the phone, she walked over to the rust upholstered recliner and dropped down in it, stretching her legs out in front of her.

"Nah," she said. "Bruce is right here. Ain't left the house. Don't talk to nobody."

She nodded into the phone. "Like I told you before. The police come by. I said I ain't seen him. They come back with a warrant and tore through the house. I said I figured he done left town."

Bruce rolled over onto his side and watched her with a worried face.

"I don't know what they know," Nell said into the phone.

Bruce tried to communicate with a frantic gesture, but she waved at him in dismissal.

"How would I know what the kid's saying? They got her in a foster home."

Covering the phone with her hand, Nell nodded at the pizza crusts on the carpet. The cat was nosing around the box, sniffing it. "Pick that up," she said to Bruce, her voice a hoarse whisper.

Into the phone, she said blankly, "You want me to do what?"

The voice crackled though the cell phone. The cat jumped on Nell's lap, and she rubbed its head.

"We been watching. Been keeping a close lookout. You really think I need to go?"

After a moment, she ended the call with a weary sigh. Bruce sat up on the couch. "What he say?"

"He wants to know if you're keeping your head down. Maybe I should've told him you're getting pizzas delivered to the house. When you're supposed to be long gone. You don't watch it, he's gonna stick you in that hut behind the plant again. Where they do the real cooking."

"Some pimple-face kid brung it. He don't know me. What about Ivy?"

Wearily, she dropped into her recliner and pushed the foot-rest to an upward position. "We got to keep tabs. He says they're taking her to the Baptist Church, letting her talk to the preacher there."

"Huh. So what?"

She closed her eyes. The cat tiptoed up and settled on her chest.

"He wants me to stop by the church. Make sure she sees me. So she'll remember what's what."

Bruce hooted. "Mama's going to church! Damn!"

She opened her eyes. "I'd rather go to a goat-gutting."

Chapter Twenty-Two

AFTER A PROTRACTED Larry Paul strategy meeting on Thursday afternoon, Elsie left Madeleine's office and pulled the door shut. Chuck Harris's adjacent office was bustling with activity.

Doug, the traffic attorney, was lounging in the open doorway. His suit pants were wrinkled and his tie loosened, revealing that he'd unbuttoned the top two buttons of his white poly-cotton oxford shirt. "How am I supposed to cover two courtrooms at once?" Elsie heard him say.

She walked up beside Doug and popped her head into Chuck's office. "What's cooking in here," she said.

Breeon stood next to Chuck; they were focused on his computer screen. Without looking up, Chuck said, "We're trying to cover tomorrow's court schedule."

Breeon held a printed sheaf of papers in her hand. She pointed to a line on the first page and said to Chuck, "I'm in Rountree's court on a sentencing hearing at nine o'clock. Then I have a probation violation set for *State v. Breckenridge*. It'll take a while; the defendant hired Yocum, and he's fighting it. I can't help you out on the third floor tomorrow morning."

Elsie stepped inside the room. "Sounds like the Friday docket is rocking."

They ignored her. Chuck said, "Bree, I'll cover Carter's court until you're done. We've got Doug in Division 1. Doug, if another judge's bailiff pulls you out of Division I, you'll just have to deal."

Elsie tried to catch Breeon's eye; but she was studying the hard copy of the court docket, frowning. Elsie said, "Wish I could give you a hand."

"You and Madeleine will be in Callaway's court." Chuck's tone was frosty.

"God, I know; that will be a real love fest, right? I'll sit beside Madeleine with a gag over my mouth. She won't let me say a damn thing."

No one responded. Chuck clacked the keys on his keyboard. In the doorway, Doug pulled his gray necktie from its Windsor knot and shed it altogether, stuffing it into his trouser pocket.

"It's almost five o'clock. I'm heading upstairs, going to get ready to blow. Okay, Chuck?"

"Sure," Chuck said, pushing the chair away from his desk. "See you tomorrow, man."

Elsie walked across Chuck's office and dropped into a seat in the corner. "I'm meeting Ashlock at the Baldknobbers. Let's all run over there and have a beer. What do you say?"

Chuck and Breeon made eye contact. Elsie saw it and nearly squawked with surprise, hiding her shock with a cough. Chuck and Breeon had never established any personal kinship during his first year as chief assistant. Both Elsie and Bree had been righteously disgruntled by his appointment to the position, since both of them had more extensive trial experience than Chuck. What they lacked was political clout; and Chuck had political connections through his father, a big-time Republican in Kansas City, Missouri. Both women knew that Madeleine gave the job to the person who could provide the most political benefit.

Chuck answered Elsie first. "No Baldknobbers for me, thanks. I'm exhausted. Pretty tough running the office by myself, since you and Madeleine have confined yourselves to the Larry Paul case. I am wore slick."

Elsie eyed him as he sat behind his desk. His auburn hair was gelled into place; his shirt still appeared freshly pressed, and his tie looked bandbox fresh. His clothes bore no sweat stains or ketchup marks; his head showed no evidence of hands tearing through his hair in frustration.

But Elsie donned an expression of deep sympathy and said, "Then it's doubly important for you to come out tonight. So you all can relax and unwind."

Chuck opened a desk drawer and pulled out a set of keys. "Sorry, Elsie; but I think we should avoid that kind of thing for now. I can't be a party to any conversations about the murder case, since I'm possibly a state's witness. Madeleine doesn't want me to be tainted." His jacket hung from a wooden hanger on a hook near the door; he shrugged into it.

Elsie crossed and uncrossed her legs as she tried to frame the right response. In an encouraging voice, she said, "No need to stress over it, Chuck. You're not a part of our case in chief; Madeleine told me so. You can't shed any light on the actual murder. You just witnessed a prior incident of abuse. She may not use you at all."

She watched him, hoping to see a nod or smile; positive acknowledgment of some kind. But he turned his back.

"No need to stress. Right. Thanks." His voice was gloomy.

Giving her head a shake, Breeon left Chuck's office and walked down the hall, fanning herself with the paper copy of the Friday court docket. Elsie quickly departed Chuck's domain and followed a couple of paces behind Bree.

"Bree! Hey, big sis." Bree turned to acknowledge Elsie's voice and Elsie jerked her thumb in the direction of Chuck's office. "What's up with Mr. Kansas City? He's playing like he has a case of PTSD."

A shadow passed over Bree's face. "Back off Chuck, okay? He's having a tough time."

"You mean because he has to run the dockets? He wanted to be chief assistant. Isn't that supposed to be his job?"

Bree's voice dropped to a whisper. "He's struggling, Elsie. Torn up with regrets, about what he witnessed and how it led to murder just days later. He and Lisa have split up over it. I've been telling him," and she paused to look around the hallway, "He should get counseling. Professional help."

"Wow. I didn't know." The notion of Chuck suffering a clinical case of angst didn't fit his profile; but maybe she didn't know him that well. She caught Bree's eye and offered up a big grin, hoping to lighten the atmosphere. "You want to meet me at the Baldknobbers? I'll buy you a beer."

Breeon made a face, wrinkling her nose and pulling down the corners of her mouth. "That's not my favorite venue."

"Yeah, I know that; but Ashlock and I are meeting there. And I'd love to get to chat with you. We haven't talked in days and days."

"That's true." Breeon turned a doorknob and entered her own office. "Not since you got busy with the Larry Paul case."

"About that—I'd like to run some stuff by you, pick your brain," Elsie began, but Bree cut her off.

"Sorry. Not interested."

Elsie's mouth fell open in surprise. "You won't help me? Won't even talk to me about the case?"

"Nah. Don't think so."

Elsie struggled with feelings of injury as she watched Breeon pack up her briefcase. After a tense moment of silence, Elsie said, "But you're my best friend. And my best coworker, for that matter."

Bree gave the clasp of the briefcase a decisive click. "I don't believe in what you're doing. I'm opposed to the penalty you're seeking in this case. So—if I won't take the case myself, out of principle, how would it be any different for me to provide you with assistance?"

Elsie's eyes stung. She and Breeon had formed a bond that dated back to her first days in the office, when she'd been a green lawyer fresh out of law school. Breeon had taken her in hand from the beginning, showing her the ropes; helping her with her first witness interviews and examinations; providing copies of motions and jury instructions. She always had her back. Until now.

Elsie tried to keep her voice even. "If I promise to stay away from shop talk, will you come on out with me?"

"Hmmm. Don't think so." Breeon avoided Elsie's gaze. "I need to go to the grocery store. I'm pretty much out of everything. Got a growing girl to feed."

Elsie knew she couldn't trump the working mother card. Breeon was a devoted mother. But on this occasion, the grocery excuse rang false. *Betcha she has a house full of food,* Elsie thought darkly, as she turned to make her way out of the office. She checked her phone for messages; Ashlock had texted an hour ago.

Running late, he said.

Aw shit, she thought. *I'm drinking alone.*

Again.

Chapter Twenty-Three

WHEN ELISE PULLED up to the gravel parking lot of the Bald-knobbers bar, she had her pick of parking spots at the front door. She pulled her car directly under the sign depicting a grinning hill-billy in a straw hat, smoking a corncob pipe. Years ago, a local joker had blacked out several of the hillbilly's teeth and added a mustache. The management never bothered to correct the modification.

She wasn't surprised to see that the joint was hopping. The empty parking lot out front was deceptive. Many patrons chose to park their vehicles in back, behind the bar, lest their cars or trucks be visible to passersby. In a small town, people didn't want to be associated with a barroom.

She slid into a booth, greeting Dixie, the longtime barmaid, with a wave. Dixie bustled over, her curly gray hair damp with sweat.

"You're busy, girl. They're working you tonight," Elsie said.

Dixie pulled a woebegone face. "This place is going to kill me, I swear. You want a Corona?"

Elsie started to nod, then reconsidered. "Gin. Gin and tonic."

"Call gin? Or the house rotgut?"

Letting out a weary sigh, Elsie said, "Tanqueray. It's been a hell of a week."

Dixie returned to Elsie's booth in a wink and set a tall tumbler in front of her. "We got a two-for-one special until seven o'clock, but we're running out of short glasses. I made you a double in a big glass. That suit you all right?"

"Fine by me." She took a gulp and closed her eyes, waiting for a hint of a buzz.

"Well, look who's here."

Elsie's eyes popped open. Sliding into the booth across from her was Claire O'Hara, waving a long cigarette. "Remember me?"

"Sure," said Elsie, instantly wary.

Claire dropped a pack of silver Marlboro 100s onto the wooden tabletop and reached for the black plastic ashtray that sat beside the salt and pepper shakers. "Mind if I smoke?"

Elsie regarded Claire through the smoky haze that filled the bar. "It's okay." One cigarette wouldn't alter the Baldknobbers experience. Though a recent nonsmoking ordinance had been enacted in the city of Barton, existing barrooms were exempt.

Claire gestured at Elsie's cocktail with her cigarette. "The Larry Paul case already has you sucking down the hard stuff. Drinking your martini out of an iced tea glass."

Elsie bristled. She made a show of toying with the cocktail straw and pushing the glass away, as if she didn't care for the beverage. "It's happy hour," she said, affecting an air of nonchalance. "And it's not a martini," she added. Not quite, she thought.

"How are you sleeping these days?" Claire's knowing smirk sent a shiver down Elsie's back. Involuntarily she shuddered, but tried to cover by tossing her hair over her shoulder.

"I don't know what you're talking about."

"Big fib." Claire took a deep pull on the cigarette, leaving a scarlet ring around the filter tip. "You're having some crazy nightmares."

How does she know, Elsie wondered. Elsie had battled insomnia in the past week. Afraid her face would give her away, she bent over the gin and tonic, stirring it frantically with the cocktail straw. She lifted the glass and took a swallow from the rim.

Dixie passed by the table. "What can I get you ladies?"

Claire stubbed the cigarette in the ashtray. "I'll have a club soda with lime. Bring my friend another of whatever she's having."

Elsie said, "Really, I don't need—"

But Claire waved her objection away. "It's on me. A friendly gesture. From one barrister to another." As she lit another cigarette, Elsie studied the jewelry on Claire's hands, the bangle bracelets circling the wrist of the left hand and two big rings on her right, one with a diamond cluster, the other a square-cut emerald.

Claire noticed. "I like shiny things. Just like a crow." She waggled her pinkie, the finger adorned with the emerald. "I just picked this baby up in New Orleans. On Royal Street. They wanted a fortune for it. But I have negotiating skills." She puffed. "An advantage of the profession."

Sitting across from Claire made Elsie nervous. To fortify herself, she knocked back the tall cocktail in record time. She was glad to see Dixie arrive with fresh drinks. When the waitress tried to take away the near-empty glass of gin, Elsie snatched it, tipped it back and drained it dry first. Then she took a sip of the fresh one. It was stronger.

Elsie leaned back in the booth. The gin was starting to do its job. She even found herself warming up a hair to Claire. *Hair to Claire,* she thought with good humor. *That rhymes.*

"What are you doing at the Bald? You're hanging around McCown County pretty late. Don't you know that we don't like the sun to set on a city slicker's face?" Elsie grinned at Claire, only half joking.

Claire barked a laugh. She turned in her seat and peered around the bar. Even for a Thursday night, it was crowded; the pool table had a circle of players and onlookers, dressed in jeans and T-shirts. All of the booths were occupied, and only a table or two sat empty. At the bar, men perched on stools, their generous derrieres hanging over the sides. The volume of the bar noise was increasing as the patrons drank.

Elsie looked around, too, hoping to see Ashlock walk through the door. *Rescue me,* she thought. *Come on come on come on.*

"I've got a date."

Elsie turned back and focused on Claire. She lifted the gin and gulped at it before asking, "Local boy?"

Claire smiled with the mystery of the Sphinx. "Kind of." Nodding at the front entrance, she beamed. "Here he comes."

Elsie twisted around in the booth. Josh Nixon was making his way toward them, his jacket hooked over his shoulder.

Claire's smile showed all of her teeth, like a piranha. She patted her red pouf of hair. *She's got it bad,* Elsie thought. Josh Nixon set all the local hearts a-flutter.

Josh stood at the end of the table. "Sit down," Claire said, scooting over to make room.

He eyed Elsie before turning back to Claire. "I thought we were going to talk."

"We are." Claire patted the vinyl upholstery. "Sit down and relax."

The sight of Josh's ambivalent expression gave Elsie an overwhelming desire to laugh. She could feel a snort working its way up her chest; to stifle it, she bent her head over her cocktail and sipped though the straw.

Nixon sat by Claire, keeping a hands-breadth distance between them. As he pulled his tie from his collar, he asked, "What are we drinking?"

Claire rattled the ice cubes in her glass. "The defense bar is drinking club soda. I'd advise you to follow my lead. We don't have the local police force in our pocket."

Elsie considered biting the bait, but didn't want to launch into battle; she was beginning to enjoy the gin's magic. When Josh ordered an iced tea, she raised her glass to Dixie as a signal.

"Have you heard the news? About me and Mr. Nixon?" Claire was looking at Elsie expectantly, her fuchsia lips curled in an insinuating smile.

"You're engaged," said Elsie, deadpan. *I am so fucking funny,* she thought, though a voice somewhere at the back of her head sounded a warning: *You think you're funny because you're drinking gin.* The voice sounded like her mother. She shook her head to dismiss it.

Josh didn't laugh, but Claire did, throwing her head back and crowing till her red pouf shook.

"Oh please. He should be so lucky." She reached over and squeezed his forearm. He moved it away. "We're cocounsel, girl."

Elsie stared at Josh. "On what?"

"*State v. Larry Paul,*" he said. His eyes flicked to the side.

Befuddled, Elsie toyed with her straw, using it to pierce the lime in her cocktail glass.

"How does that work?" Elsie asked. She pulled the lime off the cocktail straw and sucked on it. Claire O'Hara was not part of the Public Defender system; as a private defense attorney, she was not in a position to participate in the defense of an indigent defendant. "Who's paying you?" Because that was the million-dollar question. Claire O'Hara was well known for her ability to exact "Mr. Green" from her clients. Ms. O'Hara never gave it away for free. And the Missouri Public Defender's Office was flat broke.

"Pro bono, baby." Claire lifted her glass and shook it again. It no longer rattled; the ice had melted. But it set off the fire in her diamond ring. Elsie blinked.

"You are taking on a death penalty case for free. For nothing."

"For fun." Claire crossed her arms on the table and leaned forward, placing her cleavage right in Elsie's range of vision. Though she knew she should look away, she stared in fascination. "Madeleine and I go way back."

Oh shit, she thought. But it was no surprise that other women lawyers might have a vendetta against Madeleine Thompson. The cast of characters in the Larry Paul case was growing increasingly more complex.

"You think the judge will let you do that?" she asked.

"Judge Callaway? He invited me. We're old pals. And it just doesn't seem right, all that attorney general power at the prosecution table, and poor little old Josh, just sitting alone."

Josh looked distinctly uncomfortable. Elsie pulled a face, conveying disbelief. "What does your office in Jefferson City say about this?"

He didn't get the chance to answer. Claire said, "Oh, they're so busy. They were really appreciative. Their capital murder team is buried right now. What is it about prosecutors in Missouri? So hungry for blood. 'Off with their heads!' "

Dixie delivered Nixon's iced tea, and he nodded in acknowledgment. "Claire, there's a booth in the corner that's emptied out. We can talk over there."

He stood and said to Claire, "You ready?"

"Oh yeah," Claire said, scooting down the cushion to follow where Nixon led.

As Claire rose from the booth, Elsie gave her a big smile. "See you in court," Elsie said.

Claire leaned down and whispered in Elsie's ear. "You've got a big chunk of lime pulp in your teeth."

Elsie dug in her purse, hunting for a mirror, but couldn't find one. She'd left her makeup bag at home. She sucked her teeth; she could feel the lime, but it was stuck so tightly she couldn't dislodge it. Draining the last mouthful of her drink, she swished it like mouthwash, but made no headway.

Diving into her purse again, she located her phone and checked her messages: nothing from Ashlock. She glanced at the clock over the bar. She'd been waiting for almost an hour, even taking into account that the clock was set ten minutes fast, registering "bar time." She dashed off a quick text: *Where u at? Bored AF.*

Rubbing her tongue over her teeth, she decided to visit the bathroom to battle the lime pulp. A weathered sign that hung over the entrance to the Baldknobber restrooms read, YOU DON'T BUY BEER! YOU RENT IT! She figured the adage applied to gin as well.

Making her way to the bathrooms in the back, she bumped into a young man bent over the pool table, aborting his attempt to shoot a striped ball into a corner pocket. He shot her an angry glance. It occurred to Elsie that she might be losing her equilibrium. It was always the first skill to go, when Elsie drank spirits. Balance first, power of speech last. It had occurred to her on many occasions that she'd be better off if it was the other way around. She tried to estimate the number of shots she had consumed in the past hour. Four? Maybe five?

She gave a toothy grin in the mirror, and decided, in her gin euphoria, that she liked what she saw. "Girl, you're looking good," she said aloud, and pulled out a lipstick. She unfastened her pink silk blouse and removed her bra, stuffing it into her knockoff Tori Burch handbag, her genuine "*Toni* Burch." Then she buttoned her blouse back up, but only partway. Elsie checked herself out in the mirror again, studying her reflection in profile. She would never be considered a willowy figure, but carrying extra weight had its charms.

Full of good cheer, she exited the bathroom and nearly bumped into Dixie, who was carrying a tray loaded with beer bottles. Stepping out of danger, Dixie gave Elsie a sharp once-over. "Things are heating up around here, I reckon," she said, with a meaning look at Elsie's blouse.

"Yeah. I think you slipped me a mickey."

Dixie hooted, her face wrinkling with laughter. "Oh you'd hate that, all right." She ducked by Elsie and headed to a table beside the pool table, holding the tray aloft.

The front door of the bar opened, briefly illuminating the room. Squinting at the doorway, Elsie identified the silhouette; Ashlock had arrived at last.

She made a run for the entrance. "Ash!" she cried, throwing her arms around his neck. Pressing her unbound chest to his, she gave him a lingering kiss.

They parted. He held her at arm's length, looking first at her breasts and then into her eyes.

"Oh shit," he said. "Gin."

Elsie sighed, smiling like the Madonna. "Yeah, baby. Gin."

Chapter Twenty-Four

SHORTLY BEFORE NINE o'clock the next morning, Elsie checked her appearance in the mirror on her office wall. Scrutinizing her face, she thought no one would detect that she'd been buzzed the night before. A slight pallor was corrected by a careful application of cosmetics. No lingering pulp could be seen in her teeth.

After her enthusiastic greeting at the Baldknobbers, Ashlock had hustled her out of the bar in a hurry; despite her protests that she was fine, absolutely fine, he drove though the McDonald's near her apartment, ordering a Big Mac meal to go. When she invited him up to her place, offering to share her french fries, he declined at first. But the display of her cleavage worked as a charm, and he decided to come inside for a minute.

The minute had stretched into a frenzied interlude on her living room sofa. Recalling it, Elsie smiled with smug satisfaction. She loved it when Ashlock lost control. As a rule, he was so tightly wound.

The Big Mac from the night before felt like a boulder in her belly. She swallowed some coffee, but it didn't provide any relief.

She heard Stacie shout outside her office door. "Elsie! The attorney general is here! Madeleine wants you!"

Elsie's office was across the hall from Stacie's domain, the reception area, and the receptionist generally didn't bother picking up a phone to communicate with her.

Clutching her coffee, Elsie walked down the tiled floor of the hallway to Madeleine's office. Shortly they would appear before Judge Callaway on recent defense motions in *State v. Larry Paul*; and though Elsie knew she would be the silent partner, she had dressed for success, donning a new suit she had picked up at J.C. Penney.

The door was open, but she knocked on the wooden frame, anyway.

"Ready for me?" she asked brightly.

Sam Parsons sat in the armchair closest to Madeleine's desk, reviewing hard copies of the motions. Madeleine was sipping coffee from a porcelain cup with a gold rim.

Elsie took a seat on the sofa near Parsons and set her Styrofoam cup on a nearby table.

Madeleine stared at Elsie over the rim of her cup. "What is that?"

Instinctively, Elsie sucked her teeth. "What?"

Setting the cup into the saucer with a clank, Madeleine removed her reading glasses, letting them dangle from a beaded chain. "Oh my Lord. Come over here."

Elsie walked up to Madeleine's desk. Madeleine waved at her to come closer, and snaked her manicured hand into Elsie's armpit. Elsie felt a tug.

Madeleine displayed her find; she twirled the price tag, which dangled from a plastic string. "You would walk into court like that? With the tags hanging from your clothes?"

Parsons looked up from his paperwork. "Hey! It's Minnie Pearl," he said, laughing.

"Who's Minnie Pearl?" Elsie asked Madeleine; but she was studying the tag.

Madeleine poised her glasses on her nose, as if she thought her eyes deceived her, and reread the numbers on display.

"Fifty-nine dollars?" she said in a shocked whisper.

Elsie flushed. "It was on sale." She turned on her heel and walked back to the sofa. It was uncharitable for Madeleine to mock her new suit on the basis of price; of all people, Madeleine knew Elsie's pay scale. And though it was true that Madeleine was a fashion plate, by McCown County standards, her top-drawer clothing was made possible by her wealthy husband, the John Deere distributor for three southwest Missouri counties.

Samuel Parsons checked his watch and pushed out of the arm-chair with a grunt. "Showtime, ladies." He spat lightly into the palm of his hand, rubbed his hands together and slid them over his hair. Elsie looked away, struggling to keep her face a blank. She didn't know men used saliva as hair gel. She hoped he wouldn't attempt to shake hands with her this morning.

They walked the short distance to Judge Callaway's court-room in single file, with Parsons in the lead and Elsie bringing up the rear. He held the door open for the women. As Elsie walked through, he winked and whispered, "Nice suit."

Frowning, she hurried to the far counsel table and took the end chair. After her experience with the defendant in Judge Carter's court, she determined that she'd keep a safe distance from Larry Paul. If he intended to suck his finger in court again, he'd have to make it through several other bodies before he could reach Elsie.

She didn't want spit rubbed onto her new suit. Even if it did cost fifty-nine bucks.

The door opened and Josh Nixon walked in, accompanied by Claire O'Hara. Madeleine had been arranging her pens in an even row beside her files. When she saw them, she stopped short.

"What are you doing here?" she asked Claire, her voice sharp.

Claire gave an easy laugh. Dropping her briefcase at the defense table, she walked up to Madeleine and rested her derriere on the prosecution table directly atop Madeleine's ink pens. She looked down the bridge of her nose at Madeleine. "Counsel for defendant appears in person," she said in a throaty voice, then turned to Elsie. "How's your head, kiddo?"

Madeleine turned to Elsie with a jerk, but she melted back into her seat with an innocent face.

Elsie was spared the ignominy of Madeleine's cross-examination because the bailiff, Emil Elmquist appeared, slamming the door behind him as he called, "All rise! The Circuit Court of McCown County is in session, the Honorable Judge Callaway presiding."

Elsie stood. Claire slipped off the tabletop and cruised back to Josh Nixon, swinging her hips. Judge Callaway slipped into his seat on the bench, adjusting the folds of his black robe. "What are we getting done here today, counselors?"

Josh Nixon spoke. "Your honor, my client isn't present."

Judge Callaway and his bailiff exchanged a look. "We'll let him stay where he is this morning, Mr. Nixon."

"Your honor, we have important motions pending."

The judge inclined his head; the overhead light reflected a silver circle on his bald head as he flipped through the paperwork. "Mr. Nixon, we can certainly attend to the motions, guaranteed. Mr. Paul doesn't need to appear. He is amply represented today by the

Public Defender's Office, and also by Miss Claire O'Hara." To his clerk, the judge said, "Be sure to note Miss O'Hara's appearance for the defense on the record."

Madeleine stood. "Your honor, what is the purpose of Claire O'Hara's appearance in court today?" In her hand, she held one of her many pens; Elsie watched her clench it with her bony fingers.

Claire swung toward the prosecution table with a gleeful expression. "Counsel for the defense appears. And the purpose—which should be fairly obvious, even to you, Madeleine—is to provide representation for the accused."

The pen jerked in Madeleine's grasp. "The defendant claims to be indigent. The state public defender has been appointed to represent Mr. Paul."

The judge focused on Madeleine with a determined countenance. "And the public defender will be assisted by Miss O'Hara."

"But your honor—"

"Mrs. Thompson. This is a death penalty case. You've made that clear." He turned to the defense. "Take up your first motion."

Elsie watched as Madeleine took her seat, placing the ink pen neatly beside her file, and then clenching her hands together in her lap, so tightly that it looked painful. *Maybe having the role of the silent partner in* State v. Larry Paul *isn't so bad,* Elsie thought. *This case ain't gonna be no hayride.*

"Which motion shall we take up first? Mr. Nixon? Miss O'Hara?"

Elsie peered over to the defense table, curious to see which attorney would act as spokesperson and take the lead. Claire turned to Nixon with a smug smile and gave him a wink, slightly inclining her head in his direction. Nixon stood.

Mama is letting Sonny drive the car, Elsie thought. Her lips twitched with amusement; she pressed them together.

"Your honor, the defense has filed a motion for change of venue. If you want to schedule it for an evidentiary hearing, that's fine; but there's no doubt what the outcome will be."

Judge Callaway ran his hand over his bald pate, making his shrine ring glisten under the overhead light. "The case will be tried in McCown County."

Elsie blinked in surprise. She turned to speak with Madeleine, but she was whispering to Parsons in urgent tones.

"What about that? We're best off in McCown County, aren't we? That's what I want."

Parsons said, "You want reversible error? You want to try the damn thing twice?" Elsie leaned in closer, to listen; but Nixon spoke again, leaving the counsel table and advancing on the bench.

"Your honor, my client can't get a fair trial in McCown County."

"Of course he can."

Nixon's face began to flush. "The jury pool in this county is contaminated. My client is entitled to a jury that is fair and impartial, twelve people who haven't heard about the facts and made up their minds already."

From the defense table, Claire O'Hara added, "A jury that will base its verdict on the evidence alone."

The judge sighed, tugging at the sleeves of his robe. "Simmer down. He'll get a fair trial. We'll hold the trial in McCown County. We can import the jury from another county in Missouri."

"Josh!" Claire hissed at him from the defense table. He walked over, and they huddled together.

At the prosecution table, Elsie scooted close to Madeleine. "What do you think?"

Madeleine ignored her. "What do you make of that?" she asked Parsons.

He grimaced. "We sure as hell don't want to start out this case with reversible error. But if he brings in a jury selected in a different community, we should be okay. It's been done."

Josh spoke. "St. Louis. We want the jury to come from St. Louis."

Judge Callaway smiled, beaming down at Nixon as if he'd cracked a witty joke.

"St. Louis? Really, Mr. Nixon?"

Claire rose and sidled up to her cocounsel. "It's a valid suggestion, your honor. St. Louis is one of the largest cities in the nation and a safe distance away from here. A murder in southwest Missouri wouldn't receive much attention in the St. Louis media. The jury pool would be excellent for our needs."

"I don't think our taxpayers in McCown County would approve of importing a bunch of city mice from St. Louis to decide matters here in the country. I was thinking, I don't know—maybe we'll bring them in from over there in Springfield."

Nixon threw his file on the counsel table. Claire reached over and grasped his arm, as if to restrain him. "Judge, that's only thirty miles from here," she said in a reproachful tone.

"That's so. Wouldn't be too much inconvenience for any of us." The judged leaned over the bench. "Mr. Nixon, if you continue to throw your papers and files in the courtroom, I'll have you removed. Next matter?"

Claire stepped up with a confidence that Elsie admired, in spite of herself. "Motion to dismiss, your honor."

Elsie leaned her head on her hand, anticipating a speedy decision in the State's favor.

The judge gazed down benevolently on Claire's red head; it occurred to Elsie that they might share some history.

"For what cause?"

"The State has filed two counts of murder in the first degree: Count One for the death of Jessie Rose Dent, Count Two pertaining to her unborn child. We ask that Count Two be dismissed, because there is no statutory basis for it."

At the prosecution table, Parsons and Madeleine looked at each other. Elsie leaned close and whispered, "Case law."

Claire continued. "The defense acknowledges that many states have, in fact, passed legislation to criminalize the killing of an unborn child. Twenty-eight states have enacted those statutes. However, Missouri is not one of those states."

Elsie whispered, "State Constitution."

Madeleine turned her back to Elsie. "I know that," she whispered, affronted.

On the bench, Judge Callaway stuck a finger inside his collar and scratched his neck. He said, "These are uncharted waters for me, ladies and gentlemen—not gonna lie. First time this kind of murder has been prosecuted in McCown County."

Parsons spoke at the prosecution table in a harsh whisper. "Madeleine, if you lose Count Two, you are screwed. No jury is going to care squat about the mother."

Madeleine turned to Elsie with a deer in the headlights expression. "Stand up," she said.

Elsie jumped to her feet.

"Judge Callaway, it's well known that the Missouri State Constitution states that life begins at conception."

"That's immaterial. It's not part of the Missouri criminal code," Claire countered.

Elsie walked around the counsel table and stood before the bench. "Of course it's material. The State Constitution is the highest state law in Missouri. And the evidence will show that the unborn child was only a few weeks from his due date."

"The criminal code has no provision for this," Claire said, before Elsie cut her off.

"Judge, there's precedent in Missouri case law. The case of *State v. Larry Paul* isn't a first; defendants in Missouri courts have been tried and convicted of murder of the unborn. The issue has been resolved in Missouri appellate courts."

"Well, good then. What's the case name?" The judge picked up a pen and poised it over the file, prepared to write.

Elsie froze. "Beg your pardon?"

"The name of the Missouri case you refer to. That resolves this issue."

She couldn't remember. Elsie closed her eyes, urging her brain to produce the answer, but her mind was blank. She turned on her heel, looking to Madeleine and Sam Parsons for assistance. "Case name?" she whispered.

Parsons nudged Madeleine. "Isn't she supposed to cover research?" Madeleine was regarding Elsie with poorly concealed contempt. The sight of Madeleine's twitching left eye sent a chill through her. Elsie wheeled back around to face the judge.

"Your honor, may we submit written suggestions in support of our position?"

Sighing, Judge Callaway closed his folder. "Have them ready at nine tomorrow morning. I want the suggestions e-filed, but bring a hard copy to my clerk." He pushed his chair back and stood. "I like to mark them up with an ink pen. I'm old school. Or just plain old."

"Judge, you're not old. You're a classic," Claire said. She had the nerve to shoot him a wink.

Elsie couldn't top that. She slunk back to the counsel table with a brave face. Madeleine stood and leaned in toward her; Elsie wanted to back away, but didn't dare.

"You'll bring the brief to me before you submit it."

"What if I don't get the suggestions done till tonight? I have other stuff to do this afternoon."

"Then bring them to my house. Tonight. Am I clear?"

"Can't I just e-mail it?"

Madeleine moved in so close, their noses almost brushed. "Hand-delivered. I don't want you to claim a technical glitch. To-night."

Elsie held her breath. It smelled like something rotten festered in Madeleine's gut.

Chapter Twenty-Five

ELSIE PULLED INTO the long driveway of Madeleine's home and snatched up a file from the passenger seat. Not bothering to lock her car, she followed the redbrick walkway to a fourteen-foot door of carved oak. Through the leaded windowpanes of frosted glass, Elsie could see lights on in the hallway. She screwed up her courage and pressed the doorbell.

Nothing. She rang again, and pressed her eyeball to the peephole in the front door. When the center went from light to dark, she knew Madeleine was inside. The massive door creaked open, just wide enough for Madeleine to stick her head through. "Where have you been? What took you so long?"

The plastic smile of greeting on Elsie's face disappeared. "I didn't have any trouble finding the case law, but I searched for law review articles to support our position. Then I drafted suggestions from scratch. It took a while."

"You should have been prepared in advance. I can't believe you froze on the case citation in court. How hard is it to remember a case name?"

She sidestepped to the opening in the door; in the gloom of the night, she could barely see Madeleine's face. "You want me to go over it with you?"

Madeleine huffed out with irritation, and Elsie caught a whiff: booze breath. Wine, maybe. A lot of wine.

"Let's do it tomorrow," Madeleine said.

"Sure, whatever. Parsons said he wants to meet up in your office at nine? Or eight?"

"Eight. Eight fucking o'clock."

Elsie blinked; was she having aural hallucinations? Or had Madeleine just said *fuck*?

"Okay, then. Here you go." Elsie thrust the file holding the sheaf of pages through the crack in the door; thinking Madeleine had it in hand, she let go.

"Fuck. Goddamn it," she heard.

Alarmed and more than a shade curious, Elsie grasped the doorknob and pushed the door wide. Madeleine was on her knees, balancing a crystal goblet in her hand as she scrambled to gather pages scattered in the marble entryway. The liquid in the goblet sloshed down the side of the glass.

Madeleine looked up. "Are you going to help me?"

"Yeah, sure." Elsie knelt and scooped the papers into a pile. "You want me to put these back in order? I didn't number them."

Madeleine sighed, pushing a wayward lock of hair out of her eyes. "Come on."

Elsie followed her though the entryway into a great room with soaring ceilings, with a glass wall of windows looking out onto the wooded countryside. They made a turn into the kitchen. Madeleine made a beeline for the wine bottle that sat on the kitchen island. She refilled her glass, her hands moving with exaggerated care.

Elsie peeked at the label: *Mersault*. It was French, she was pretty sure—not that she'd know from personal experience.

Shifting her attention to the copy of her brief, Elsie said, "We're not going to have a problem with this issue; case law is absolutely on our side. We don't have a criminal statute in Missouri addressing murder of an unborn child, but with our State Constitution declaring life begins at conception, it's a given. In Missouri, the unborn have protectable interests in life, health, and well-being. Here's the citation: Section 1.205, Revised Statutes of Missouri. And there's a case on point from the Western District: in *State v. Holcomb*, they tried and convicted a man for the murder of a pregnant woman and her unborn child. He was the father of the baby, just like Larry Paul. And the conviction was upheld by the Missouri Court of Appeals in the Western District. They cited two Missouri Supreme Court cases—"

"I know all that."

The hell you do, Elsie thought. She observed Madeleine covertly. Her speech wasn't slurred, but she was even more waspish than usual. Elsie sighed; it had been a rough day, all around. She decided to reach out.

"You want to talk about it?"

"What, this brief? I actually know how to read—are you aware of that?"

"Come on, Madeleine. It was a rough ride in court today. And now we've got that defense toad Claire O'Hara to contend with. This is a tough case to deal with. You want to talk about that?"

She could see the hesitation in Madeleine's face. Finally, she gave her head a shake and rolled her eyes. "You want a glass of wine?"

"Sure," Elsie said, settling onto one of the upholstered raised seats at the island. "Love it."

As Madeleine walked to the cabinet, Elsie admired the goblet she'd been drinking from: faceted cut crystal. She bet if she flipped her fingertip against the rim, the glass would ring like a bell. Not that she'd dare.

"Here." Madeleine sat an ordinary wineglass in front of her, the kind that could be thrust into a dishwasher without concern.

Madeleine filled the glass and Elsie took a sip. "Oh my God, Madeleine, that's fabulous."

"I expect it compares favorably to the swill you drink at the Baldknobbers Tavern." Madeleine pursed her lips to sip from her own glass. "But you're right. It is divine."

Her hair fell into her eyes again, and Madeleine pushed it back with a careless hand. Elsie had never seen her in this state; garbed in a pair of striped pajamas, with disheveled hair and a naked face. She kind of liked it.

"Madeleine, I'm not so sure that Sam Parsons is going to be of any benefit to us. You know, you could tell that guy to bug off. Get in his car and drive back to Jefferson City."

Madeleine tutted, making a scornful sound. "It's not that simple."

"Madeleine, we don't need him."

"But I asked him. I asked him to come. I implored the office. Used up a couple of favors."

"So?"

Madeleine lifted her chin and stared at Elsie. "You know nothing about politics." Her eyes were red; whether from drinking or crying, Elsie couldn't guess.

"I know how to try a case. You and I will team up and get it done. He's an out-of-towner; you know that doesn't sell around here. And an unnecessary player, an obstacle." She paused. "Not to mention an asshole."

"You think it's so easy. Pick a jury and put on a show. I have other things to weigh. My burden is different than yours."

Elsie opened her mouth to speak, but Madeleine cut her off.

"It's so easy for you. You have no idea."

Elsie wanted to say that she didn't think her job was particularly easy, but Madeleine turned away at that moment, to rise and walk over to the fridge. She pulled on the stainless steel door and stared at the interior. "I should eat something."

Elsie watched as Madeleine stood before the open fridge for long moments. Finally, she pulled out a plastic container and tossed it onto the granite top of the island. Fishing in a kitchen drawer, Madeleine said, "You have no idea."

Elsie said, "How's that?"

"What I went through. I graduated law school in 1983." She gestured at Elsie with a spoon. *"Nineteen-eighty-three."*

Elsie cleared her throat. "Yeah. That's cool."

"It was harrowing. Harrowing." Madeleine pulled the top off the container and dipped the spoon inside. Elsie peeked at the contents: hummus. With fascination borne of horror, she watched Madeleine eat a glob off the spoon.

"Aren't you supposed to put that on crackers?"

Madeleine responded with a look, but her eyes were glazed. She swallowed.

Elsie sipped her wine, savoring it. "You were the first, Madeleine. The first woman to practice law in McCown County. That's really cool."

"They treated me like an interloper. I wasn't a member of the club."

"Well, that just makes it more impressive."

"They made up rules to keep me out. The necktie rule." She laughed, a humorless bark. "I came for my first appearance in court, all dressed in a navy suit and white silk blouse. It had mother-of-pearl buttons. They said no attorney could appear in court without a tie."

Elsie felt a kernel of new respect for Madeleine. "That's bullshit."

"They went into chambers and brought out a tie—some decrepit monstrosity. Made me tie it around my neck before I could speak a word in court."

"That is incredible. That sounds like a Title VII violation. You should've threatened an ethics complaint."

"Nobody cared. Nobody." She pushed the hummus to the side and set the spoon down with a clatter. "I was trying to live my father's life, but it was too hard."

Elsie's brow wrinkled. "Your father wasn't a lawyer."

Madeleine sat up straight. "He was a judge."

She knew she should back down, but facts were facts. "He was a county commissioner, right?"

"But they called them judges. In the 1980s, commissioners were referred to as judge."

"Yeah, but it was a courtesy title. He wasn't a real judge."

"Oh, shut up." Madeleine took a dainty sip from the goblet.

Elsie followed suit. Swallowing, she said: "Madeleine, it's a compliment. I'm just saying that you went further professionally than your father did."

"I wanted to be my father. Live his life, make him proud. It was too hard. Impossible, actually. You don't understand." She refilled her glass, emptying the bottle. "What he really wanted was for me to become Miss Missouri. I tried and failed. Became a lawyer; what a trip to hell that was. So I got married."

As if on cue, a hum of the garage sounded. Elsie craned her head to look at the door that opened off a mudroom beside the kitchen. Donald Thompson walked through the door, garbed in muddy camouflage.

"Hey," he said, running his hand though disheveled gray locks. Nodding at Elsie, he said "You're Elsie, right?"

Elsie nodded. "Nice to see you, Mr. Thompson."

"I'm Donny, honey. Call me Donny." He bent down and buzzed his wife's cheek. "Hey, there."

She waved him off. "Donald, you're a mess."

He laughed, a boisterous bark, baring shiny white teeth. Donny must use Crest White Strips, Elsie marveled. She didn't know a man in McCown County who fell prey to such vanity. She looked away, lest she be caught staring.

"Got a buck," Donald said.

"Oh, Lord."

He laughed again, filling the room with the sound of his mirth, as he reached in the refrigerator for a bottle of beer. "Got anything to eat?"

"I didn't expect you." Madeleine's voice conveyed a chill; Elsie was used to hearing the frosty tone in meetings at the office. "You didn't drag that thing home on your truck, did you? Tell me you didn't."

The bright teeth flashed. "Yep I did!"

"Dear Lord—is it in my driveway?"

"It's in *my* driveway."

Elsie heard the emphasis on the possessive; she was growing uncomfortable. She began to slide off her chair.

"You take that wretched corpse and deliver it to those people at Smokey Dean's so they can process it and package it."

"I'll do it. When I'm ready." He opened his Budweiser and walked away, swigging from the bottle. Before leaving them, he said, "Lay off the wine, Madzie; makes you bitchy. You'd be better off popping those Xanax you like so much."

Elsie bent down to pick up her purse. She was eager to depart, embarrassed to have witnessed the scene. Elsie knew her father would never address her mother like that in front of a stranger—or in private, for that matter. Madeleine's lot was not one to be envied, Elsie decided, for all her crystal stemware and fancy house and French wine. Tentatively, she pushed her legal brief a few inches closer to Madeleine.

"We can talk about the unborn child cases in the morning, if you want. I'll get there early," Elsie said.

Madeleine nodded, a bare movement of her chin.

Elsie added, "Whatever time works best—I'd be glad to get there at seven-thirty, if that's good for you."

Madeleine didn't meet her eyes. She mouthed the word "fine."

As Elsie headed from the kitchen into the great room, Madeleine's sharp voice stopped her. "Do you need to call a cab? Are you in any condition to drive?"

Without looking back, Elsie let herself out through the front door. She resolved that she would gouge her own eyes out before permitting herself to feel sorry for Madeleine Thompson ever again.

Chapter Twenty-Six

No BREEZE FILTERED through the open windows in Judge Callaway's chambers, but the people assembled in the judge's office didn't complain, or even comment about the temperature. They knew better. Judge Callaway had an appetite for fresh air and a prejudice against central air-conditioning that was famous in McCown County. The windows of his office, and the adjoining courtroom, remained open from April through October.

The freshly printed pages Elsie had prepared with such care the night before lay unheeded on the judge's desk. She had proudly presented hard copies to the defense, as well as to the judge, but no one was flipping through her written suggestions. It was a new day, with a new wrinkle in *State v. Larry Paul*. A hot new day, Elsie mused.

Of the seven individuals crowded into the chambers, six were sweating. Only the judge looked comfortable, with no beads of sweat on his forehead, no telltale ring round the collar of his white shirt.

The jailer of McCown County, Vernon Wantuck, appeared to be suffering the most from the temperature of the crowded office.

A man of considerable girth, he had a red bandanna in his hand and was using it to mop his face and the back of his neck.

With a weary sigh, Vernon Wantuck spoke. "We got to get him out of there, Judge. Get that old boy out of our county lockup. That Larry Paul, he has got to go."

Near the window, a beefy middle-aged man stood with his arms crossed, a sheriff's badge pinned to his chest. "Ditto that, judge," said Shelby Choate. He had served as the county sheriff for twelve years. His no-nonsense, no-frills approach to law enforcement made him a popular candidate with the voters in McCown County.

Claire O'Hara and Josh Nixon sat together, at the right end of the judge's desk. Madeleine's chair was between theirs and the jailer. Elsie stood behind Madeleine; no other seats were available. And Sam Parsons was absent, stuck in traffic that morning on highway I–44.

Josh Nixon leaned into Claire O'Hara. She whispered something in his ear, but Elsie didn't catch it.

"Your honor, we have to have access to our client. Larry Paul has Sixth Amendment right to counsel, and the right to assist in his defense. How can he exercise his rights if you send him away?"

Wantuck grunted, shifting his weight in a chair that was a tight fit. "Call him on the damn phone."

The sheriff's eyes narrowed; the lines on either side of his mouth deepened. "You're in the presence of ladies, Vernon. Watch your mouth. And offer Ms. Arnold your seat."

Elsie shook her head. "I'm fine, really."

Wantuck made no movement to leave his chair. Sherriff Choate shook his head in disgust. "I don't see how you can let a woman stand when you got a seat. Vernon, you must've been raised in a barn." His eyes cut to Josh Nixon. "Wouldn't expect any better from a defense attorney."

"Ouch," Claire said, flashing a feral smile at the sheriff. "Shelby. You wound me." She winked at him. The sheriff frowned.

Claire leaned forward in her chair, her eyes darting from the judge to Madeleine. "Come on, boys and girls; I've got things to do today. Let's get back to our client: the unfortunate Mr. Paul. He's got to have his medication."

Sheriff Choate spoke, his frown deepening. "We can't afford it."

Josh said, "The county is responsible for his welfare. You're the ones who have him locked up in the county jail. Being held without bond, at the prosecutor's request."

Madeleine wiped her upper lip with a dainty finger. The heat was affecting even her. "The defendant has been charged with two counts of murder—"

"We know the charges," Nixon said. "And it doesn't matter what you've accused him of. While he's in county lockup, he's the county's responsibility."

Elsie knew that Nixon was right. She studied Judge Callaway's face, trying to predict what he would say; but he was a hard man to read. His face was relaxed, almost tranquil, as he surveyed the room through eyes that were partly closed.

Shit, Elsie thought. *He's going to fall asleep. He's not listening to a word they're saying.*

But she was wrong. The judge said, "So who has looked into this medication. This—what do they call it? A drug cocktail? For AIDS?"

Vernon Wantuck groped in his shirt pocket and pulled out a sheet of paper folded into a small rectangle. "The Public Defender's Office up in Jeff City sent me a letter. A demand. This is it right here." He pushed the paper across the judge's desk. "Just looking at it made me cross-eyed."

"We don't have the money," Sheriff Choate repeated.

The judge picked up the wrinkled paper, which appeared to be slightly damp. He pursed his lips and blew out a shrill whistle.

"What did I tell you," Wantuck said.

"We're prepared to file an action in Federal Court if the county won't accede to our demands for Mr. Paul's care," Josh Nixon said.

Judge Callaway tipped his chair backwards and swiveled it, turning his back on the room and placing his feet on the open windowsill behind his desk. He crossed his feet at the ankle. *Just look how worn out his shoes are,* Elsie marveled. She wondered how many times the judge had the battered black wingtips resoled.

He was a thrifty man.

"You can go file in Federal Court, that's a fact. Go running up to Springfield, crying tales about us here in McCown County." The judge's voice sounded thoughtful. They couldn't see his face.

After a pause, he spoke again. "Of course, nothing happens very fast in Federal Court."

Elsie glanced at Josh, interested to see how he would react to the judge's pronouncement. A flash crossed his face; he sat up straight in his seat. "Nothing happens fast anywhere in the court system. We all know that. That's just how it works."

"Oh, I don't know." Judge Callaway fell silent, then uncrossed his feet and let them drop to the floor. "Ladies and gentlemen, we need to pack up and get to Greene County."

Claire O'Hara smiled, then resumed a poker face. Nixon shook his head. "What for?"

"We need to pick a jury. Time to move the wheels on this old wagon."

Madeleine was breathing hard; Elsie could hear it. Madeleine's voice had a faint tremor when she said, "Mr. Parsons isn't here. He's stuck in traffic; there was a wreck on the highway. I have to check with Mr. Parsons."

"Well, he better get down here, then. If he's going to help you out. The presiding circuit judge in Greene County is an old friend of mine. I bet he can accommodate our jury selection with a couple of weeks' notice." He studied his desk calendar, then lifted his eyes to Madeleine. "We're going to get this case tried. Are you ready?"

When Madeleine didn't reply, Elsie's voice rang out. "The State is always ready, your honor."

Madeleine turned on her with a look of horror. Elsie responded with a shrug. It was an automatic answer.

"That's what I always say," she whispered.

Nixon rose to his feet. "This is an action taken by the court to deprive my client of his rights."

But Claire O'Hara grabbed Nixon's arm and pulled him back into his chair. "Settle down, kiddo. Don't get your panties in a wad." Josh turned on her with a look of indignant disbelief, but she silenced him with a queenly wave of her jeweled hand. "I'm good with this, Judge. Totally good with it."

"We're not ready," Josh said.

When she answered, her voice was harsh. "We'll get ready." Regaining her flirtatious banter, she said, "I hate to talk strategy in front of the enemy, sweetheart. But during jury selection, we can knock the law and order types off the panel with a deer rifle. Easy pickings. If we drag our feet, Greene County will forget. In a couple of years, it'll be Larry who?"

"That settles it, then. I'll be in touch with counsel for the prosecution and defense as soon as Greene County gives me a date.

They may have a panel of prospective jurors called in for next week, for something that could plead out. They can give us the panel, and we'll pick them over; and once we've got our jury, I can clear a time for trial on my docket." He smiled, sanguine. "That should take care of everything."

"What about our demand for medication? For our client?" Josh was hot, his voice was rising.

"Oh, that." Judge Callaway shut the case file in front of him and tossed it to the side of his desk. "I think I'll take that under advisement, for now." When Nixon opened his mouth to speak, the judge cut him off. "You're all free to go. I have other business this morning." He swiveled in his chair, turning his back to them, and propped his feet in the windowsill again.

As the group shuffled out the door, Elsie noted that the back of Vernon Wantuck's trousers were wet. Butt sweats, she surmised. Major butt sweats. Glad she hadn't been sitting on that soggy cushion.

Chapter Twenty-Seven

ELSIE AWOKE, HER heart beating with terror. The worn T-shirt she slept in was soaked with perspiration.

Sitting up in bed, she willed herself to calm down. It was just a dream. A bad, bad dream.

The memory of the nightmare was beginning to fade, though her heart still raced. The image was still clear, though: she'd been at the prison in Jefferson City, the state capital. The old maximum security facility. Sitting in the gas chamber.

She shuddered. During a brief internship with the state attorney general's office in her third year of law school, she'd been invited to tour the old prison—including the gas chamber, used to execute Missourians on death row prior to the move to lethal injection. The tour guide explained that the chamber was a two-seater, to accommodate any prisoners who wanted to die together.

The laces on Elsie's Converse tennis shoes had come undone during the tour. As a joke, she'd flounced onto one of the seats in the gas chamber and tied her shoe.

It didn't seem so funny now.

The dream continued to fade, but she knew that in the nightmare, she and Larry Paul had been seated side by side in the gas chamber. Madeleine was standing nearby, asking whether they had any last words. Larry Paul stuck his finger in his mouth; in the dream, Elsie knew he intended to wipe the finger on her arm, as he had done in court. She called out to Madeleine, trying to explain that it was a mistake; she only sat down to tie her shoe.

In slow motion, the door to the chamber shut with a clang. She could see Madeleine dropping the gas pellets, preparing to execute both of them: Elsie and Larry Paul. She tried to jump from her chair, but couldn't move.

Larry Paul wiped his finger on her. Then he smiled and said, "That's not how you catch AIDS."

Sitting up in bed, Elsie took deep breaths, inhaling through her nose and blowing the air out. The thought she'd been suppressing took hold and refused to be silent.

I don't want to be a part of this case, she thought.

She squeezed her eyes shut, and spoke it aloud. "I want out. Out of this fucking case."

Hugging her knees, she buried her face in the quilt that covered her. The fabric was soft, and it gave a measure of comfort. It was an old quilt, stitched in a faded wedding ring pattern, made long ago by her mother's grandmother. Elsie ran her hand over the nubby surface, trying to gather her fortitude and face her fears.

Breathing slowly in and out, she tried a technique she'd seen on *Oprah* once, or maybe *Dr. Phil.* Imagine the worst-case scenario. In an instant, she scrambled out of bed, gasping. So many horrific scenarios had jumped out at her that she couldn't bear to contemplate them.

She grabbed the tattered heirloom quilt and dragged it into the living room. Huddled on the sofa, she reached for the television remote. Clicking through the stations, she visited one infomercial after another, and finally hit the Mute button and picked up a legal pad from the coffee table. Turning to a fresh page, she scrawled:

Advantages of serving in State v. Paul.

Elsie tapped the pen. Couldn't think of any. Not one.

She divided the page with a stroke of the pen and made a second column: *Disadvantages of serving in State v. Paul.*

She started writing feverishly, muttering aloud, oblivious to the kitchenware offered for sale on the television screen.

I have no power. No discretion. Hate my cocounsel. Hate the opposing counsel. Suspicious of Claire O'Hara. Toting the weary load of Ivy Dent.

Breathing fast again, she studied the list, knowing that the real reason hadn't yet been addressed.

She wrote:

I don't want to kill anybody.

Unable to sit still, she jumped up and shuffled into the kitchen, still wrapped in the quilt. Opening the refrigerator, she surveyed the contents. A Styrofoam carryout box stood beside a small collection of condiments, many past their expiration date. On a lower shelf, a partially full twelve-pack of Diet Coke sat beside a fresh six-pack of Corona in bottles.

Clicking on the overhead light, she opened a cabinet, and rummaging behind instant oatmeal packets and Special K, she hit pay dirt: Pop-Tarts. Strawberry. Frosted.

"This is good stuff," she said. "This will help me get my shit together." She had read somewhere that ingesting sugar heightened test performances. She hoped it might improve cognitive abilities and emotional stability.

Juggling the Pop-Tart from hand to hand after it came out of the toaster, she sat again at her list. Determined to write something on the pro side of the paper, she bit down on the rectangle of cardboard pastry before it had a chance to cool down, and burned the tender flesh behind her front teeth.

Bearing down with the pen, she wrote in capital letters.

DOMESTIC VIOLENCE.

Female Homicide Victims: 3 out of 4 women murdered by husband/boyfriend.

She willed herself to recall the hideous image of Jessie Dent, lying in a pool of blood. And the baby who died before he drew breath.

And Ivy. The girl had lost her whole family in one fell swoop, at the hands of Larry Paul.

Probably better off, a voice whispered in her mind. Elsie shook her head to banish the thought. "Shut the fuck up," she said to the voice. An image of the child's face, wary from exposure to disaster, floated into Elsie's conscience. She whispered aloud, "I don't see how I can fix it, kiddo. Your life is a train wreck. But it's out of my hands."

In the kitchen chair, her shoulders shuddered involuntarily, sending a shiver all the way down her spine. She grasped the pen to continue.

Trial experience, she wrote; but scratched it out with a stroke of the pen. She had years of trial experience; it was no particular gain in this case. Even the initial triumph of a major death penalty assignment had faded to ash in the past weeks. The price she was paying was high. Too high.

She broke the Pop-Tart into pieces and ate them, trying to think of a compelling reason to justify her aversion to working on *State v. Paul*, but her eyes kept drifting back to the core of her anxiety. She didn't want to be part of a proceeding that ended with someone's death. Even though he had caused two deaths, by his own hand.

It was one thing, believing in the worth of the death penalty from a philosophical point of view. But she was learning that being an inside player in a death penalty case was too close for comfort.

I can't do this, she thought; and began to tear up. Before the tears rolled, she shook her head, hard, and blinked them back.

"Get over yourself," she said sharply. She picked up the pen and wrote one last line.

It's my job.

She dragged the quilt back to bed and lay down, but the dark comfort of sleep eluded her. After long minutes of waiting, she returned to the kitchen, still dragging the quilt along with her. She reached for a Corona inside the fridge and popped the top with a bottle opener and drank it, staring at the list on the kitchen table. Then she drank another one.

After that, she managed to drift back into a troubled sleep.

.

Chapter Twenty-Eight

SUNDAY MORNING WAS cloudy. Angry overcast skies threatened rain, but Nell Stout hadn't bothered to bring an umbrella along. The one she had in her closet at home was in pitiful shape, the spines broken.

After parking the white Buick, Nell ran a hand over her gray hair, pulling it back into an elastic band and tucking stray locks behind her ears. She uncapped a Maybelline lipstick, purchased for the occasion, and rotated the rearview mirror to apply it.

She drew a pink ring on her mouth, surveyed it in the mirror, and frowned at the reflection. Shaking her head, she wiped the lipstick from her mouth with the back of her hand.

Nell walked into the entry of the Riverside Baptist Church, looking furtively around her, as if she feared someone would jump up to block her path and ask her to leave.

"Good morning!" A smiling man with moussed hair extended a folded bulletin to her. "Glad to have you with us today."

She took the paper he offered, not bothering to respond. In

the sanctuary, her eyes darted around the space, looking for her target.

At first, she didn't find what she was seeking. Nell took a seat at the end of a back pew, to sit and wait. A young woman sitting beside her, wearing a maternity dress, tapped her arm.

"Ma'am? Sorry, but if you don't mind, I'm saving that seat. My mom is running late."

Nell turned her head and gave the woman a look. She didn't speak, didn't bother to smile.

The young woman snatched up her purse and moved to a different pew.

Nell waited, scouring the room with her eyes. Finally, as the men serving as deacons were lined up at the doorways on either side of the sanctuary, a family of four arrived, moving down the center aisle with haste, to find their seats before the service began.

Nell stood, watching the family shuttle into a spot near the altar. Waiting, she rested her hands on the pew in front of her.

"Excuse me? Can you sit, please? The service is about to begin."

She ignored the usher at her elbow, a man wearing a jacket and a bow tie. Moving with a decided tread, she walked the crimson carpet down the center aisle to the beat of the drums pounding in the praise band.

At the pew where Ivy sat with her foster family, Nell paused, turning to peer down the row, as if she might join them.

At the altar, the pastor invited the congregation to stand and join in the "Hymn of Adoration."

Nell locked eyes with Ivy. The child ducked her head and tried to hide behind her foster mother.

Nell walked around the front of the sanctuary and slid in

a spot on the side, to the right of Ivy's pew. She looked at the person standing next to her, a short woman with a frowzy gray permanent wave. Nell broke into a sharp laugh and nodded at her seatmate.

"Hey there, Dixie," she said with a lopsided smirk.

Dixie, who had been singing the hymn, stopped in midnote to gape at Nell. Nell grinned, revealing the gap that showed her missing molars.

Dixie snatched up her purse and started to shuffle past Nell.

"Hey. Don't mind me."

Dixie ignored her, brushing past Nell into the aisle and heading up the aisle at a near-run. While the hymn continued, Nell chuckled. Remembering her aim, she leaned forward and caught sight of Ivy. In violation of the minister's order to stand and sing, Ivy sat in the pew; her knees were pulled up to her chin, her eyes locked on Nell.

Nell winked at her. Ivy's head dropped to her knees.

IVY SLID HER eyes toward Nell Stout to see whether she was still keeping watch.

She was. The black gaze was fixed on Ivy. She squirmed under the scrutiny, as if it burned her. Nell was a devil who could see into her mind and heart.

The preacher was talking. Ivy transferred her attention to him, hoping for distraction from her pursuer. She stared at his head; the bright lights in the ceiling reflected off of his thin golden hair.

"Brothers and sisters, I extend an invitation—on behalf of our savior, Jesus Christ. Is anyone ready to enter the fold?"

There was palpable shifting in the congregation, as people turned in their seats to see who might rise and respond.

"Who is ready to have their sins washed away? Washed in the blood of the lamb?"

Ivy sunk down in her seat, uneasy with the public display. Her foster mother cut her eyes at her and gave her a nudge, but Ivy ignored her. She was thinking.

"Who believes? Who will be saved by faith alone? For brothers and sisters, you can't be saved by works; don't think that your good deeds will count for you on the Day of Judgment. You must believe; you must be born again."

A disheveled man in a worn jacket and dirty jeans rose from a back pew and made his way down the aisle.

"Welcome, brother! All are welcome!"

As Ivy hunkered down in her seat beside Holly Hickman, the foster mother nudged the girl again, looking at her with an urgent expression. Ivy remained in her seat until a shove from the foster mother set her in motion.

With a look of resignation, Ivy nodded at Holly. It was the smart thing to do, she thought. The safest thing—though as a rule, she shied away from being a show-off, drawing attention. But maybe today was the day to make an exception.

Slowly, the girl rose and made her way to the pastor, literally dragging her feet. It was hard to go before so many people, to have so many pairs of eyes fixed on her back. But the preacher smiled, as if he'd been waiting for her. He disregarded the shabby man he had greeted moments ago, and reached out to Ivy with both hands.

With a radiant face, he said, "Let the little children come to me and forbid them not; for theirs is the kingdom of heaven."

Ivy paused. Maybe it wasn't so smart, after all, putting on a show with Nell watching. She tensed, looking like an animal poised to retreat; but the pastor bounded over to her and grasped her hand before she could escape.

"This is the sheep that was lost, and we have found her. This little lamb will be redeemed in our church this very day."

He led her up to the baptistery, a large tub at the front of the sanctuary.

"She was born into sin, into the worst kind of iniquity. But every man, woman, and child can break free of the chains that bind them, and enter the fold."

His wife appeared as if by magic, with a plastic poncho. She slipped it over Ivy's head. The pastor lifted her up, her legs dangling off the floor.

"Ivy, do you accept Jesus Christ as your Lord and Savior?"

Her face was contorted with fright, but she nodded.

"Say 'I do.' "

"I do," she mouthed.

"Do you reject Satan and his temptations?"

This time, with the second question, he let her frantic nod suffice. He set her inside the baptistery, then followed, climbing into the tub with alacrity. Covering Ivy's nose and mouth with his hand, he announced, "Ivy Dent, I baptize you in the name of the Father, and of the Son, and of the Holy Spirit."

He plunged her backward into the water and held her in place, though her writhing arms and kicking feet were visible, splashing the water from the tub.

When he raised her up and released her, she gasped, reaching out and grabbing hold of the tub. She shook her hair like a puppy, blinking her wet eyelashes.

The pastor spread a hand on her head. "How do you feel?"

"Good."

He laughed, and the congregation joined in. "So you weren't scared down there in the water?"

"I was scared. But then I seen a beautiful angel in a white dress. And I didn't need to be scared no more."

"A vision! From the mouth of babes." The preacher's voice was happy—but he turned on Ivy with a look that was suspicious and unbelieving.

She meant to give the man what he wanted. Ivy had managed to make it through the first six years of life by figuring out what people in charge wanted from her, and either delivering it, or staying out of the way. And the enemy was present, seated right in the church. Ivy needed God on her side. Or, at least, the Reverend Albertson.

So she tried another tack. "And I knew Pastor Albertson would take care of me and not let me get water up my nose. So I wasn't afraid so much."

The smile returned. Ivy felt a wave of relief; she had made him happy the second time around. He held out his large, soft hand, and she clutched it, holding on for dear life. It was clear to her that one of her primary jobs these days was keeping the preacher happy. If she played it right, he might stand between her and Nell Stout.

And Smokey.

Chapter Twenty-Nine

SUNDAY NIGHT, ELSIE bent over a file on the scarred wooden tabletop at the Baldknobbers. With a pen, she crossed out a line and scrawled in the margin, her handwriting nearly illegible.

Dixie walked up with a platter and set it beside the file. "Burger and fries."

Elsie straightened in the booth, looking hungrily at the cheeseburger. "Thanks, Dixie. This will give me strength. I need something to inspire me. Like grease, and salt."

Dixie slipped into the booth across from her. "Could've gone for inspiration this morning." She pulled a pack of Winstons from the pocket of her apron and lit one.

Elsie squirted mustard on her hamburger bun. "What are you deviling me about?"

"I'm saying we missed you at church this morning." She blew out a plume of smoke and added. "Ashlock was there."

Elsie pulled a face. Pushing her papers safely out of the way, she grasped a ketchup bottle and shook it. "Don't hold your breath waiting to see me back at Riverside Baptist. That place does nothing for me. Dixie, this ketchup's almost empty."

"Just squeeze a little harder." She rolled the cigarette in the ashtray. "I thought maybe you were thinking about joining, with Ashlock being such a regular. Now that he's got his boy with him and all."

Elsie chewed a french fry. "Joining up at Gay Bash Baptist? No way. How often does Reverend Albertson weigh in on the sin of same-sex relationships? Once a month? Twice?"

Dixie waved a hand through the smoke cloud she'd created. "Honey, he's a Southern Baptist preacher. What do you expect?"

"So why do you warm a seat in there?"

"Oh, I'm too old to change." She grinned at Elsie, her face creasing with mischief. "Besides, he's pretty cute."

"That sanctimonious nut job? Oh please." Elsie gave the cheeseburger a vicious bite.

"He's got attendance way up at Riverside. We're getting lots of new members, young people with kids. He's got the magic. Has folks running down the aisle for the chance to get saved." She took another hit from the cigarette. "He baptized your little witness today."

"Who?"

"You know. Little girl with the glasses. The one whose mother got murdered by her boyfriend."

"You mean Ivy Dent?" Elsie was talking with her mouth full. She swallowed and said, "Ivy's just six years old. Are you saying she went forward to be saved?"

"Yeah. Poor little shit." Dixie stubbed out the cigarette in the ashtray.

"That preacher is summoning six-year-olds with an altar call?"

"Hey, I was about six when I was saved. It was in a river, though. At Turnback Creek." She shivered. "Damn, that water was cold. Scared the dickens out of me." She stood up. "You want another Diet?"

"Yeah. Please."

Elsie consumed the cheeseburger meditatively, thinking about her young witness's emotional state. When finished, she pushed the plate away and pulled her notes back in place. She had no time to worry about Ivy now; she was trying a second-degree burglary case on Monday.

Madeleine, meanwhile, would be heading to nearby Greene County with Sam Parsons, to pick the jury for the Larry Paul case. As Judge Callaway predicted, his friend on the Greene County bench had worked a miracle to accommodate Callaway's request, offering up a jury panel on Monday that would otherwise be dismissed. Judge Callaway and the lead counsel for both sides would spend the next couple of days in Springfield, picking over the prospective jurors to find a dozen who would decide Larry Paul's fate.

Elsie's exclusion from the jury selection process ruffled her feathers. The makeup of the jury could determine the outcome of any case. She had offered to seek a continuance for the burglary trial so that she could assist in the selection, but Madeleine had brushed away the offer, assuring her with little grace that they needed no help from Elsie. A mean corner in Elsie's head harbored a hope that Claire would smack Madeleine around in the Greene County courtroom, though she knew that she should be ashamed to entertain the notion. She and Madeleine were on the same team.

When Dixie returned with a red plastic tumbler fizzling with Diet Coke, Elsie said, "So Ash was there today."

"Oh, honey, everybody in town was there. Saints and sinners." A look of distaste crossed her face. "Jesus Christ. Nell Stout. Never thought I'd see the day she'd darken the door of a church house. When she slunk in there today, I thought for sure that lightning would strike."

"Who's that?"

"Nell Stout. Works for Smokey Dean's, over at the commissary where they butcher the hogs."

"Smokey Dean's Barbeque?"

"Yeah. I've known her since I was a pup." Dixie shuddered. She repeated, "Never thought I'd see the day."

"Well, maybe she saw the light." The name Stout rang a bell; but Elsie didn't have time to think about it. She would be heading into trial in fourteen hours. She picked up her pen and bent over her file, hoping Dixie would get the hint. Dixie started to say more, but halted before she spoke. Turning slowly, she walked away, muttering, "Nell Stout. In the Lord's house. I'll be dawg."

Chapter Thirty

On Tuesday afternoon, Elsie sat at the prosecution table and held her breath as the jury in her burglary case exited the jury room and filed into the jury box. They had been deliberating for nearly three hours; this was a close one, with an unsympathetic victim, and she was by no means certain of the outcome. She scanned the faces of the twelve Missouri citizens, looking for a sign. Most avoided eye contact. *Oh shit,* she thought. Then she caught the foreman's eye, and he gave her a barely perceptible smile. Every muscle in her body relaxed. That was good, very good.

When Judge Rountree read the verdict aloud, and pronounced that the jury found the defendant guilty, it came as no surprise to Elsie. Mission accomplished.

She gathered her papers and some scattered exhibits as the courtroom emptied out. There wasn't much of a crowd; the man on trial had been a small-time burglar, with no family to speak of and no cheering section. Even the victim, a middle-aged drunk who owned a run-down motel on the highway, hadn't waited around for the verdict. The reporter for the *McCown County Record*, the local newspaper, had disappeared after Closing Argument. Elsie supposed she might cruise into the Prosecutor's Office on Wednesday and ask about the outcome. *This verdict won't be the pinnacle of my career,* she thought, but she was grinning a little, nonetheless. She liked to win, and the defendant was good for it. Of that she was absolutely sure.

She also liked to be absolutely sure. And the defendant, a persistent offender, would be heading directly to prison. No passing go, no collecting two hundred dollars. Not this guy.

And no lethal injection.

The thought crept into her mind unbidden; she pushed it away, unaware that she was literally shaking her head. *Not gonna think about Larry Paul today,* she thought. *I'm taking the day off from State v. Larry Paul.*

Two cops who had investigated the burglary and testified for the prosecution were waiting in the courthouse hallway as she walked out with her files.

"Score!" said Deputy Joe Franks; he lifted his hand for a high five. She had to juggle her files to slap his uplifted palm, and almost dropped her load. He said, "Hey, you were great in there today. I liked your closing: getting their minds off the victim, and making them focus on the crime. Good argument."

Franks was no investigative genius, but he did solid work and made a respectable appearance on the witness stand. In light of their joint victory, Elsie decided to forget the injury of being called a heavy load during Larry Paul's first appearance.

Matching his jovial tone, she said, "If they'd been focused on our dirtbag 'witness for the prosecution,' the defendant would be doing a victory dance in the streets this very minute. Why can't I ever get a Pollyanna type as a star witness? Could you guys work on that?"

"Prosecutors always plead out the good cases." Franks shrugged. "These weak cases are the ones that end up on trial. For all that, you've got a pretty long string of victories. How many guilty verdicts in a row does this one make?"

"Oh, who knows," she replied, with a smile that was the slightest bit smug. "It's not like I'm keeping score or anything." Elsie knew every detail of her trial record by heart.

Joe Franks's companion, a young deputy named Beauregard, broke in. "Joe, aren't you going to talk Elsie into joining us?"

Franks said, "Come on out for a victory drink at the Bald. I'll buy your first beer. You can pick up the next round, since you're a rich lawyer."

"Oh please, spare me," Elsie said, with a lifted eyebrow. "McCown County pays all of us with food stamps, Joe."

Deputy Beauregard put a hand on her shoulder, and Elsie turned her attention to him. "Franks is a damn tightwad," he said. "You'll be like a celebrity tonight. Come and drink with us. I'll let you put the quarters in the jukebox."

"You're a real prince," Elsie said. "Will you pick the songs out for me?" She gave him a flirtatious grin. Beauregard was cute, a high-testosterone specimen whose exploits led to whispers of awe among women in the courthouse regarding the size of his penis. If not for Ashlock, Elsie would jump him in a New York minute.

"You can play anything you want, as long as Patsy Cline sings it."

"I tend to sing along with the jukebox when I'm drinking."

"Yeah, I heard that," Deputy Beauregard said.

Oh hell, she thought. Maybe she should cut out the singing at the Baldknobbers. But she was getting an itch to join them. It was only Tuesday, but she had burned the midnight oil through the past weekend. "Well, maybe I'll head that way after work," she said.

As she walked away from the deputies she saw Breeon, sitting on the far end of the wooden bench outside Judge Rountree's chambers, marking on a sheaf of papers with a Sharpie.

Elsie paused. "Hey there."

Breeon looked up. "You all wrapped up in there? I need to talk to Rountree."

"Yeah, just got the verdict." She shifted the files she carried to her right arm; the left was aching from the load. "They found him guilty."

Breeon's face broke into a smile. "I bet they did. No surprise there."

The words warmed her; the Larry Paul case had built a wall between them, and she missed their customary camaraderie. Elsie sat down on the bench beside Breeon, balancing the files on her lap.

"What have you got going with Rountree?"

"Nothing much. Received a motion on a parole violation; I want to set it for hearing."

Elsie continued before silence became uncomfortable. "How's Taylor?"

Breeon shook her head, letting loose with a sound that was a cross between a laugh and a moan. "That girl. What a monster. Do you know what she said to me this morning?"

Elsie smiled; this was a familiar refrain. Safe territory. "Tell me."

"I was trying to get her out the door—harder to do with every passing day, I swear. You know what she said? 'Chill your tits.' Jesus, that child. Really—'chill your tits.' "

Elsie snorted. "What did you do?"

Breeon rolled her eyes, the epitome of the long-suffering mother. "I read her the riot act. What would your mother have done?"

"Same thing. Marge was a screamer, not a hitter."

"I guess I'm following in her footsteps. Damn—does that mean Taylor is going to turn out like you?"

Elsie laughed, the sound carrying a shade of a false note, as she wondered whether Bree was actually trying to make an unflattering parallel. Determined to battle past the iron curtain that had separated them since Elsie's assignment to the death penalty case, she pressed on.

"Joe Franks and some county guys are going to hit the Baldknobbers, to celebrate. Beauregard is going—the hottie who works for the county. Want to run over there after work?"

Breeon looked away from Elsie's gaze. Elsie could see her turning the invitation over in her head. "Huh. It's a Tuesday."

Elsie scooted closer to Bree on the bench; their arms brushed. She sang, slightly off-key, " 'Club going up on a Tuesday.' " She paused, unsure of the next line to the song.

Breeon ceded a laugh, but just a small one. Encouraged, Elsie continued: " 'Girl in the club and she choosy.' "

"That's not it."

"What? What did I get wrong?"

" 'Got your girl in the cut—' " Breeon began, then stopped, waving a hand as if she was shooing away a fly. "Whatever. Doesn't matter."

"Okay, my rap singing needs work. Want to go out? It'll be fun."

"Better not. Taylor will be looking for a hot supper." She fell silent, and then added, "Probably needs me to help her with her homework."

Elsie could spot the lie. Taylor was the smartest kid in her eighth grade class; if she had any homework, she would burn through it without any assistance from her mother. She almost tried to cajole Breeon into joining her, then stopped. No point in forcing the issue. If Bree didn't want Elsie's company, that was fine. Just fine.

"Okay, then," she said, standing and hoisting the files, hugging them to her chest. "See you later. Good luck with all that home-work."

Breeon nodded, still not meeting her eye, and Elsie turned to go. *Fucking Larry Paul,* she thought.

Elsie carried the armload of files through the front door of the Prosecutor's Office. In her mind, she battled the kneejerk funk triggered by Breeon's rejection, trying to retain the adrenaline high from her guilty verdict.

Stacie swiveled in her chair, clutching the phone to her chest. "You gotta talk to Tina Peroni."

Elsie turned on Stacie, still distracted by the jury trial and her thoughts about Breeon. "I just got out of court. I'll call her in a little bit."

"No, she's on the line. You have to talk to her now." Into the receiver, Stacie said, "I'll transfer you."

Struggling to tamp down the irritation that was quickly re-placing her victory buzz, Elsie dumped her files on the desk and picked up the ringing phone.

"Yeah? Tina?"

"You have to go see about Ivy."

Elsie dropped into her chair and leaned backwards, closing her eyes. "I just wrapped up a jury trial."

"Sorry to bug you, honest. But I'm over in Christian County and I can't get away, and all hell's breaking loose over at Ivy's school. The foster mother called, saying there's some crisis and Ivy can't go home on the bus."

The adrenaline lift had deserted her. Elsie slipped her aching feet out of her high heels. After spending the day on her feet in court, her toes felt like bloody stubs. She propped her left foot onto her desk to examine the damage, and was amazed to see that it looked fairly normal. "Tina, what does this have to do with me? She has foster parents."

"The dad's at work and he won't go. The mom is home with the baby; he has some kind of stomach bug, she doesn't want to take him over there." A desperate note came through the phone. "Elsie, I don't have anyone else I can call. My supervisor is out of the office. Please. Ivy knows you. Go over there and see what's happening and take her home. Okay?"

Elsie let out a harried breath. *No rest for the wicked,* she thought, stuffing her feet back into the torture chamber of footwear.

"I'm on my way."

"Oh, God—thanks, Elsie. Get in touch as soon as you deliver her home, okay? It's got me worried."

"Yeah." With an effort, Elsie pushed out of the chair, teetering on the high heels. Next time she bought a pair of shoes that felt a little tight when she tried them on at Shoe Carnival, she would walk away. Even if they were half price and looked like something you'd see on a red carpet.

Elsie drove across town and pulled into the parking lot of Ivy's school. Mark Twain Elementary School was a sturdy Depression-era structure built of brown brick and granite. Air conditioner units jutted out of various windows like warts. The grounds were neglected, and the outdated playground equipment looked utilitarian and forlorn.

Elsie wound through the chain link fence that surrounded the playground and made her way to the entrance. By the time she climbed the stairs to the principal's office, she was limping.

Spying the main office, she opened the door and walked up to the wooden counter. A secretary sat at a desk behind it; she was fishing in a box of Band-Aids while a young boy stood by, blood dripping from his elbow. She looked up at Elsie, her face harried.

"Are you with the Children's Division?"

Elsie shook her head. "The Prosecutor's Office."

"Oh," the secretary said, with a short laugh. "I know you; you're Marge Arnold's daughter. We worked together at Keet Middle School, before I transferred over to Twain. Are you here about," and glancing at the child next to her, she dropped her voice to a whisper. "Ivy?"

Elsie nodded. The secretary carefully placed the Band-Aid over the boy's cut, then nodded on the direction of the principal's office. "Just walk on in; they're all back there. And tell your mama that Shirley said hello."

Elsie tapped on the closed door and entered. "Okay if I come on in? I'm Elsie Arnold, from the Prosecutor's Office; Tina Peroni asked me to stop by."

The principal, a pretty woman in her thirties with short dark hair and red lacquered fingernails, sat behind a gray metal desk. The small room was crowded, with books and binders stacked on the floor. The walls were plastered with children's drawings and homemade cards celebrating Principal's Day. An open bag of Funyuns lay on her desk, next to a jug of Red Diamond sweet tea. "Sorry, everything's a wreck," the principal said. "I spend the lunch hour in the cafeteria with the kids, so I grab a bite when I can." The principal shoved the Funyuns into a desk drawer. "So, I guess Tina told you we had a situation?"

Elsie nodded. "She said. Didn't give me any details." With

mounting confusion, Elsie studied the three people seated in the office.

Ivy sat beside the principal; next to her sat Reverend Albertson. He was holding Ivy's hand, patting it.

Elsie pasted an encouraging smile on her face. "Hey, Ivy. It's Elsie, from the courthouse. Are you okay?"

Ivy didn't answer. The principal stood, extending a hand. "Frances Key, Ms. Arnold; I'm the principal. Tina called and said we could expect you. Do you know Reverend Albertson?"

Elsie and the preacher exchanged an unfriendly glance. "Yeah. So, Ms. Key, Tina said you had a problem over here today."

"Take a seat."

"I can stand, thanks," Elsie said, hoping to communicate her desire to swiftly get to the heart of the matter.

Ms. Key darted a look in Ivy's direction, then pointed to a box on her crowded desk. Elsie stepped closer to look. It was a package of Trojan condoms, with a sticker on the cellophane wrapper that read, *For Ivy.*

Elsie looked from the box to the principal. Ms. Key was chewing the inside of her cheek; it looked to Elsie like a painful exercise. "Can you just tell me what happened?"

The principal turned to Ivy, whose hand was still clasped in the preacher's tight grasp. "Ivy, please tell Ms. Arnold about the box."

Ivy shook her head.

The principal softened her voice. "Please, Ivy."

"I don't know nothing." Ivy looked down, avoiding eye contact. Elsie saw her glance at the box of Trojans and cut her eyes away.

Reverend Albertson spoke; his voice holding a note of command. "Ivy. Tell the lawyer."

He said lawyer like it's a dirty word, Elsie thought.

THE WAGES OF SIN 193

Ivy looked up. Elsie crossed her arms on her knees, crouching so they were eye level. "You can tell me, Ivy."

Ivy's eyes flickered to the right. "At recess, by the swings. The box was laying there. With my name." One of her legs swung, with a new canvas shoe, the lace untied. "I can read my name."

"Who found it? You?"

"Everybody seen it. It was by the swings." The shoe swung back and forth, the shoe string flapping.

"Who put it there?"

Ivy shrugged. Elsie persisted. "Do you know who did it?"

When the girl didn't answer, Elsie turned to the principal for illumination. "Do you know what's going on here?"

The principal opened her mouth to respond, but Ivy spoke.

"I don't know nothing." Elsie watched Ivy, trying to read her demeanor. Her face was closed. She didn't look like she'd been crying. But she seemed to be locked behind a wall of secrecy. Elsie had encountered that wall with young witnesses before. It was hard to break through.

The principal said, "There's been some trouble. Some teasing by the other children in class. All these things we've heard on the news—" Her voice faded, but it was clear that she referred to the murder case and the courtroom drama involving Larry Paul.

"The sins of the mothers," sighed Reverend Albertson. Elsie shot him a piercing look, then turned to the principal.

"Ms. Key, you think this was a first grader's prank? Because I don't see how a six-year-old would be buying a box of Trojans."

The principal looked at the offending box, distress evident in her face. "But who else could do such a thing? Teasing a child like that?"

"You call that teasing?" Elsie said.

The preacher interjected, "Shaming, perhaps. That would be the better word."

Elsie tried to get Ivy's attention. "Ivy? Who gave this to you?"

The girl looked up, her eyes hollow. "Nobody give me nothing."

"Who showed it to you, then?"

"It was by the swings."

Ms. Key broke in. "Her teacher questioned the class. No one saw anything, until she was holding the box. Then an older boy knew what the box was for, and there was a scene." She sighed. "Bedlam."

Elsie sat back in her chair. "So it's just an unsolved mystery. Well." Picking up her purse, she pulled put her car keys. "Unless there's anything else to discuss, I guess we'll head out. Ivy, Tina Peroni said I'm supposed to drive you home." She stood, and the principal did likewise.

Ivy remained rooted in her seat. "I want preacher to take me."

The smug look on his face lit a contrary flame in Elsie's chest. "Hmm. Well, you know, Ivy—Tina's your social worker, and she put me in charge. So let's get your backpack and stuff. Got to hit the road."

The principal pawed through papers on her desk. "I wonder if I should have you sign a form."

Ivy and Reverend Albertson remained seated, side by side. He'd resumed patting her hand. "I'll take care of you, Ivy."

Ivy nodded, avoiding Elsie's eye.

Elsie was growing impatient. "Come on, Ivy; I'll have you home in a flash."

"I'm going with preacher. He's supposed to keep an eye on me."

With a frustrated exhale, Elsie surrendered. "Fine. I'll let Tina know."

She watched the preacher lay a hand on the child's head. Ivy narrowed her eyes, but tolerated the caress without protest, her face closed.

Elsie turned to go, ignoring the warning buzz in her head. Something was off, but she didn't know what it was. Ivy's demeanor was unreadable today. She didn't know whether to attribute the girl's stony behavior to the condom box, or the principal's office, or the influence of Reverend Albertson. There was an underlying vibe that troubled Elsie.

She shook it off; she'd done her part. It was time to head to the Baldknobbers. She deserved a drink. She needed one.

Chapter Thirty-One

ON WEDNESDAY AFTERNOON, Nell Stout drove the Buick down Delmar Street, keeping a close lookout. She had her orders. No time for waffling. Nell was a soldier, had been one all her life.

When the yellow school bus pulled up to the street corner Nell hit the brake and waited. She reached over to the passenger seat and clutched the black ski mask that she'd been instructed to bring. She saw that the price tag still dangled from it, identifying it as a purchase from the dollar store in a neighboring community. Nell pulled it off with a jerk. She'd been laying out money all week; trifling amounts, but it added up. She'd bought the condoms two days ago, the ski mask last weekend. Money didn't grow on trees, she thought; and wondered whether she'd be reimbursed for the purchases, as well as her time and trouble.

None of this was her fault. She hadn't told Larry to go at Jessie with that bat. When he'd whined about the baby in Nell's presence, she'd advised him to hush his mouth. And she'd told her boy, Bruce, a hundred times or more to keep his rod out of that woman's tail. *Don't lose your head over tail,* she'd said. She hoped to goodness he'd had the sense to wear a rubber. Everybody knew that woman was trash. Considering what they all knew, it was no wonder that Smokey pulled her out of the meatpacking plant and put her to work selling product instead. They said you couldn't catch it from food, but Nell wasn't so sure.

Nell watched as the schoolchildren filed out of the bus. A double handful of kids emerged from the open door, jumping down the steps onto the curb. She knew who would appear first: kids from the upper grades, with permanent teeth and cocky attitudes. She put her car in Park and waited for the little ones, the last to descend. Finally, Ivy walked down the steps of the bus, clutching the rail.

Nell put the Buick in gear and trailed Ivy, not worried whether the child was aware of the tail. The hour of reckoning had arrived. It wasn't her decision, not her call. She was working under direct orders from the Big Boy.

A Ford Escort turned down the corner and tore down the street, slowing as it reached the ambling cluster of schoolchildren. The car pulled directly in front of the Buick, its brake calipers squealing with the effort. The window of the Ford rolled down. "Ivy!" the driver shouted.

The child looked over at the driver, her face closing with apprehension. Nell drummed her fingers on the steering wheel, debating what to do next.

"Ivy," the driver repeated in a friendly, singsong voice. Nell cursed under her breath as she caught a glance of the driver's face in the Ford's side mirror. It looked like that prosecutor, the one that the Big Boy hated like poison. The one everybody in town knew was blowing the big detective at the police department. Big Boy swore she would try to bring him down one day.

With a dogged expression, Nell covertly watched as Ivy approached the Ford and leaned into the passenger side window. The girl was talking to the lawyer, and Lord only knew what she might reveal. Big Boy said he wasn't about to let the operation fall apart on account of a white trash kid. There was too much at stake.

Stretching her arm to the glove compartment, Nell reached inside and pulled out a Smith & Wesson .357 revolver. She inhaled deeply. This was a fly in the ointment, complicating what should have been a simple execution. She let the gun rest in her lap and pulled out her phone, pondering whether she should text for advice, knowing he wouldn't like it.

Nell was torn. The presence of the lawyer was a wrinkle they hadn't prepared for. She could still bide her time and follow through, though it would be a whole lot harder to pull it off. The lawyer was a risk. A big fat risk. Not just to Big Boy, but to Nell personally. She had survived to the ripe old age of sixty by keeping her head down and dodging catastrophe. Watching the car ahead, she was inclined to abort the mission. To play it safe.

But she was a mother. She loved her son. And she was loyal, no question about that. Loyal to the Big Boy, just as she'd been loyal to his daddy.

With one hand on the gun and the other on the phone, she waited for inspiration.

ELSIE HAD NOT planned to meet Ivy after school. Her work hours didn't mesh with the end of the school day. After spending two days in trial, she had played a frantic game of catch-up on Wednesday. Moreover, time spent with Ivy was no joy ride. The sight of the girl's grim face behind the broken glasses could kill a buzz on Christmas morning. That child would wipe the smile off Ronald McDonald.

But while sitting behind her desk at the courthouse that afternoon, Elsie couldn't quit thinking about the condoms. As she stared at the computer screen, she would recall the image of the box of Trojans, plastered with a yellow sticker bearing Ivy's name.

"I'm not your mama," she would mutter, as if it was Ivy's fault that Elsie fought to banish the image from her head.

But she kept envisioning the girl, her shoe untied, her hand caught in the preacher's grasp. Elsie could sense the power the man held over Ivy, and she didn't like it. It was easy enough to understand that a recently orphaned child would attach herself to an adult who offered her kindness. But she worried that it was unhealthy, and moreover, she wondered about Albertson's motives. Because his brand of Christian charity was suspect, in Elsie's book.

She wasn't getting any work done. Elsie logged onto Twitter, but no one had posted anything diverting, and she didn't dare to initiate a tweet; Madeleine frowned upon the staff dawdling on social media during work hours.

She turned back to her desk, sorting through the Larry Paul files and putting the folders in order. The file bearing the investigative photos spilled open, and she was confronted with Ivy's unsmiling image, behind the broken glasses. It was a copy of the very photo that once made Chuck Harris wet his pants.

Elsie stuck the file on the corner of her desk. "Fuck a duck," she said. She checked the clock: it was just past 3:00 P.M. Elsie bowed to the inevitable. She would seek out Ivy, check and see whether she was okay. Once Elsie determined that all was well with the girl, she could get that picture out of her head.

She slipped out of the courthouse without a word to anyone. Ordinarily, she would have checked in with Breeon, and asked her to cover for Elsie's departure. But that Wednesday, she didn't even pause beside Breeon's office door. The strain in their friendship grew heavier with every day that Elsie continued to serve as counsel in the Larry Paul case.

Driving down the street to Ivy's foster home, she scoured the sidewalks for schoolchildren, trying to determine whether Ivy might be home.

She planned to wait at Ivy's foster home, but she saw the school bus stop down the block. Elsie was driving too fast. *Slow down— watch out for kids,* she reminded herself, as she pulled in front of an old Buick and rolled the passenger window down. Ivy was stepping off the bus. Elsie called to her.

She saw the child's reaction. Ivy's face puckered; she dropped her chin and looked at Elsie over the broken glasses. Elsie sighed. When was someone going to do something about those glasses?

She leaned across the passenger seat and spoke again, smiling like a clown. "Hey, Ivy! Can I walk you home?"

Ivy didn't answer. She was staring at the Buick behind Elsie's Ford. Elsie also shot a glance in that direction, following Ivy's gaze. A quick movement in the front seat, so fast that it was a blur, made her look twice. Was the driver hiding, she wondered. The afternoon sun reflected off the windshield. She couldn't be sure.

But she had a bad feeling. She beckoned to Ivy.

"How you doing, Ivy?"

Ivy tore her gaze from the Buick and looked at Elsie with trepidation.

Elsie tried again. With a light voice, she said, "I was in the neighborhood. Just thought I'd say hi." To reassure her, Elsie added, "No court business. Nothing like that."

Ivy didn't speak. Elsie cut off the engine and exited the car, crossing to meet the child on the curb. "How about if I walk you home? That okay with you?"

Ivy slid her hand into Elsie's. Elsie gave it a squeeze, gratified by the gesture of trust. Ivy headed toward her yellow house at a brisk pace, almost a run: Elsie had to move quickly to keep up. She saw Ivy look over her shoulder.

Elsie glanced back; the Buick was still there. "Do you know that car?" she asked Ivy.

Ivy pulled at Elsie's hand, heading for home. "I don't know nothing."

When they reached the steps of the yellow house, Elsie saw the Buick zoom down the street, passing them by so fast she couldn't get a look at the driver. She stepped off the sidewalk, trying to read the rear license plate.

The car didn't have one.

Chapter Thirty-Two

ELSIE STOOD IN the lobby of the Barton Cinema Palace on Friday night, clutching a bucket of popcorn in one hand and a jumbo drink in the other. A clock over the entryway showed that Ashlock was late again. She wanted to check her phone, but her hands were full.

The size of the popcorn tub made her self-conscious; but the high school concessions worker informed her that the jumbo size was five cents cheaper than the medium combo. It made economic sense to order it. Besides, she would share it with Ashlock. And his son.

When Ashlock called her in the afternoon to suggest they see a movie, she was delighted. It sounded like an excellent escape, a date night where they might sit in the dark, holding hands. Maybe make out, like a couple of teenagers, if they nabbed a seat in the back of the theater.

Then he dropped the bomb. "*Jurassic World* is playing. There's a showtime at 7:20."

Elsie made a horrified face at the phone. "Dinosaurs?"

"Yeah, Burton wants to see it. It's supposed to be a good show."

Elsie had swallowed back her negative response: that she didn't like dinosaurs or action adventure films. And that three people was an odd number for a Friday night date. With false cheer, she agreed to meet Ashlock and Burton at the theater. He had to pick Burton up after debate practice at school, so he might not be able to swing by and pick Elsie up at her apartment.

"No problem," she'd said, trying to keep a cool note out of her voice. *I am going to be a good sport,* she thought as she ended the call. *Just gonna go with the flow.*

But as she stood in the crowded lobby, her resolve to be a good sport disappeared. When Ashlock and Burton finally made their way into the theater, she had to restrain herself; she wanted to bite his head off.

"Sorry," he said. "We're a little late."

"Yeah, you're late. They're already showing the previews."

"Well, that's good. We haven't missed anything. But I didn't mean for you to buy your own ticket."

"I don't mind laying out seven dollars. What I do mind—" she dropped her voice, because Burton had taken a step backwards, as if trying to distance himself. "What I do mind is standing around here like an idiot, not knowing when you were going to show up."

He frowned at Elsie, then looked over at his son. "You want anything to eat, Burton?"

"I got popcorn. To share," Elsie said.

Burton tilted his head, studying the pictures of concessions. "I could go for a pretzel."

Elsie closed her eyes and willed herself to stay silent. *Not a pretzel. The pretzels take forever. When I'm in line behind a guy who orders a pretzel, I want to throttle him.*

Ashlock handed Burton a ten-dollar bill, then took Elsie by the elbow. "We'll go on in and get our seats," he said.

The theater was packed. They had to wade to the center of the second row to find three adjacent seats. Elsie set her jumbo Diet Coke on the floor and put the popcorn bucket on the armrest she shared with Ashlock. "I got this to share," she whispered.

He stared into the bucket. "Did you salt it?"

"Yeah. Salted the hell out of it."

"Shhhhhh," sounded from someone behind her.

Ashlock dropped his voice. "I'll let you have it. I'm cutting back on salt."

She pinched her lips together and pulled the bucket onto her lap. Burton found them; balancing a soft pretzel on a paper plate, he scooted down the aisle to join them in the seat that Ashlock saved. As Burton crossed in front of Elsie, he kicked her drink. The plastic lid slipped off when it fell sideways onto the floor, flooding Elsie's feet.

"Sorry," he whispered as Elsie leaned over to right the cup. The woman on her left stood and deserted her seat, muttering.

"You want me to get you another one?" Ashlock asked. Elsie shook her head. Maybe she could take a nap. If she fell asleep, she might enjoy herself.

She slid down in the theater seat, resting her head against the cushioned back. Watching the activity onscreen through hooded eyes, she entertained a hope that the dinosaurs might tear off Chris Pratt's clothing, because he was looking good. Kicking the ice cubes underfoot out of her way, she stretched her legs and fell into a light snooze.

Her rest was broken when Ashlock let out a piercing shriek.

She sat up with a jerk, knocking a layer of popcorn from the bucket. Turning to Ashlock, she clutched his arm. "Are you okay?"

He shook his head with a sheepish grin. Elsie glanced at the screen; apparently the monster dinosaur had popped onto the screen unexpectedly, to give the audience a scare.

Turning back to Ashlock, she saw him focused on his son. Burton was laughing so hard that it choked him; he wiped tears from his eyes. "You squealed like a girl," he said, when he could catch his breath. Ashlock nodded in acknowledgment, covering his face in mock shame.

Burton punched him in the shoulder. "Real tough guy. Dad, you're showing your true colors."

Ashlock whispered something in reply that Elsie couldn't quite catch, but as she watched the interaction of Ashlock and his son, she had a change of heart. With new eyes, she focused on Ashlock and Burton taking in the film together, laughing, whispering plot theories of what might happen next. With a feeling of remorse, Elsie wondered: why on earth would she begrudge Ashlock that? He shared a bond with his son like the one she had with her parents—particularly with Marge. It was a gift. No one should create a divide between something so precious.

She was smiling when Ashlock glanced her way. "What you thinking about?" he asked.

She couldn't tell him the turn her thoughts had taken. So she leaned in and whispered, "You're even cuter than Chris Pratt."

Ashlock rolled his eyes at her extravagant claim. Burton must have overheard it, because he choked on his pretzel.

Ashlock whispered, "Wish you'd set that bucket in the

empty seat by you. I'd like to hold your hand. I might get scared again."

She tossed the popcorn aside and slipped her hand in his. He gave it a squeeze. Then she rested her head on his shoulder, not minding the wooden armrest that dug into her flesh. *This is nice,* she thought. *This works.*

Chapter Thirty-Three

A FRESH OCTOBER breeze rattled the screen door at the Battered Women's Center of the Ozarks. Elsie breathed it in with pleasure as she presided over the front desk of the facility, housed in an old hotel on the wrong side of the tracks in Barton, Missouri.

Elsie had served as a volunteer at the BWCO since the prior winter, when she went to trial in *State v. Taney*, a hard-fought incest case. She didn't resent dedicating two Sundays a month to work the front desk at the women's shelter. As a prosecutor, she had seen firsthand the need for refuge that the building provided.

She walked to the screen door and opened it, looking at the hard blue sky overhead. The past four weeks since the jury selection had flown by, bringing a change of weather along with the approach of the Larry Paul trial. Madeleine's ordinary mood had declined with the temperature, transforming her everyday pique to wild-eyed hysteria. Elsie would have liked to lean on Ashlock, but his paternal duties kept him busy—and though she was learning to accept that with grace, she still missed the support. And Breeon remained taciturn and distant. As the leaves turned to vibrant autumn hues, then fell, Elsie approached each day with listless dread, and found that it was increasingly difficult to sleep without a nightcap or two. Or more.

She had always loved October, the change in the colors of the sky and landscape, the cool mornings, the air as crisp as a Jonathon apple. But this year, she anticipated the season with a mix of impatience and trepidation. On some days, she wanted the trial date to hurry up and arrive, so she could get it behind her.

On other days, she wished a truck would run over her.

As she stared at the ancient, crumbling storefronts that faced the old hotel, she reflected that a major bodily injury sounded increasingly tempting. Maybe the truck could just roll over one leg. That would put her in the hospital, free her from the Larry Paul case. But it wouldn't kill her.

And sometimes, she thought that the Larry Paul case would. Kill her, that is. Because the case itself was a killer; it was screwing her up. Maybe. The thought had whispered in her head repeatedly over the past weeks, that maybe she wasn't really cut out to handle a death penalty case.

The ring of her cell phone interrupted her dark thoughts, and she walked to the desk to pick it up. When she saw the caller's name, she smiled.

"Hey, Ash," she said into the phone. Elsie sat on the desktop; it was a century old, but held her weight better than the vinyl-topped metal desk at the courthouse. "What you up to?"

"Sunday afternoon at the grocery store. Got stocked up for the week."

"Well, that's using your head. No one will call you Old Mother Hubbard."

She liked the sound of his voice in her ear. It was warm and strong, and had a calming effect.

"Yeah, well. Burton's a skinny kid, but he'll eat me out of house and home."

"Growing boy," Elsie responded.

Ashlock said, "Are you still at the Women's Center?"

"Yeah. But it's been quiet. Which is a good thing."

"Yes, ma'am—on a number of levels. Glad to hear no one's having to run for shelter today. Did you get some work done?"

"In fact, I did." Elsie's eyes shifted to her briefcase, which had the direct examinations for her witnesses in the Larry Paul case. She had gone over them twice that afternoon as she sat in the empty hotel lobby, and they were fine-tuned. "I've got all my exams for trial. Did my laundry last night. So I'll have clean panties to wear for the jury."

"That's always a plus."

"So I've got a great idea." She scooted off of the desk and circled it as she talked. "Let's get something to eat tonight, since our Sunday jobs are done. Something fat and fabulous. It feels like chili weather. Let's go to Casper's Chili Hut."

She heard the pause, anticipating the disappointment that was coming. "Well, you know my new Sunday routine. Burton and I will be heading to Riverside Baptist."

She cleared her throat. "Didn't you go this morning?"

"We did."

The silence lingered until it was just short of uncomfortable. "Um. So if you've had your sins washed away once today already, why do you have to do it again? Rinse and repeat?"

"Elsie, we've been through this."

"Yeah. Yeah, I know." She chided herself for making it difficult for Ashlock. She knew his time with Burton was important. More than important; it was paramount.

"My ex had a set of conditions."

"Right, you've told me. I get it, Ash, I honestly do." She sighed into the phone. "It's been kind of lonely lately, that's all."

"Still rocky?" His voice was sympathetic, and she wished she could literally lean on his shoulder, right at that moment.

"Yeah." She dropped into the wheeled wooden rolling chair and swiveled in it, pushing it across the floor with her feet.

"With Breeon?"

"Uh-huh. We never hang anymore. Not even lunch. Or coffee."

"The two of you will get past this, Elsie."

"Lord, you'd think so." She checked the hour on the grandfather clock that ticked off the minutes in the corner, still keeping time behind a broken face. It was nearly four o'clock; time to go. She picked up her pen and dropped it into her purse, saying, "I'm sure going to be glad when the next week is done."

"I bet. Hey, Elsie; why don't you come on tonight with Burton and me? I'll pick you up at six."

"No. Thanks, but no."

In an encouraging voice, he said, "It's not bad on Sunday nights. They feed you a Sloppy Joe. And the service is short."

"You remember? I swore I'd never set foot in Albertson's temple again. Can't go back on an oath."

"You'll see your little witness, Ivy." He huffed a laugh. "Seems like those Hickmans are at church every time they unlock the doors."

At the mention of Ivy's name, Elsie tensed. Ivy was the only crucial, high-impact witness that Elsie would examine at trial. Her other examinations were necessary witnesses who packed no punch: the records custodian at the hospital; the x-ray technician who x-rayed the deceased mother and child; the police officers who made up the chain of custody for the admission of physical evidence from the crime scene. Those direct exams would be routine.

But with Ivy, nothing was ever routine.

Ashlock continued, "Don't you want to run into her? Wish her luck, saying 'see you this week.' "

"I saw her at the courthouse last week; we did a run-through. We're good."

"Got a new member at Riverside you'd be interested to hear about."

The screen door swung open. A middle-aged woman with a long gray braid entered. Elsie smiled and waved; the woman was her replacement at the front desk. Elsie shouldered her purse and briefcase; moving the phone away from her mouth, she said to the woman, "No activity today. All quiet."

"Good," the woman replied.

Elsie walked out with the phone at her ear. "Why would I care who joined?"

"Old schoolmate of yours. Dean Mitchell."

"No! You're shitting me."

"It's true. Joined up this month. Don't you want to come watch him singing hymns?"

"Shit. I hate Dean Mitchell. Hate him worse than your gay-bashing preacher. Didn't I tell you Dean Mitchell held my head under at the pool?"

Ashlock laughed into the phone. "I believe you mentioned that."

Elsie's Ford was parked on the street. She unlocked it and threw her bags onto the passenger seat. Frowning, she said, "I hate his guts. I don't want to see his face."

"Girl, you sure can hold a grudge."

Elsie considered the statement as she started up the car. It was true, she decided. Rolling down the driver's side window, she rested her elbow on it and let the engine idle.

"I think it's a family trait. I got it from my mother's side."

"Hey, Elsie—so why don't you head over and see the folks? I bet Marge and George would love a visit. Wouldn't be surprised if she'd feed you supper, to boot." Elsie considered the temptation of a home-cooked meal, but discarded the notion. She was a little too keyed up to be good company; and her mother's good intentions and advice might grate on her, in her present mood.

"Better not. I think I'll drive-through Little Hong Kong and get some cashew chicken. Spend my evening with the *Sister Wives.*"

Ashlock laughed. "Elsie, for a smart woman, you have the worst taste in television. Dang near shameful."

She scoffed. "You're heading off to spend your time with Little Smokey Mitchell and Reverend Albertson. Who's got the shitty taste?"

"Okay, I get it."

She smiled; her voice took on a teasing note. "Ash, maybe I should add: you gotta lotta taste—it's all in your mouth."

"That's an old line. Elsie, try to relax and ease up tonight. I miss you, baby. See you tomorrow."

"Okay." She hung up and tossed her phone into her open purse.

She had just pulled away from the curb when the phone rang again. What did he forget, she wondered, scrambling to pick up before the call went to voice mail. Keeping her eyes dutifully on the road ahead, she answered.

In a saucy tone, she said, "So you decided you want to tie me up and fuck me instead of going to church."

There was no response on the other end.

Elsie said, "Ash? You there?"

She heard an intake of breath, followed by a cackle. "You are such a trashy bitch."

Elsie gasped. She looked at the phone in her hand, but the number wasn't one of her contacts. "Who is this," she said, switching to her most dignified courtroom voice.

The laughing voice on the line made her cringe. "It's Claire, hon. Claire O'Hara."

Elsie gritted her teeth. "Well, I sure do apologize, Claire. Thought you were someone else."

"I'm so disappointed! I thought you were lusting after me."

"No, nope. Not." Elsie fell silent. *Tell me what you need so I can end this call,* she begged silently.

"Oh, I'm teasing you. I know you're banging Robocop. Everybody in southwest Missouri knows that. But I didn't know you're into bondage. That's kinda spicy."

"It was a joke." She saw the Hong Kong Inn and signaled a right turn. "What can I do for you, Claire?"

"Well, since we start up tomorrow, I just wanted to check and see that you've provided us with all the information we're entitled to."

Elsie pulled into the drive-through and up to the station to place her order. She braked, frowning into the phone. "I don't understand. You and Josh have discovery; you've had access to our file for weeks."

"Oh, I know that. I'm just wondering if you have any little secrets you're not sharing."

"Secrets? Like what?"

"Other statements. Witness summaries."

Impatience made Elise's chest knot up. "I don't know what you're digging for, Claire, but I'm too busy to fool with this right now."

A voice came from the metal intercom box: "Welcome to Little Hong Kong. Please place your order."

Elsie tried to cover her phone with her hand, but without success. She bristled at the sound of Claire's laughter.

"You're one busy lady—yes indeed. Important business at Little Hong Kong. Top Secret."

"Place your order, please."

"Just a minute, okay?" Elsie pleaded to the voice inside the metal box. Turning her head away from the car window, she spoke in a harsh whisper. "We don't have any secret, undisclosed witness statements. I don't even know what you're looking for."

"What about Ivy?"

"You've got her statement and deposition, for God's sake."

"Hmmm. I was wondering. Do you have any handwritten notes? From your meetings with Ivy?"

The question took her by surprise. Elsie did have notes from her encounters with Ivy, where she recorded her observations and jotted strategic points. But she was not about to share her notes with the defense.

"That's my protected work product."

"You think? There's a man's life at stake, and you want to haggle over what you will and won't reveal? Haven't you been in trouble with the ethics commission before?"

"That was all bullshit. Josh Nixon knows that."

The box hummed again. "We need you to place your order. There are cars lined up behind you."

In fact, four cars had pulled behind Elsie, and a glance in the side mirror showed that at least one of the drivers was visibly unhappy with her.

"I want the cashew chicken special with fried rice," she shouted into the box; then turned back to the phone. "Back off, Claire. I'm not the green kid you slapped around in court four years ago. You can't bully me. I'm not taking any shit off of you."

Claire sighed. "I guess we'll find out what kind of lawyer you've become. Gonna find out this week. Enjoy your cashew chicken."

She hung up. Elsie pulled her car to the pickup window. The brown paper bag they handed to her was warm and fragrant.

But she had a sour stomach.

Chapter Thirty-Four

It was six o'clock in the morning. The big day had arrived. Elsie stood under the shower, trying to pump herself up. As the warm water pelted her face, she counseled herself: *It's almost over. A week or two, depending. Then you won't have to think about it anymore.*

As Madeleine had instructed, Elsie pulled her car into the parking lot of the Kinfolks Kafe diner, directly across the square from the courthouse. She checked the time on her phone: eight o'clock on the dot, she noted with relief. She wouldn't be met with a hairy eyeball for running late.

She hurried in through the back door, and saw Madeleine and Parsons sitting in a booth near the kitchen door.

"Morning," she said, trying to hit the right note, conveying a can-do attitude mixed with solemnity. How did you greet your coworkers when you were walking into a death penalty case? She didn't want to appear too jocular.

Madeleine looked her up and down. Elise felt self-conscious; she had to stifle the urge to glance down and see whether her bra strap was visible.

"Go look out the front door. Check the courthouse. Then report back." Madeleine's eyelid twitched.

Elsie walked the short distance to the front entrance of the Kinfolks, tugging at her zipper and adjusting her bra as she moved down the aisle. The morning sun blinded her; she had to shield her eyes to make out the activity in front of the courthouse.

At first, it looked like any Monday in October at the McCown County Courthouse. A lawyer mounted the steps, swinging a brown leather briefcase. Two county employees smoked a cigarette by a side door, chatting lazily and dropping ashes on the pavement.

But two local TV vehicles pulled to the curb, one after another. As the reporters alighted carrying cameras and equipment, a large unmarked van that was parked nearby came to life. The doors slid open and people poured out, carrying signs.

Elsie fairly ran back to the table. "Things are heating up."

Parsons smiled. "Are my people here?"

"I saw a big van unload when the TV mobile units arrived. It's a big old van, probably holds a dozen or more people." She glanced at a coffee carafe of black and gold plastic sitting on the table. "Can I have a cup of that coffee?"

"No. No time." Madeleine clutched her purse and slid to the end of the booth, but Samuel Parsons leaned back in the seat, smiling like the Cheshire cat.

"No need to rush, Madeleine. Let's all have another cup of coffee. Give the pot a chance to bubble and boil over there at the courthouse."

Elsie looked at Madeleine for the order to stay or go; but she saw her relent, saw it in the drooping of her shoulders under her silk jacket. Elsie reached over, picking up a clean coffee mug from an empty booth nearby. She scooted in beside Madeleine and poured a cup. She and Madeleine sat in tense silence.

Parsons didn't appear to suffer their first-day jitters. "This will be a breeze to kick off. Jury selection is behind us, so we just jump right in." Parsons folded his arms on the table and leaned toward Elsie. "You got your Opening Statement ready to go?"

Rather than answer, Elsie dove into her bag and pulled out the neatly handwritten pages. The top of the first sheet read "OS."

Parsons's eyebrows shot up. "You don't do it on the computer?"

"I've told her. I've told her time and again that any professional should create a Word document when preparing arguments or examinations. You compose and make a record of it at the same time. She never listens." Madeleine's eye twitched again. She gave her eyelid a delicate rub with a pinkie finger, as if she needed to remove a speck.

A small metal pitcher of milk, sweating with beads of moisture, sat near the coffeepot. Parsons reached for the milk and poured a measure into his coffee cup. "What TV stations are out there?"

"One of the Joplin Stations," Elsie said.

"Joplin always gives us good coverage," Madeleine said. She pulled a silver compact out of her purse and opened it, studying herself in the mirror.

"What about Springfield? Is Springfield out there?"

"Maybe. I couldn't see." Elsie leaned out of the booth in an attempt to peer out the front window, but her view of the street was blocked.

Parsons stirred his coffee with a battered spoon. "We need KY3. KY3 from Springfield. Their audience is huge."

"Joplin's stations go out to four states," Madeleine said. She sounded defensive.

"Yeah, but KY3 has a better market."

"Oooh," Elsie said, with mock awe. "The Queen City."

Parsons looked at her in confusion. "Huh?"

Madeleine answered. "Springfield. It's the Queen City of the Ozarks."

Elsie met Madeleine's eye and they broke into genuine laughter. Elsie waved a hand in apology. "Sorry, Sam. In out-state MO, we like to have a little laugh at Springfield's expense. They think they're such big shit over there, third largest city in the state."

"So cosmopolitan in Springfield. They have a mall. And four Walmart Supercenters." Madeleine flashed her a wink from the non-twitchy eye. It occurred to Elsie that the sisterhood of small-town Missouri was one of few connections she and Madeleine shared.

Parsons sipped the last swallow of his coffee, holding a hand over his tie to protect it from a stray drip. "Let's roll, ladies."

They strolled across the street to the courthouse entrance, Parsons and Madeleine shoulder to shoulder, Elsie a pace behind. They hadn't proceeded far when Elsie heard Parsons whisper, "What the hell?"

Peering around Madeleine, she saw the people surrounding the van: a dozen or so, as she estimated. But they didn't look like any Right to Life supporters Elsie had ever seen. They were assembling posters of another kind. She caught a glimpse of one: DOWN WITH THE DEATH PENALTY. It depicted a hypodermic needle with a large X painted across it.

Standing alone, at the end of the courthouse steps, was a woman holding a sign that said, END ABORTION NOW.

Parsons made a beeline for the anti-abortion protester. Elsie heard him ask, "Where's your friends?"

The woman shrugged, a helpless movement of her shoulders. Then the cameras—both of them—moved in, and the death penalty opponents made a dash for the press.

"Move," Elsie said. "Now."

She gave Madeleine a shove, almost causing her boss to trip up the stone steps. The three of them ran for the door, followed by a reporter with an outstretched microphone, shouting, "How does it feel to be part of a death penalty case?"

The deputy in charge of security was a new hire; when they reached the door, he instructed them to empty their pockets and send their bags through the metal detector.

Madeleine scowled at him, her eyes ablaze. In a high-pitched shriek, she said, "Get. Out. Of. My. Way."

Oh shit, Elsie thought, *she's losing it.* Glancing over her shoulder, she saw that the reporter had captured it on camera.

Parsons tugged at her elbow. "Come on," he said, and they bypassed the elevator, heading up the stairs at a brisk trot.

On the second floor, Claire O'Hara leaned over the rotunda railing, laughing as she watched their procession. "That was quite a show. Brava," she called. Her voice echoed in the vaulted space.

Madeleine's fingers shook as she pressed the security code buttons for entrance in the back door of the Prosecutor's Office. Once inside, she marched back to her private office, unlocked the door, and hurled her briefcase against the wall. It connected with her law school diploma, knocking it to the floor.

Parsons turned to Elsie; they exchanged a look. "Does she get like this often?" he asked.

Elsie opened her mouth to answer, then clamped it shut.

Parsons shut the door behind him. Elsie sat in her customary seat on the couch, but he remained standing, watching Madeleine with a wary eye as she fiddled in her purse and pulled out a prescription pill bottle.

"You'll have to excuse me, Sam. I'm not myself this morning." She shook a small tablet into her hand and dry-swallowed it. "Get me water," she said to Elsie.

Elsie slipped through the door, glad to have a reason to escape. As she pulled it shut, she heard Madeleine say in a wavering voice, "I think this death penalty issue is getting to me, Sam."

The admission bolstered Elsie's spirits. The specter of Larry Paul's execution was certainly boring into her. Twice, in the previous night, she had resorted to staring at the gory photos of Jesse Rose and her unborn son, to bolster her resolve and give her strength to make it through the night. When the images didn't provide the relief she sought, she added an additional step to her regimen: she poured a shot of gin and downed it. Liquid valium, she thought, jumping to her own defense. Not everyone could resort to the luxury of Madeleine's pill bottle.

In the reception area, she met Stacie, stowing her lunch in the community office refrigerator. "Hey, Stacie. Do we have any bottled water around here? It's for Madeleine," she added as an afterthought, hoping it would add weight to the inquiry.

Stacie blew her wispy bangs out of her eyes with an impatient explosion of breath. "What am I, a convenience store?"

Elsie interpreted that as a negative. She peered through the glass door into the rotunda, debating the wisdom of a dash to the courthouse snack bar. But the hallways were already filling up, with spectators for the Larry Paul trial by the looks of it.

She dodged into her office and opened the small fridge where she stowed her personal stash. Elsie had refilled it on Friday, as a necessary preparation for trial. It contained twelve cold cans of Diet Coke. She grabbed one and ran down to Madeleine's office.

When she entered, Elsie saw that Madeleine and Samuel Parsons were bent over her handwritten Opening Statement, as if checking if for errors. Elsie's jaw clenched. She'd presided over more trials in the past four years than Madeleine and Parsons combined.

She set the Diet Coke on the desk by the Opening Statement, giving Madeleine a look of resentment. "Drink this," she said. She bent over and snatched up the pad with her handwriting, flipping the pages back into place and smoothing them with a possessive hand.

Chapter Thirty-Five

ELSIE SAT AT the end of the prosecution counsel table, in the spot farthest from the jury and closest to the courtroom door. Strategically, it was the weakest spot in the trial court. The prosecution should be seated at the table beside the jury box, to initiate an unspoken bond with the group of twelve (fourteen in this case; they had seated two alternates, and no one but the judge knew which two these might be) through physical immediacy.

But the prosecution team had wasted precious minutes that morning, lingering in Madeleine's office as Parsons wrangled on the phone with his absentee Right-to-Life constituency. While the prosecutors loitered, Josh Nixon and Claire O'Hara set up camp at the prime table.

That made two battles lost by the prosecution and won by the defense that morning; and court had not yet convened for the day.

Elsie smoothed the skirt of her best suit; not purchased on sale at J.C. Penney, but a graduation gift from her mother and dad over four years ago. It was no longer the cutting edge of fashion, even for McCown County, and it was growing increasingly difficult to fasten the zipper in back. She managed to create additional space around the waist by leaving the button undone and securing the waistband with a large safety pin. Under her jacket, no one would know.

Judge Callaway's courtroom was large, by McCown County standards. In addition to the space devoted to court business— the judge's bench, the witness stand, the jury box and counsel table— there was a generous gallery for public spectators, benches built a century ago to accommodate fifty people. Today the benches were full, seating reporters, onlookers, and curiosity seekers. No witnesses were seated inside: the defense had invoked the rule prohibiting witnesses from being present in court when they were not giving testimony. All of the witnesses for the State were roaming the halls of the courthouse, except for one. Ivy was seated at Elsie's desk in her office, attended by Tina Peroni.

At least we won't deal with her shit-for-brains foster mother today, Elsie thought. Holly Hickman had begged off, claiming that her husband worried that the baby would catch something at the courthouse, exposed to so many people.

The bailiff opened the door and ushered the jury into the room. Elsie stood as they made their way to the jury box, taking careful note of the attitudes and expressions of the four men and ten women. Several of the women looked nervous; a middle-aged man appeared to be supremely self-conscious, probably unused to being the focus of so much attention. The youngest panelist, a bearded college student in his early twenties wearing a maroon Missouri State University T-shirt, smiled as he made his way to his seat.

Oh please God—let that boy be an alternate, Elsie prayed. He was a walking Not Guilty vote. She could already read it on his face.

It took the jury a few minutes to settle into the jury box. When it had been designed in the 1900s to accommodate twelve citizens, people were smaller. The fourteen twenty-first-century jurors were a tight squeeze. Elsie was glad to see that jurors hailing from the Queen City of Springfield were just as fat as the home folks in Barton, Missouri. Maybe fatter. The thought was painfully interrupted when the safety pin enlarging her waistband popped open and jabbed her in the back.

During the judge's reading of instructions to the jury she struggled under her jacket, trying to fasten the pin. When Madeleine turned on her with a wild-eyed stare, she gave up the attempt and folded her hands on the counsel table. *Maybe the pain will keep me on my toes,* she comforted herself. As long as she didn't start to bleed, she should be okay.

She pulled out the pad that held her Opening Statement and scanned the first page. While she concentrated, Madeleine elbowed her. She looked up.

Madeleine was passing a sheet of paper to her. She jerked her head in Sam Parsons's direction, apparently to indicate that it was a communication from him.

Elsie stared at the words on the paper, wondering what Parsons thought she'd omitted in her Opening. It was surely a matter of some importance, for him to interrupt as she was poised to begin.

The paper, in handwritten caps, said USE THIS. Underneath was a typewritten paragraph. It began with the following words:

"Ladies and gentlemen of the jury, a trial is like a jigsaw puzzle."

She swiveled her head to face Parsons, her eyes bulging with a look that conveyed: *are you kidding me?* The puzzle metaphor was so tired and passé, even law students scoffed at it in their trial practice classes.

He nodded at her with insistence, pointing at the puzzle shtick again.

She slid the page to the side. Opening Statement was the job that fell to the low man. Unlike Closing Argument or voir dire, no one ever claimed that a trial could be won or lost on the basis of Opening Statement. But she was prepared to make her very best showing, and she'd be damned if her speech would incorporate a boring three-minute comparison of evidence to pieces from a puzzle box.

Judge Callaway spoke from the bench. "Is the State ready to proceed with Opening Statement?"

Elsie rose. "We are, your honor. If it please the court."

When he nodded, she approached the jury box, clutching her legal pad. The old-time lawyers, like Billy Yocum, didn't require notes; when they spoke to juries, it was always off the cuff. Elsie knew that some young trial layers attempted to mimic the extemporaneous style, but she didn't dare. She still needed the security of a script to refer to when she was interrupted by defense objections, to ensure that she had covered all of her bases.

She stood up straight. The safety pin pierced her spine. "Ladies and gentlemen of the jury," she began.

She didn't smile.

"I'm Elsie Arnold, Assistant Prosecutor of McCown County; my cocounsel in this case, as Judge Callaway told you earlier, is County Prosecutor Madeleine Thompson and Sam Parsons, from the State Attorney General's Office. And the defendant in this case—"

She paused to turn on the defense table to point a literal finger of accusation at the defendant. "Is Larry Edward Paul. He has been accused of two separate counts of murder in the first degree."

She let her gaze linger on Larry Paul, knowing that if she stared at him, the jury would follow her example. For trial, he was dressed in his orange jail scrubs, which surprised her; she would have expected his attorneys to scrounge up more suitable garb for his courtroom appearance. His hair was trimmed and his beard was gone; Paul was fresh-shaven, revealing a dimple in his chin that could rival the dent in Ben Affleck's face.

But the cold blue eyes were the same she had encountered before; though this time, his courtroom manner resembled a case of shell shock.

She turned back. In a voice conveying deep solemnity, she said, "Ladies and gentlemen, this is what the evidence will show."

Elsie took a deep breath, and let it out. "Jessie Rose Dent was twenty-six years old. She was the mother of a daughter, Ivy—a six-year-old. Jessie Dent was expecting her second child. She was eight months pregnant; the evidence will show that the unborn child had reached thirty-six weeks' gestation." Elsie paused. "It was a boy."

The jurors' eyes were glued to her. She was glad she had disregarded Parsons' advice. She'd still be halfway into the puzzle piece explanation, and many of the jurors might be staring out the window by now.

"Jessie Dent lived in a trailer in McCown County, Missouri, right inside the city limits of Barton. She had been a working mother, employed at a local meatpacking plant until her swelling, due to pregnancy, rendered her unable to work."

She walked to the other end of the jury box, trailing her fingers down the wooden railing. "She lived with the defendant in that trailer. For a period of two years, she had lived with Larry Edward Paul. He was her boyfriend, her partner." Her voice intensified.

"DNA evidence will show that the defendant, Larry Paul, was the father of the baby she carried—the unborn son in her womb."

A middle-aged woman with iron gray hair sitting on her head like a helmet nodded at Elsie, as if instructing her to continue. *Score,* Elsie thought.

"On the sixth of September of this year, at approximately ten o'clock in the evening, Jessie Dent and her young daughter, Ivy, were at home at the trailer, with the defendant and a friend of his, named Bruce Stout. We'll provide evidence that the defendant took a baseball bat and beat Jessie Dent with it. The coroner will testify that she suffered massive skull fractures, which caused her death; and that she also suffered internal injuries. Because the coroner's examination revealed that in addition to blows to the head, Jessie Dent sustained repeated blows to her abdomen—her belly—with a blunt instrument." She leaned forward, scouring the jurors with eye contact. "Her unborn son died with her."

Elsie was on a roll; but she couldn't help but wonder why the defense table was so quiet. She had anticipated a dozen objections by this juncture, had jotted notes of how she might respond to the protests of the defense counsel. She was tempted to glance over at Josh Nixon and Claire O'Hara, to gauge what they were planning; but she steeled herself to resist the urge. She must retain her focus and keep it aimed at the jurors in the box.

Elsie gained more momentum as she talked, dropping nuggets of what the jury could expect: medical evidence from the coroner, fingerprints, hair, and DNA evidence from the state crime lab; eyewitness testimony from Ivy; and toxicology reports showing that the defendant's blood had .15 alcohol as well as methamphetamine.

Silence still reigned at the defense table.

She took a step back; it was time to cut the snakebite and suck the poison. "But ladies and gentlemen, those are not the only shocking facts in this case. The evidence will reveal other disturbing truths. Toxicology reports will also show that Jessie Dent, the victim, had traces of alcohol and drugs in her system. And in addition, she was HIV positive." She paused. "Though her son was not." She repeated it, to make certain they understood. "The baby did not have AIDS."

Now that she had bloodied her victim, it was time for the final punch.

"When the police came to the trailer after an anonymous call to 911, they found Jessie Dent's battered body in a pool of blood. A bloody baseball bat lay beside her. The police found the defendant, Larry Paul, passed out in the bedroom. He had blood on his hands and body. It was the blood of Jessie Dent."

Why didn't they object? Emboldened by their silence, Elsie was using language she knew was inflammatory, referring to the defendant as "passed out" rather than "asleep." But she dismissed the concern; her adrenaline was pumping, and she forged on.

"Detective Ashlock questioned the defendant. Detective Ashlock, the head of the Detective Division of the Barton Police Department, will testify that the defendant confessed to killing Jessie Dent. He admitted that he beat her to death. That he meant to do it, had been thinking about it for months, as she grew larger and larger with his baby."

She leaned into the jury, all but invading the space of the jury box.

"Because he didn't want the baby to be born, you see. The defendant told the detective he didn't want to be stuck with it. He was afraid—" and she dropped her voice, for effect. "Afraid he'd be made to pay child support."

Done, she thought. She looked at the jurors a final time, from one end of the jury box to another. She nodded. "That, ladies and gentlemen, is what the evidence will show."

As Elsie walked the short distance to her seat, the thought pounded in her head: What was the defense doing? Where were the objections? Claire and Josh Nixon had permitted her to get away with murder: she'd delivered an Opening Statement that had bordered on Closing Argument. They should have been on their feet, shouting her down. If the situation was reversed, Elsie would be on them like a duck on a June bug. Like flies on shit.

Though it was tough, she resisted the urge to turn her head and glance at them to try to read their faces. But that would be an admission of the defense table's power. She strode by them, keeping her eyes straight ahead, on her own cocounsel.

Sitting, she flipped to a blank page and wrote without looking down. *WTF???* She pushed the pad in front of Madeleine. She and Madeleine exchanged a look. Madeleine lifted her shoulders.

Judge Callaway spoke. "Mr. Nixon, Ms. O'Hara, are you prepared to give the Opening for the defense at this time or do you wish to reserve it for later?"

Nixon stood. "We're ready, your honor." He adjusted his tie and strode to the jury box. Like Elsie, Josh Nixon carried a legal pad. The hand that held it trembled slightly.

Elsie stared at the back of his head as he faced the jury, clearing his throat. He didn't bother to get a haircut for trial, she noticed with surprise. But Josh was a public defender; the rules were different for attorneys who wore the black hat. If a prosecutor appeared before a jury with shaggy hair, Madeleine would have his head on a platter like John the Baptist.

"Ladies and gentlemen of the jury, my client, Larry Paul, has been charged with the murder of his girlfriend and his unborn son."

Nixon paused. The silence stretched for long seconds. Elsie had an urge to fidget; she repressed it, clenched her hands together in her lap.

"The prosecution just outlined evidence that will be presented in this case, the evidence that will support the State's accusation."

Again, he stopped. Elsie heard Parsons whisper to Madeleine, "What's his problem? Does this guy know how to try a case?"

"Ssshh," Elsie said with a hiss. She scooted to the edge of her seat.

Josh Nixon took a deep breath. "The penalty under law for these charges is either life imprisonment without possibility of parole, or death by lethal injection. The prosecution has indicated that they will ask you for the death penalty."

Parsons rose, resting his fingertips on the table before him. "Objection! Your honor, these comments are premature. This is not the punishment portion of the trial. Defense counsel is out of order."

Josh Nixon didn't turn, just swiveled his head. "How is the comment out of order? Is this not a death penalty case?"

Parsons stepped away from the table, approaching the judge. "Is this argument? I'm stumped."

The judge said, "Mr. Nixon—" but Josh cut him off, facing Parsons and saying: "If you are not asking for the death penalty, we'd all like to know that right now. Right this minute."

Josh Nixon's complexion had reddened and his voice shook with emotion. Elsie's heart rate started to increase as the tension mounted in the courtroom.

Parsons's face wrinkled with frustration. "Ask that counsel approach the bench."

Claire O'Hara called out from the defense table, where she sat with her arm draped over the back of Larry Paul's chair. "What for? What do you want to talk about that this jury can't hear?"

Parsons wheeled around and shot daggers at her. "Judge, I ask that Ms. O'Hara be censured."

She laughed. Crossing her legs, she swung a foot encased in a candy-apple-red high-heeled shoe. The sole of the shoe was shiny and black. *What does a pair of shoes like that cost*, Elsie wondered. She was certain that Claire didn't acquire them at Shoe Carnival.

Claire adjusted the bracelets on her wrist and asked, "What are you afraid of, Parsons?"

Parsons clenched a fist. "Objection!"

Claire sighed with dramatic weariness, and slowly stood. "Your honor, this is just Opening Statement, and we're already at a standstill. I entreat you: tell Mr. Parsons to sit down so that Josh can give his opening to the jury."

"Sit down, Mr. Parsons."

His mouth went agape, then Parsons recovered and said, "He can't talk about punishment in this phase of trial, your honor."

Callaway nodded. "Mr. Nixon," he began, but Nixon interrupted the judge a second time.

"It's no secret, Judge. This jury was examined on the death penalty during voir dire, back in Greene County. They know they are here to decide whether my client will be executed."

The timbre of his voice raised during the speech. Judge Callaway lifted a hand to halt him, and spoke as a man used to giving commands.

"Confine your statements to the evidence that will be presented in this stage. You may continue, sir."

Nixon returned his attention to the legal pad that rested on the ledge of the jury box. He flipped two pages, examined the text, and set the pad down again.

"Ladies and gentlemen of the jury, sometimes people think defense attorneys try to trick jurors. That we set out to deceive you, pull the wool over your eyes. Ladies and gentlemen, I promise you, with all honesty in my heart, that is not my intention."

Elsie stared at his back, her face wearing a skeptical expression that she hoped some jurors would note. But she was hiding her internal surprise. She'd gone to trial against Josh Nixon before; this was not his standard defense presentation.

"You'll understand just how open, how up front we are determined to be, when I tell you: we do not contest the evidence that Ms. Arnold outlined in her opening."

Elsie's jaw went slack. Never, in the most outlandish speculation she might have entertained, would she imagine that Nixon would open with a blanket admission. He had essentially admitted his client's guilt. And he did not appear to be following up with some justification or rationale that would excuse the defendant's action or shift the blame elsewhere. Elsie, in her Opening, had painted a detailed picture of Larry Paul's murder of mother and child; and Larry Paul's defense attorney stood before the jury to agree with her version of the facts.

Then in Elsie's mind, the parallel surfaced. In the Boston marathon bomber case, the defense counsel tried the same tactic. They waved the white flag from the outset, and then begged the jury for mercy, to spare the man's life.

But it didn't work, Elsie thought. The jury in Boston recommended death. Why would Nixon duplicate a losing strategy?

Josh continued, pacing in front of the jury box with his hands thrust into the pockets of his trousers.

"So now that I've established that I'm shooting straight with you, I'll tell you something else the evidence will show. My client, Larry Paul, is a dying man."

The room was so quiet, Elsie could hear the buzzing of the large clock on the wall as its hands ticked off seconds.

"Regardless of what you do, whatever you decide as a jury in this case, my client has a death sentence already."

Every eye in the room focused on Larry Paul. As he sat in the wooden chair at the counsel table, his uncuffed hands clenched the arms of the chair with the grip of a man hanging onto a lifeline with his last vestige of strength.

His face was pasty white, but scarlet patches stood out on his face and neck. He drew a breath that rattled.

He looked like a dying man. If the defense was blowing smoke, they had everyone fooled. Including Elsie.

Chapter Thirty-Six

Late that afternoon, Elsie stood near the witness stand, holding a large manila envelope in both hands. She gave her witness, an x-ray technician, a small smile before asking: "On the morning of September seventh of this year, did you have occasion to take x-rays of a deceased woman named Jessie Dent and her infant son?"

"I did."

"Where were the x-rays performed?"

"At Barton Memorial Hospital, here in Barton, Missouri."

She handed him the manila envelope. "I hand you what's been marked for identification as State's Exhibit 31 through 36. Do you recognize it?"

The young man examined the envelope and confirmed that the exhibit contained x-ray pictures that he had taken of the injuries to Jessie Dent and her unborn son.

"How do you know?" Elsie asked.

He held up the envelope and pointed. "These are my initials, that I signed on that occasion; and I dated it."

The witness had a husky build, and was dressed in his scrubs from the local hospital. Elsie knew without checking that Madeleine wouldn't like his garb. She always wanted State's witnesses dressed in clothes that they would wear to a funeral: somber, respectable attire, to impress the jurors with their solid respectability. But the man worked at the hospital, Elsie thought. Dressing in hospital scrubs would add weight to his testimony, not detract from it.

Not that any of Elsie's witnesses could make or break the Larry Paul case.

Madeleine and Sam Parsons had divided the juicy parts between them. They were examining the coroner, the officers who responded to the scene, Detective Ashlock, the forensic technicians from the crime lab. Elsie got the grunt work: the chain of custody witnesses. The x-ray technician, laying the foundation for the coroner to discuss what the x-rays revealed. And Ivy, of course.

But Ivy might not be testifying in the State's case in chief, after all. This trial was broken down into two parts. In the first, evidence was presented so that the jury could decide whether Larry Paul was guilty or not guilty of murder.

If they found him guilty of murder, the second stage of trial would begin. The jury would determine punishment, and the prosecution and defense would provide evidence and argument as to which penalty the defendant should receive: life or death.

The tech in the green scrubs had identified and authenticated all of the x-rays to be used in the prosecution's case. Elsie turned to the bench and said, "Your honor, the State offers State Exhibits 31 through 36 into evidence."

Judge Callaway looked over at the defense table. "Any objection?"

Josh Nixon rose partway out of his chair. "No objection, your honor." He sat back down.

Elsie nodded at the witness. "No further questions."

As she sat, the judge asked the defense, "Cross-examination?"

"No questions for this witness," Josh Nixon replied.

The judge nodded at the man in green. "You are excused."

Elsie peeked at the defense attorneys on the way back to her seat; but they sat poker-faced. Nixon's only tell, his one indication of nerves, was the drumming of the fingers of his left hand on the tabletop. Claire O'Hara was cool as a cat, nodding at the jury with a satisfying half smile, as if to indicate that everything was proceeding exactly as planned.

When Elsie settled back into her seat, she whispered to Madeleine, "This is nuts. Are they setting themselves up for a claim of ineffective assistance of counsel? Is that the master plan?"

"Be quiet. And be grateful. No one can mess up this case. Not even—" Madeleine paused, but Elsie bristled at the implication. *Yeah—not even Elsie,* she thought. *Not even me.* She could have cited her win/loss record for Madeleine's benefit, because it was impressive. But it would be a futile effort. Madeleine couldn't be won over. She had placed Elsie in a box, years ago, and she liked keeping her within its confines.

Parsons was calling the doctor to the stand. He would discuss his findings in the autopsies and give his opinion of cause of death. The coroner would describe and point out for the jury what the x-rays revealed.

Elsie studied Dr. Gray. He was a good doctor, a generous soul; serving as coroner was a sideline to his practice, and he did the duties out of loyalty to McCown County. The doctor was not a fashionable figure; his thinning hair was shaggy on his neck, and the untucked white shirt he wore was wrinkled. Gray fuzz sprouted from both of his ears. But he had a loyal following in the county. Elsie's mother refused to see anyone other than Doc Gray when she was ailing.

Parsons established the doctor's expertise, eliciting testimony regarding his educational background, medical license, and hospital privileges. Then Parsons said, "Please describe the condition of Jessie Dent when you examined her. And if you will, sir, please refer to State's Exhibits 14 through 24." He handed the doctor the stack of glossy photographs, blown up to 12 x 14 images. Elsie knew what they depicted. They were gruesome.

"The deceased woman—Jessie Dent—suffered external trauma: to the head, the back, and the abdomen. The observations can be seen in these pictures by the bruising and contusions here—" and he pointed to an area on the photograph "—and here."

"Will you mark those areas, Doctor? Circle them with a pen?"

Doc Gray did so, marking on the glossy photos with a careful hand.

"Were x-rays taken of the deceased, Jessie Dent, to your knowledge?"

"They were. I ordered them."

"What did the x-ray of Jessie Dent reveal?" He handed Dr. Gray the large manila envelope.

The doctor slipped the first x-ray from its envelope and held it up to the light. With the blunt end of his pen, he said, "This x-ray reveals a skull fracture; you can see it here." He tapped gently with the pen.

"Do you have an opinion as to the cause of Jessie Dent's death?"

"I do."

"What is that opinion?"

"The skull fracture resulted in a subdural hematoma, which caused her to die almost immediately. Of course, the other injuries almost certainly would have killed her, anyway. But the skull fracture is, in my opinion, the cause of death."

"What are the other injuries you refer to?"

"Her abdominal injuries—I refer to her ruptured spleen."

"So the deceased had a ruptured spleen, in addition to a skull fracture."

"Yes."

"And the ruptured spleen could have caused her death, on its own?"

"Oh yes, indeed. More slowly of course. But the injury to the skull was the fatal blow, as they say."

"Is the ruptured spleen depicted in an x-ray?"

"It was." Doc Gray fumbled with the envelope before pulling out a second x-ray. "This one—it says State's Exhibit #33."

"Doctor, did you also have occasion to examine the deceased's infant son?"

"I did."

"Please describe the condition of the deceased's unborn son when you examined him."

"There was no fetal heartbeat. No respiration. We attempted a delivery by Caesarian Section, but the child—the baby boy—was dead."

"Did you see evidence of bruising or injury to the fetus?"

"No, not that kind of injury. No."

"But Doctor, if the mother of the child sustained the grievous injuries to her abdomen that we see in State's Exhibit #23 and #24, how is it possible that the child didn't exhibit similar bruising, contusions?"

"The trauma to the mother's belly was grievous. But inside her womb, the baby was in a bag of fluid—amniotic fluid. That bag of fluid provided a buffer, you see. The boy was afloat."

"But he died."

"Because the mother died. While he was in utero."

Parsons said, "Let's go back to the injuries that Jessie Dent sustained. What might have caused the injuries you described?"

"The injuries, the contusions and bruising I observed were consistent with blows from a blunt object."

"Like a baseball bat?" Parsons asked.

Elsie tensed for the objection from the defense. The question was premature; Parsons hadn't asked it correctly, hadn't laid the proper foundation. She mentally corrected Parsons, asking the proper questions in her head: *Doctor, from your expertise, observations, and examination, did you form an opinion as to the manner of death? And what is that opinion?* But silence still reigned at the defense table.

"The skull fractures you described. Could they also have been made by the baseball bat?"

In her head, Elsie anticipated the reaction from the defense. *Objection: leading. Objection: the prosecution has not laid the proper foundation for the witness to offer an expert opinion.* She glanced again at Claire O'Hara. Claire caught the look and winked at Elsie, while toying with her bangle bracelets.

Parsons handed Dr. Gray the photos. "Are those pictures fair and accurate representations of the deceased Jessie Dent and her son on the date of your examination?"

"They are."

Parsons held up the photos. "Your honor, the State offers State's Exhibits 14 through 24 into evidence."

Claire spoke. "No objection."

Judge Callaway blinked. "Don't you want to take a look at them first, Ms. O'Hara?"

"No need."

The judge cleared his throat, as if he was debating whether to say more. "Photos can be inflammatory at times, Ms. O'Hara."

"Judge Callaway," she said, rising slowly and putting her weight on the balls of her feet. Elsie peeped again at Claire's high-heeled shoes. Just as shiny as a candy apple at the county fair. "We want this jury to have all the information they need to decide this important case."

Josh Nixon's fingers were drumming again, making a rapid beat on the wooden tabletop. *Pretty sure this is Claire's idea,* Elsie thought. Nixon generally put up a whale of a fight. Claire O'Hara must be calling all the shots. Since Josh joined forces with Claire, Elsie detected a change in his demeanor. Claire had pulled out the lion's teeth and cut his claws. It was unsettling to see Josh under Claire's thumb. Elsie decided that she liked the old Josh Nixon better, the one who sometimes kept her off-balance with his defense advocacy.

Larry Paul turned to Nixon and whispered, just loud enough for Elsie to overhear. "I want to see them pictures."

"We don't need to. Lower your voice," Nixon said.

Larry Paul dropped the register of his voice, but Elsie could still make out his words when he said, "I want to get a look at the baby. My boy." He shook his head and his eyes welled up. "I never got to see what my boy looked like."

You motherfucker, Elsie thought, a tide of color washing over her face. *You ought to be dead.*

But just as the thought took shape in her head, Elsie's heart began to race. She began her breathing trick again. Inhale, exhale. Slowly.

Chapter Thirty-Seven

AT NOON ON Wednesday, they sat around the desk in Madeleine's office, making strained conversation and keeping an eye on the clock. Due to the defense strategy of silent surrender, the State had rested their case that morning. The defense called no witnesses, and the lawyers went straight to argument. As Elsie sat with Madeleine and Sam Parsons, the jury was deliberating on the question of Larry Paul's guilt or innocence.

The Greene County jury didn't make them wait long. Sam Parsons had just finished his cheeseburger, delivered with bad grace by Stacie, when the knock came on Madeleine's door.

Judge Callaway's bailiff Emil Elmquist didn't wait for an invitation. He opened the door and announced, "We've got a verdict."

Elsie took a final swallow from her can of Diet Coke. It was lukewarm; she'd been nursing it for the past hour. Parsons wiped his hands on a napkin. "Let's roll," he said.

Elsie was beginning to despise that expression.

Madeleine pulled out a lipstick and opened her silver compact.

Her hands were shaking; the touch-up took a minute. "What do you think, Sam?"

"If we didn't get a guilty verdict, I think I'll retire and go to work for your hubby, selling tractors. Come on, ladies; this one was a walk in the park."

Privately, Elsie agreed; but the ease with which it had gone down nagged at her. Something wasn't right.

The television cameras focused on them as they made their way to the courtroom. With a shade of petulance, she assumed she'd barely be visible on the evening news, blocked as she was by the figures of Madeleine and Parsons, marching ahead of her. Maybe she wouldn't even watch tonight.

She probably would.

They sat at the counsel table. Claire O'Hara and Josh Nixon were already in place, awaiting the arrival of their client. When Elsie walked in, she saw Claire cross her legs. Her skirt was short; she looked like she was heading to a nightclub, rather than a funeral. She wore the candy-apple-red shoes. They were a lone pop of color in the somber courtroom.

Claire winked at them. "You all nervous?"

Parsons made a reply, but Elsie didn't take note of it; she was looking at Josh Nixon, who sat in silence at the defense table, toying with a pen. His face was pale, covered with a sheen of sweat. She felt a moment's sympathy. He was gambling with his client's demise.

But she thought of Jessie Dent, and the photos in her file. *Fuck Larry Paul.* She sat down.

Madeleine and Parsons were huddled in a whispered conference. Elsie leaned in to listen.

"When we present our evidence for the punishment phase, we lead off with the kid," Parsons was saying.

Elsie frowned. "No," she said in a loud whisper. "Save her for last."

Madeleine turned to her. "Please. Your breath."

Elsie pulled back, mortified. Madeleine was probably right. She hadn't consumed anything but coffee and Diet Coke all day; her nerves were strung too tight to contemplate food. She reached into her briefcase; she should have a container of Tic Tacs. She found it in a corner, beneath a handful of pens. She pulled out the plastic box. Empty.

Emil Elmquist held the door to the courtroom open as four deputies ushered the defendant into court. The four uniformed officers represented a substantial portion of McCown County's manpower. Elsie hoped that the 911 line wasn't lighting up with calls for assistance outside the city limits. She wasn't sure anyone would be available to come to the rescue.

Larry Paul had been shackled like an animal. He was trussed so tightly that he was forced to shuffle along with baby steps. *I won't look at him,* Elise thought; but when he passed in front of the prosecution table, her eyes focused on his face, in spite of her intentions.

He was terrified.

The blank passivity he'd exhibited in trial was gone, replaced by a slack-jawed expression of fear, his face clearly reflecting an acute awareness of his situation.

She looked down. Reflexively, she reached for the folder with Jessie Dent's photo, to provide yet again the justification for Larry Paul's death, but made herself pause. Elsie folded her hands on the table in front of her.

This is my job. This is how it's supposed to be.

The door to Judge Callaway's chambers opened. "All rise,"

Emil said, and Elsie stood. A murmur sounded from the collective group of onlookers in the public gallery.

"Be seated." The judge turned to Emil. "Bring the jury in."

Though the pronouncement of guilt was highly predictable, given the conduct of the trial, Elsie's pulse quickened. Jury verdicts could be capricious.

As the jury filed into the jury box, she peered over to see who led the way. The middle-aged juror with an iron gray helmet of hair held the verdict forms in her hands. In Elsie's experience, it was an unusual sight; McCown County juries generally selected a man to be their foreman.

Elsie focused on the gray-haired juror's face: it was grim. *We're okay,* she thought.

"Have you reached a verdict, Ms. Foreman?"

"We have, your honor," the woman said.

Judge Callaway gave his bailiff a nod. Emil took the papers from the foreman and handed them to the judge. He adjusted his reading glasses and read silently, then said, "As to Count One, we the jury, find Larry David Paul guilty of murder in the first degree, as submitted in instruction number thirteen."

He shifted to the second page and read, "As to Count Two, we, the jury, find Larry David Paul guilty of murder in the first degree, as submitted in instruction number fourteen."

Elsie became aware of a wheezing noise beside her. She glanced over; Madeleine was hyperventilating. Elsie studied her face with anxiety; was she going to pass out, she wondered.

She gripped Madeleine's hand. "Chill," she whispered. "We won."

Madeleine nodded without looking at her. She didn't repeat her complaint about Elsie's halitosis.

As the judge instructed the jury about the next phase of the trial, determining punishment, Elsie tuned him out. Her thoughts were fast and frantic.

Ivy, she thought. Got to get Ivy through this in one piece. Ivy was the key to the punishment phase. She could bring the crime to life, demonstrate the violence from a child's perspective, show the jury the effect the killing had on the victim's survivor.

If Elsie could walk her through it. Ivy was the key to success or to failure. The girl might fall apart.

Elsie was so busy thinking about the potential pitfalls of Ivy on the witness stand, she didn't even give a thought to Ashlock's testimony.

Chapter Thirty-Eight

LATER THAT DAY, Ashlock sat erect on the wooden chair in the witness stand. He wore his good navy suit and the paisley tie Elsie picked out for him at Dillard's in Springfield. She'd made a special trip out of town for the purchase, as the only local clothier in Barton, Missouri, was Walmart. She eyed him with satisfaction, thinking he cut a dashing figure.

Madeleine stood at the podium by the jury box. "State your name, please."

Her voice wavered. *Oh, Lord, she's nervous,* Elsie thought, as her boss coughed delicately into her fist to disguise her discomfiture.

"Robert Ashlock."

"And your occupation?"

"Chief of Detectives, City of Barton Police Department."

"Detective Ashlock, you have testified that you responded to the scene of the Jessie Dent homicide on September sixth of this year."

"That's correct."

"And you made an arrest for the homicide, based on the evidence at the scene." Her voice was growing stronger. *Come on, Madeleine,* Elsie urged, trying to send supportive vibes.

"I did. I arrested Larry Paul," he said, and pointed at the defense table, "the criminal defendant in this case."

"In the course of your investigation, did you review the defendant's criminal history?"

"I did. I read his rap sheet. Also, I was familiar with Larry Paul, as a police officer in Barton for eighteen years."

"Does he have a criminal history?"

"He does. Misdemeanor assault, property destruction, minor drug offenses."

Check. Elsie had the Missouri statute in front of her, that listed mitigating factors a jury might consider to spare a defendant from the death penalty for the crime of murder in the first degree. She drew a line through subsection (2) (1): No criminal history.

Madeleine continued, "To the best of your knowledge, does the defendant have a history of emotional or mental disturbance?"

Claire O'Hara jumped up. "Objection. The witness has not been qualified to make that determination."

Judge Callaway appeared to consider the point. After a moment, he nodded. "Sustained."

Madeleine turned to the prosecution table with a deer-in-the-headlights face. Elsie waved her over. In Madeleine's ear, "Did Larry Paul exhibit any behavior consistent with—"

Madeleine picked up the ball. "Detective, did the defendant exhibit any behavior that suggested emotional or mental disturbance?"

Ashlock paused before answering, wiping a hand over his face. "He appeared to be under the influences of inebriating substances. Other than that, no. No, he did not."

Madeleine looked at her notes, then focused on Ashlock. "From what you observed at the scene of the crime, was there any indication that Jessie Dent consented to her murder?"

A grimace crossed Ashlock's face. "No one who saw the scene, or the condition of the body, could reach that conclusion." He looked at the jury. "And the baby. The baby was a victim. He could not consent."

"In Larry Paul's statements during interrogation, did he indicate that he was acting under the domination of another person?"

"No."

"Did he, or another, claim that Larry Paul couldn't appreciate that what he did was a crime?"

"No. On the contrary—he stated that he knew it was wrong."

"Did he claim he was unable to conform his conduct to law?"

"No. He said he did it because he felt like it. She was trapping him with the baby. He wanted out before the child was born. And he was high. And once he started he didn't stop." He paused, and when Madeleine didn't speak, he added. "With the bat. He didn't stop beating her with the bat."

"And he was aware that he was hurting the baby?"

"He didn't want the baby to be born. He'd been thinking about it for a long time." He turned to the jury again. "He didn't want the child support liability."

Elsie watched the jury to see their response to the statement. The woman who was the foreman, generally stone-faced, shook her head. It was an excellent sign for the prosecution.

Madeleine said, "Detective Ashlock, was the murder of Jessie Dent and her unborn son wantonly vile, involving depravity of mind?"

Claire O'Hara shot out of her seat. "Objection. That's the province of the jury."

"Sustained."

Elsie thought that Claire was probably right on that score. It was up to the jury to decide whether the actions of Larry Paul were so horrible that he deserved the death penalty. But it was worth a try. Good to plant the "aggravating circumstances" statutory language in the minds of the jurors.

Madeleine was returning to her seat. As she lowered into her chair, Elsie took her hand.

"Good job," she whispered.

Madeleine squeezed Elsie's hand in response, and gave her a grateful look. Her lipstick was uneven, as if she'd been chewing at her lips.

Elsie half expected the defense to let Ashlock go without cross-examination; but Claire O'Hara stood and stalked him, proceeding slowly toward the witness stand.

"Detective," she said, "During your investigation, I would bet you checked out the history of domestic dispute calls to the home of Jessie Dent and Larry Paul."

Ashlock's eyes widened slightly; the question took him by surprise. It mystified Elsie, too; Claire was opening the door on Larry Paul's past abusive behavior, matters that the prosecution couldn't get into evidence. She studied the back of Claire's strawberry red head, wondering what angle the defense was playing. Maybe they were trying to establish that Jessie had threatened Larry in the past.

But that wouldn't fly. It would not save him from the death penalty for the murder of the unborn child.

Claire continued, "Jessie Dent and Larry Paul lived together in that trailer in McCown County for almost two years. Isn't that right?"

Slowly, Ashlock nodded. His guard was up. "Sounds about right."

"And in that period of time, there were eight calls to 911 for domestic assault, eight separate occasions when the Barton Police Department responded and came out to the home of Jessie Dent and my client. Is that correct?"

"I don't have the paperwork in front of me, so I can't say exactly how many—" he said, but Claire cut him off.

As she swung back to the defense counsel table, Josh Nixon handed her a sheet of paper; with a flourish, she held it up. "I'd like to have this marked as Defendant's Exhibit #1." She presented it to the court reporter, who marked it with haste.

"Detective Ashlock, I'd like for you to examine Defendant's Exhibit #1. Can you tell the jury what it is?"

Ashlock's face was unreadable. "It's a record of domestic dispute calls to Farm Road 125, the address where the defendant lived with the deceased."

"How many times was the Barton Police Department called to that address to respond to domestic assault complaints?"

"Eight times." He rested the document on his lap.

Claire leaned her rear end against the front of the defense table, assuming a relaxed pose. "How many arrests resulted from those calls?"

Ashlock didn't glance down. "None."

"None? Not one? Tell me, Detective, how many times did the Detective Division investigate the domestic abuse that was going on at the homicide victim's home?"

"The record shows that the victim was uncooperative," he said, but Claire cut him off.

"Objection! Your honor. The witness is not responsive."

She pushed away from the counsel table, walking toward the bench. "Your honor, please instruct the witness to answer the questions."

The judge nodded. "Answer the question, Detective."

Ashlock didn't flinch. "The Detective Division did not investigate the abuse allegations."

A sweat was breaking out on the back of Elsie's scalp. She finally saw where the inquiry was headed.

Claire strolled toward the jury box and leaned against it, her bejeweled hand and wrist splayed out on the railing. Making contact with them, Elsie thought. She often used the same technique.

"Detective, are you familiar with the Lethality Assessment Program?"

Elsie saw the twitch in Ashlock's jaw. "I've heard of it."

Turning to the jury, Claire said, "Maybe you've heard that it's based on the Maryland model, which was designed by Maryland Network Against Domestic Violence. Are you aware of that?"

"It sounds familiar."

"So what do you understand that the Lethality Assessment involves?"

Ashlock shifted in his seat, as if the chair had become uncomfortable to sit upon. "Police reporting to a domestic assault ask the victim certain questions. To assess the degree of danger."

Claire smiled at Ashlock, baring bleached teeth. "What is the purpose of those 'certain' questions? Do you know?"

His expression hadn't altered, but Elsie noticed that his respiration had quickened. He was breathing hard. "To assess whether the victim is at risk of being killed by the partner or spouse."

Claire dropped the smile. She gripped the railing of the jury box with her right hand. "Did your officers ask those questions, to the best of your knowledge?"

He didn't hesitate. "They did not."

Claire shook her head, somber. "No further questions."

Madeleine turned to Parsons. "What do I do?"

In a harsh whisper, he answered, "Get him out of here."

Elsie's eyes pricked; her heart went out to Ashlock as he was dismissed from the witness stand and walked out of the courtroom, his bearing erect.

Her head swung back to her cocounsel. Madeleine and Sam Parsons were staring at her. "What the hell?" she whispered.

Madeleine's face was pasty; she looked like she'd used clown white as her foundation when she applied her makeup that day. "They are implicating the Barton Police Department."

Clearly, Madeleine was right. And a small kernel of Elsie's brain applauded the move; it was brilliant. And totally unexpected.

"Get that kid up there," Parsons said in a harsh whisper. When Elsie didn't jump up immediately, he added: "Move!"

She looked through the glass panel of the courtroom door to ensure that her witness was present. Ivy and Tina were visible, sitting on the wooden bench in the hall outside the courtroom.

"Your honor, the State calls Ivy Dent to the witness stand."

The bailiff stepped out into the hall. For once, he did not shout the witness's name; Elise was grateful for that. Instead, Emil nodded at the pair on the bench and said, "Miss Dent," in a hushed voice.

Tina walked Ivy into the courtroom. The first thing Elsie noted was that Ivy wore a new pair of eyeglasses. The light brown frames sat straight on her nose and required neither safety pins nor Band-Aids. *Oh, thank God,* she thought, feeling a fervent sense of gratitude for the intervention of Tina Peroni. She was certain that the Hickman family was not responsible for Ivy's new eyewear.

Elsie took Ivy by the hand. "You'll go sit on that chair up there, right by the judge." *Just like we rehearsed,* she thought—but was careful not to add. She hoped that Tina had reminded Ivy of an important instruction that Elsie had repeated to the child multiple times: *Don't look at Larry Paul.*

Because when a child was confronted by the physical presence of the defendant, all of Elsie's careful witness preparation could be shot to hell.

Ivy sat in the witness chair. She wore a yellow dress of eyelet lace; a summer dress, probably snagged from a clearance rack, but it suited her, and added to the picture of childlike innocence she made on the stand. Her short blond hair had been tamed for the occasion; it looked like her bangs were trimmed, but it might have been an amateur effort by the foster mother; the hair on her forehead slanted upward at the right side of her head. As Elsie stepped closer to the stand, she saw a faint brown stain on the bodice of the yellow dress; it distracted her momentarily, as she mentally berated Holly Hickman. *Couldn't she have sprayed the stain with Shout before she laundered it,* Elsie wondered. Elsie's mother would never let her appear in stained clothing.

She closed her eyes for a moment, to regain her focus.

"Ivy, please tell us your first and last name."

The girl answered without hesitation. "Ivy Dent."

"Ivy, you are going to be asked to promise to tell the truth in here today. Do you know the difference between telling the truth and telling a lie?"

Elsie was standing close by the witness stand, right in front of Ivy. The child nodded, then caught herself; they had repeatedly told her she would have to speak her answers out loud.

"Yes."

"If I said your dress is yellow; is that the truth?"

"Yes."

"If I said your dress isn't yellow, it's blue; would that be the truth?"

"No. It would be a lie. It's yellow."

"Ivy, is it wrong to tell a lie?"

"Yes."

"So if you promise—" Elsie was gaining momentum, but Claire O'Hara interrupted.

"Judge Callaway, we're good with this."

Elsie swung around. "What?"

Claire has risen to a stand and was waving her hand in the air. "She's demonstrated her understanding of the oath. Let's proceed."

The judge blinked with surprise, then turned to Ivy. "Miss Dent, do you promise to tell the whole truth and nothing but the truth in court today?"

Ivy didn't answer. She was staring at the defense table, her eyes wide with apprehension.

Judge Callaway tried again. "Ivy?"

Shit, Elsie thought; *shit shit shit. She's looking at Larry Paul.* Elsie strode over to the defense table and stood directly in front of the defendant, effectively blocking him from Ivy's view.

Nixon protested. "What are you doing? I can't see."

She ignored him, staring at Ivy, willing the child to answer.

Judge Callaway frowned. "Ivy Dent, let's try again." He repeated the oath.

But Ivy wasn't listening. Her gaze was locked on the defense side of the courtroom, her eyes narrowing behind the new glasses, with a look that combined suspicion and fear.

She crossed her arms, and turned sideways in the chair, her back to the judge.

Elsie felt the blood rush to her head and pound in her ears. She walked up to the witness stand, trying to maintain an outward appearance of calm. Laying her hand on the wooden rail that separated her from the child, she spoke in a clear voice that didn't betray her inner quaking.

"Ivy."

Ivy shifted even farther away from Elsie, presenting her back to her. The tag of her dress hung out at her neck; it was a size six, Elsie saw.

"Ivy, please turn around. You're in court."

Ivy turned her head, but didn't change position. Elsie studied the child's profile for a moment, silently willing her to swing around in her seat. But Ivy made no move to face her. Elsie looked up at Judge Callaway. Their eyes met. He leaned forward, a question in his face. "Ms. Arnold?"

"Judge, we need a recess."

Claire O'Hara still stood at the defense table. "Your honor, if the prosecution is unable to proceed with this witness, let's move on."

"Just a few minutes," Elsie said. Her voice carried a pleading note. *Stop it,* she thought. *Don't sound weak.*

"The defense objects." Claire turned to the jury. "The prosecution seeks to coach the witness. If the court permits that, we'll ask for a mistrial."

Elsie heard a gasp behind her. *Shut up, Madeleine,* she thought. *Put on your damned poker face.*

The jurors were shifting in their chairs, glancing at Ivy and looking away. Elsie could read the tea leaves. She was losing ground.

She walked to the side of the witness stand and faced Ivy, placing her back to the jury. Elsie's mother was a career schoolteacher;

she affected Marge Arnold's best classroom voice. "Ivy, please turn around in your seat and answer the judge's questions."

The child's face was mulish. When she spoke, Elsie's stomach dropped.

"I don't know nothing," Ivy said.

Elsie took a deep breath. "Ivy," she said, in a gentler voice.

But the girl's arms tightened across her chest. She lowered her head and glanced away from Elsie, then repeated the prior statement.

"I don't know nothing."

Sam Parsons stood, and said in his booming voice, "The State requests a brief recess."

Claire said, with a timbre that matched Parsons's volume, "Defense objects."

Judge Callaway looked down at the child's stiff figure for several protracted moments. While Elsie waited for his decision, she could feel sweat dripping from her hairline. She thought she was sweating in her underwear. *Flop sweat,* a voice whispered in her head.

With a somber face, Judge Callaway shook his head. "Prosecution's request is denied. This witness may step down. Let the record reflect that she was unable to respond to the oath."

Elsie turned to the courtroom, intending to seek direction from her cocounsel. But Claire O'Hara caught her eye instead. The defense attorney settled in her chair, looking like the cat that ate the canary. Her self-satisfaction wasn't unexpected; she had won the round. But Claire pulled a packet of Kleenex tissues from her bright red briefcase and applied one to her nose with a hand that shook so violently, it made the bangle bracelets around her wrist jingle.

Elsie didn't have the opportunity to reflect upon the reason for Claire O'Hara's uncharacteristic fit of nerves. As Tina Peroni escorted Ivy from the room, Judge Callaway turned to the prosecution table and said, "Call your next witness."

They had no other witness. Ivy was the key to the prosecution's pitch for the death penalty. It had been Ivy's job to demonstrate to the jury the impact that was made by Jessie Dent's death.

And Ivy was no longer a player. It appeared that she had switched teams.

What did I do wrong? Elsie wondered as she slid back into her chair under the baleful eye of Madeleine Thompson. She would have wagered a fortune she did not possess that the girl would speak up in court. Ivy Dent had grit, intestinal fortitude, chutzpah. She was a survivor.

When Madeleine hissed in her ear, "What on earth was that about? What did you do?" Elsie didn't speak a word in her own defense. Because she was wondering the same thing.

Chapter Thirty-Nine

ELSIE WATCHED WITH a stoic face as the bailiff held the door open for Tina Peroni and she walked out, holding tightly onto Ivy's hand.

As Ivy's figure in the yellow dress retreated through the doorway, it was replaced by another: Bob Ashlock stood in the doorway, unable to enter, like a captive prince in a fairy tale.

The door closed on him, but he continued to stand before it, staring at Elsie through the glass panes.

She raised her eyebrows at him; he shook his head. Glancing away, she checked to see whether they were the object of anyone's attention; but no one was paying her any mind.

She looked back. He pulled his phone out of his pocket and held it in his hand, staring her down.

Her briefcase was at her feet. The phone was inside, the bell tone off. She bent over and felt for the phone, covertly checking for a message from Ashlock without removing the phone from its pocket inside the bag.

Ashlock had texted: *SPD is here.*

She looked up at him in confusion, lifting her shoulders to show that she didn't understand. Ashlock turned and walked away.

Parsons was whispering to Madeleine, so Elsie lent an ear. "She blew your case for the death penalty. You needed her to establish the impact of the deceased's death on the survivors, under the death penalty provision in the criminal code."

Who's "she," Elsie wondered. Did he blame Ivy? Because the fault should fall squarely on her own shoulders. Elsie had undertaken the task of enabling Ivy to articulate what her mother's death had wrought. It was Elsie's responsibility, her duty.

She had failed. The jury would never see what was in the child's heart.

Madeleine twisted in her seat, placing her back pointedly to Elsie. The pair at the counsel table continued to whisper.

Parsons said, "We've still got Closing Argument. Are you ready?"

"What about the defense evidence? To mitigate punishment?"

"They got nothing. We'll rest, they'll rest, we'll talk jury instructions with the judge. Then we'll close. The baby. Drive home the baby."

"And Ivy," Elsie whispered.

Madeleine turned. "Are you insane?"

Parsons followed up. "We need them to forget all about that fumble." He dropped his voice. "I never liked that kid."

A sudden wave of anger washed over Elsie; in her mind's eye, she saw the mulish face with ragged blond hair framing broken glasses: the survivor. The title was apt. Ivy was a true survivor.

Parsons was rising, resting his fingertips on the counsel table as he announced, "The State rests, your honor."

Callaway nodded, without surprise. "Defense counsel, you may call your first witness."

A flash of prognostication, fueled by Ashlock's text, struck Elsie. They've got something. Something major.

Josh Nixon stood. "The defense calls Lieutenant Vincent Boone to the witness stand."

Emil Elmquist didn't have to call the policeman's name; he opened the door and Lieutenant Boone marched in, dressed in his uniform blues.

The patch on his arm reading SPD didn't take Elsie by surprise; but it sent Madeleine into a coughing fit.

Boone took the oath and took his seat on the stand. Even a casual observer could detect ambivalence in the policeman's attitude.

Josh Nixon said, "State your name, please."

"Vincent Boone."

"What is your occupation, sir?"

Defense counsel hadn't called Ashlock *sir*, Elsie noted. It was a message to the jury, that demonstration of respect granted to one lawman and withheld from another.

"I serve as Lieutenant in the Violent Crimes Division of Springfield, Missouri Police Department."

"How long have you served in that capacity?"

"I've been with SPD for fourteen years."

"What's your educational background?"

"I have my bachelor's degree in criminology from Missouri State University."

More ways to make our local police department suffer by comparison, Elsie thought. Ashlock had done some coursework at Missouri Southern in Joplin, but had not attained a degree. No time to devote to it, she thought, mounting his defense in her head.

"Lieutenant, have your heard of the Lethality Assessment?"

Ooooh shit, Elsie thought. She suspected she could guess the direction the direct examination would take.

"Yes, sir."

"And what is the Lethality Assessment, to the best of your understanding?"

The lieutenant shifted to face the jury. "The Lethality Assessment was established in an effort to reduce homicides, and serious injuries, in domestic assault cases. It's a series of eleven questions used to determine whether the victim of domestic abuse is at risk of death."

"What are the questions, Lieutenant? Can you tell us?"

"I can, sir."

Don't call the defense attorney sir, Elsie thought, pinching her lips together in frustration. The lawman was raising the defense profile by such offhand expressions of respect.

The lieutenant didn't have to resort to notes; he recited the questions from memory.

"We ask the victim: 'Has he ever used a weapon against you or threatened you with a weapon?' "

Nixon nodded. "What else?"

" 'Has he ever threatened to kill you or your children?' "

"Go on."

"Okay, number three: 'Do you think he might try to kill you?' Number four: 'Does he have a gun or one he can access easily?' "

The lieutenant paused. Nixon said: "Continue."

" 'Has he ever tried to strangle you?' "

A member of the jury exhaled with an audible gasp. The policeman looked at her with an apologetic grimace. "Sorry. These are pretty heavy."

Nixon said, "Indeed." Elsie saw Nixon make eye contact with

the juror that gasped. The defense attorney blew his breath out in a silent whistle.

Elsie didn't like it, didn't like it a bit. Nixon and the juror were creating a connection.

Nixon turned back to Lieutenant Boone. "Next one?"

Boone took a few second to recall, raising his eyes to the ceiling tiles. "We ask, 'is he consistently jealous of you or others?' "

"Next question, please."

" 'Have you left him or separated after living together or being married?' "

"And?"

" 'Is he unemployed? Has he ever tried to kill himself?' "

"Next one, please."

The lieutenant closed his eyes briefly. "Give me one second, please."

When he opened them, he turned to the jury. "I know these questions like the back of my hand. Then I get on the stand, and I hit a blank."

Three jurors smiled and nodded.

"Ready?" Nixon said.

"Yes, sir. There's two more: 'Does he follow or spy on you or leave threatening messages?' "

Nixon cruised to the jury box and leaned on it with his elbow. "Tell us the last question you ask the victim of domestic violence."

"Do you have a child that he knows is not his?"

The gasping juror huffed again with a loud inhalation. *Ivy,* Elsie thought. Ivy was actually the defendant's Exhibit Number One.

"Lieutenant Boone, what is the purpose of asking all these questions?"

"We do it so that the officer can identify victims of domestic violence that have the highest risk of being killed by their husband or partner. Boyfriend, or whatever. Killed, or seriously injured."

Nixon still stood by the jury. "So if they're high risk, what do you do at the SPD? Just tell the women—I'm sorry, I mean the victim—that they're in danger? Or give them a referral? Or hand them a card?"

"No, sir. The officer immediately calls a twenty-four-hour crisis hotline and puts the victim in touch with The Victim Center and Harmony House." He turned to the jurors. "The Victim Center provides free counseling to victims of violent and sexual crime. And Harmony House provides a safe place to stay."

Elsie didn't know whether the defense tactic was working on the jury, but it was certainly having an effect on her. *Why haven't we done that in Barton,* she wondered. Barton had the Battered Women's Center of the Ozarks, where she volunteered.

"Lieutenant Boone, thank you for your time," Nixon said. He nodded at the judge. "No further questions."

As Nixon settled back into his seat, Elsie huddled with Madeleine and Parsons to conduct a whispered exchange.

"What do we do now?" Madeleine said.

"What do you want to do with him?" Parsons asked.

Madeleine turned to Elsie, the question in her eyes. Elsie whispered, "What the hell can we do? Attack him because Springfield has a better policy on domestic assault cases than the Barton PD? Let him go, and smile at him on the way out. We're on the same team; we are all law enforcement."

Parsons frowned; it almost looked like a pout. "I could ask for numbers. See if he can substantiate whether the Lethality Assessment has saved any lives, or if it's just baloney."

"Are you nuts? Why would you attack a procedure that's designed to keep women alive?" Elsie glanced up; most of the jurors were staring at the prosecution table. "This is taking too long. The jury is getting suspicious—like, what are we talking about?"

Madeleine stood. "We appreciate our cohort's presence today, but we have no questions of Lieutenant Boone." She shot the lawman a brave smile. "Thanks for coming, Vince."

As the lieutenant walked out, Elsie reached over to Madeleine's legal pad and wrote, *Well done.*

Claire O'Hara stood. "For our next witness, the defense calls Chuck Harris to the witness stand."

Elsie dropped the pen she'd been holding. Madeleine's face transformed from a pleasant expression to a mask of angry shock. Parsons did a double take, then turned to Elsie and Madeleine to demand: "What did she say?"

Oh fuck, Elsie thought. *Fuck me running.*

Chapter Forty

CHUCK WALKED TO the stand, pausing to shoot a desperate glance at the prosecution counsel table. For the first time since Elsie had known him, his appearance bore marks of strain. His auburn hair was dark with perspiration, and sweat stains showed in the armpits of his gray pinstripe suit jacket.

He took the oath and sat in the chair, clasping his knees with his hands. Claire approached him.

"State your name, sir."

"Chuck Harris."

"Your occupation?"

"Assistant prosecutor," he answered, then corrected himself. "Chief assistant prosecutor, McCown County Prosecutor's Office."

Claire stood inches in front of the stand, confronting him. "Directing your attention to Labor Day weekend of this year: where were you on Saturday, the Saturday of the holiday weekend?"

"Camping. I mean—I was in Mark Twain National Forest. Camping."

"Were you alone?"

"No." His nose was dripping. He paused to wipe it with his hand. "I was with my girlfriend, Lisa Peters. She's a juvenile officer."

Claire pivoted abruptly, facing the jury box. "When you were camping on Labor Day weekend, did you see anyone who is present in the courtroom today?"

"Yes. Yes, Larry Paul. The defendant."

Claire didn't look Chuck's way. She kept her eyes facing the jury. "Identify the person you saw please."

Chuck pointed. "It's the man in the orange jail uniform, sitting by Josh Nixon."

She strolled away from Harris at a casual pace, remaining parallel with the jury box.

"Was the defendant alone on that date?"

"No. A man was with him, at his campsite. A shorter guy, with a ponytail. And a pregnant woman with purple hair. And a child."

"Who was the pregnant woman?"

"Jessie Dent. The deceased."

"Was she alive when you saw her?"

"Yes." Chuck's voice caught, but he continued. "Yes, when I last saw her, she was alive."

Claire turned to face Chuck Harris on the witness stand. "Describe the interaction you observed between the defendant and the deceased."

He paused. "My girlfriend saw it. I just heard."

"Well, then, tell us what the juvenile officer reported to you." Claire glanced over to the prosecution table with a glint in her eye.

"Object, Madeleine," whispered Parsons. "It's hearsay."

Madeleine started to rise from her chair, but Elsie clutched her arm and stopped her. "Let them hear it. We won't gain anything by concealing the facts from the jury."

Madeleine gave her a hard look, then nodded and sank back down into her seat.

Chuck said, "There was shouting at their campsite. Lisa said they were angry with the deceased, because she knocked over the cooler. She told me that the defendant, Larry Paul, knocked the deceased onto the burning campfire." He paused. "I didn't see that. But when I left the tent, he had the deceased in a headlock. And I saw smoke coming off the shirt she wore."

"Okay, then—let me get this straight. Your girlfriend told you that a man was abusing a pregnant woman near your campsite. Is that right? Sound right?"

Stiffly, Chuck nodded. "Yes."

"And how far away was this? Miles away? Feet? What?"

"Just a few feet. Couple of yards."

"And then you saw the big man—the big old defendant over there—get the pregnant woman in a headlock. Saw her shirt was still smoking from the fire. That right? Have I got that right?"

"Yes."

"A couple of yards away from you, a pregnant woman, great with child, is viciously attacked. Mr. Harris—Chuck—what did you do to defend her?"

"We couldn't get a signal to call," he began, but Claire cut him off.

"I'm not talking telephones. I'm asking you, Mr. Chief Assistant, Mr. Hot Dog McCown County Law and Order: what did you do to help that woman?"

His face was scarlet. Beads of perspiration studded his upper lip. "We wanted to contact the police, but we couldn't because we couldn't dial 911."

"Oh, shut up."

Elsie's breath caught when she heard Claire speak the words. Parsons jumped up. "Objection, your honor. Counsel is badgering the witness."

Before the judge could rule on the objection, Claire lifted a hand to concede. "No problem, Judge. I'll rephrase." She studied Chuck for a long moment, pursing her lips, as though pondering what to say. Then, nodding sagely, she walked up to the stand. "So isn't it true that you saw the woman being savagely attacked, and yet at the moment it occurred, you did nothing—absolutely nothing—to assist her or defend her."

Chuck was silent.

"Answer the question, Mr. Prosecutor," she said, her voice dripping contempt.

At length, he answered. "That's correct."

She pulled her eyes away as if she couldn't bear to look at him. "No further questions, your honor."

Sam Parsons stood and attempted damage control. During questioning, he elicited testimony from Chuck that he and Lisa had driven to the nearest town, called in the information and reported it to the police. But Elsie watched the jury, searching for signs of recovery. She could read their faces.

They didn't like Chuck Harris. They judged him for his cowardice.

And Chuck was, though absentee, a member of the prosecution team, one of those who wore the white hat.

But once Claire was done with him, Chuck's hat looked dirty as a dog.

Chapter Forty-One

WHEN THE JUDGE declared a recess, Madeleine's thin fingers snaked around Elsie's forearm.

"Did you make hard copies of the jury instructions?"

Elsie nodded. "They're on my desk."

"Get them. We'll meet in my office. Immediately."

Elsie grimaced. "I really have to go to the bathroom, Madeleine," she said, but Madeleine's back was already turned, her head bent to Sam Parsons's ear.

Elsie's first stop was the second floor restroom, but the jury had beat her to it; a bailiff was standing guard. She dashed down the steps to the first floor, relieved to find herself alone in the facility. She sat in the stall with her eyes closed, relishing the quiet.

The outer door opened; she heard whispered laughter. Four feet appeared in the next stall, followed by the scent of cigarette smoke. Elsie sighed. Her break was over. If she walked into Madeleine's office with the odor of secondhand smoke on her clothes, there'd be trouble.

She trudged up the stairs to her office, passing Stacie at the reception desk. "How's it going?" Stacie asked.

Elsie responded by rolling her eyes back, pointing an index finger at her temple, and pulling the trigger.

Engrossed in performing the pantomime, Elsie failed to notice that the door to her nearby office stood open, and the room was occupied. Holly Hickman sat in Elsie's chair, rocking her baby. Ivy doodled on a sheet of paper with an ink pen. Tina Peroni was nowhere to be seen.

Elsie dropped the makeshift gun from her head and stuffed the offending hand in her pocket. "Hey," she said in a voice of false cheer. "I figured you all would go on home. Ivy's been dismissed; you don't need to stay."

Elsie anticipated that her announcement would cause a look of relief to cross Ivy's face, but she was wrong. The relief washed instead across the features of Holly, her foster mother. Ivy remained expressionless, working with increasing intensity on her sheet of white paper.

"Oh, thank goodness gracious." Holly stood, hoisting the infant to her shoulder. The movement awakened the baby; he began to fuss. "Tina called us over here to keep an eye on Ivy, but I don't think that Ivy's brother wanted to stick around here much longer."

Ivy's brother, Elsie repeated in her head, her heart softening toward Holly Hickman. "Well, Ivy, what do you think? You ready to head out? You want to go on home?"

Ivy remained in her seat, drawing circles, bearing down so hard with her pen that she tore through the paper.

Elsie stared at the black hole on the paper. "Ivy?" She lifted her eyes to the child's face. "You ready to go?"

The girl's jaw was locked at an angry angle. She didn't lift her eyes to look at Elsie. Ivy raised the pen and began punching small holes into the paper with the ball point.

"Whoa, little sis. You're banging up my desk." Elsie reached over and retrieved the pen from Ivy's grip. "The county of McCown will be jumping on both our backs if we damage government property."

The small hand that had been robbed of its weapon splayed on the sheet of paper. Without looking up, Ivy said, "You ain't no good."

The statement brought Elsie up short; the pen almost dropped from her grasp. Holly gasped and said, "Ivy! Mind your manners!"

An empty office chair sat next to the seat Ivy occupied. Elsie sat down, studying the girl with concern.

"Ivy, are you mad at me?"

Ivy didn't respond. She picked up the sheet of paper and wadded it up into a ball.

"Ivy, what's up, hon? I don't understand. Talk to me."

Ivy threw the paper ball at Elsie. It bounced off her chest.

Holly said, "That does it. You are in big trouble, girl."

Elsie turned to the woman. "Give us a minute, okay? Mrs. Hickman, do you mind waiting in the reception area? It's right outside my door." When Holly didn't move, Elsie rose and stepped up to usher her out. "Right over there. You can't miss it."

She saw a reluctant Holly through the door and closed it behind her, then turned to focus on her young witness. Ivy had regained possession of the ink pen, and was drawing circles on the palm of her hand.

"Ivy," Elsie began, in a cajoling voice.

Ivy held up her hand, displaying the inky circle. "Cootie shot. Can't get me, I got a cootie shot."

"Won't you please tell me? What went wrong? Did the court-room scare you? Because I get it; I can totally understand that. Even grownups think it's scary to talk in court. I don't want you to feel bad. It's a scary place."

Ivy muttered under her breath; Elsie barely caught it. It sounded like the girl said: "You done bad."

Perplexed, Elsie sat back. The girl's head was ducked. She had new stains on her yellow dress, the product of Elsie's ink pen. "Ivy. What did I do?"

Slowly, the child raised her head. She glared at Elsie through the new eyeglasses. Her expression reminded Elsie of something she'd seen on television; and it was not an image from children's programming. It was the steely glare of Tony Soprano.

"You done set me up."

The statement was so unexpected, so preposterous, Elsie let a laugh escape.

"Don't you laugh at me."

Elsie composed her face into solemn lines. "I'm sorry, Ivy. I'm not laughing at you; you just surprised me, that's all. I don't un-derstand. Why would you say I set you up?"

The child bent over her hand, pressing the pen to darken the ink spot on her palm.

"Ivy? How did I set you up?"

The pen stopped circling. Her head bent, Ivy whispered, "You had his bitch in there."

"What?"

The blond head raised. Her eyes squinted as if assessing the threat of danger. "His bitch. Sitting right there." The child's voice dropped. "You trying to get me killed?"

"Oh my God," Elsie said, her thoughts darting to the gallery of faces in court. Had Larry Paul planted a conspirator among the spectators, someone who could intimidate the child? Did he have a friend on the jury? The idea seemed unlikely. But nothing was impossible.

She reached out and pressed Ivy's hand, searching her face for the answer. "Who frightened you? Who did you see?"

"I seen his bitch." The voice was a whisper.

"Whose bitch? Larry Paul? Did he have a girlfriend, aside from your mom?"

The child rolled her eyes. "Not him. The Big Boy."

Elsie repeated the name, like a magpie. "The Big Boy. Big Boy who?"

Again, the whisper. "Smokey."

The light was beginning to dawn in Elsie's head. "Ivy, who is Smokey Dean's bitch?'

The eyes behind the classes surveyed Elsie with a look of disbelief. Ivy pulled her hand away from Elsie's grasp. "You don't know nothing."

As Elsie's mind raced, she looked down at her own hand. She'd held Ivy's hand with such pressure, the ink had transferred. The palm of Elsie's hand bore a black circle. A cootie shot.

Chapter Forty-Two

IVY JUMPED WHEN the door to Elsie's office flew open with a bang. A skinny woman in fancy clothes stood in the hallway, her eyes flashing fire. "Where are the jury instructions?"

Ivy watched Elsie grapple with a file on her desk, nearly spilling the papers.

"I have them right here. I proofed them last night. They're ready."

"Then what are you waiting for?"

The woman's gaze fixed on Ivy, then transferred to her foster mother, who stood in the open doorway. The fancy woman balanced her reading glasses on the bridge of her nose, and glared over the top of the frames.

"What's your name again?"

Holly placed a protective hand against her chest, holding the baby with the other arm. "Me? My name? I'm Holly."

"Right. Holly, you can go. Take the children away. You're excused." Turning back to Elsie, she said. "My office. Immediately."

Ivy stood in the hallway, watching Elsie race down behind the older blond-headed woman. She reached up to her foster mother, trying to catch her hand. But Holly shook her off.

"I've got to hold brother. And the diaper bag." Holly shifted the bag higher onto her shoulder. "Come on, honey. Let's go."

Ivy followed her foster mother down the steps of the court-house staircase, clutching a golden hand rail. Holly looked over her shoulder, regarding Ivy with a face that looked cross. "Hurry up. Daddy will be wanting his supper. And I've got to get brother down for a nap."

The big courthouse doors facing the front steps were blocked by a crowd of people with signs. Holly made an impatient noise; turning on her heel, she headed for the side exit, her diaper bag slipping from her shoulder. "Come on. Follow me."

When they exited, the late afternoon sun shone into Ivy's eyes, blinding her. She paused at the top of the stone steps that led to the sidewalk.

"I can't see," she said.

Her foster mother wheeled around on the step. "Ivy! We gotta get home."

Ivy's hand grasped a metal railing that ran along the hand-icapped ramp. She eased down the steps, taking them one at a time, until she reached the pavement.

Holly pushed a button on the traffic light. "We have to wait. You don't walk until the little man on the light says you can." After a pause, she added, "Always look both ways when crossing the street."

There wasn't much traffic on the street that bounded the west side of the courthouse. But Ivy felt a prickle of unease.

"Let's walk now," Ivy said.

"No, the light doesn't say we can go. You have to wait. It's the law."

The rumble of an idling white Buick could be heard a short distance away. Ivy's eyes had adjusted to the afternoon glare. She took a hard look at the car, and then sidled up to her foster mother.

"Hold my hand." Ivy's voice had a pleading note.

"What?" Holly peered down, her brows drawn together in a frown.

"I want to hold your hand."

Holly groaned. "Honey, I have the baby, I've got the bag; I don't have another hand for you to hold."

As Ivy inched nearer, she clutched Holly's denim skirt. Holly said, "Ivy, you're a big girl, you're in school. Let go of me. You're going to knock us all down."

Only a moment passed before a body flew at Holly, flinging her and her baby to the pavement. The attack sent the diaper bag flying, its contents spilling onto the sidewalk. Holly's screams chorused with the cries of her infant son. Vaseline and baby wipes and Pampers diapers littered the street.

The screams made Ivy's ears ring. It seemed that time had stopped, and that she was watching from a far distance as her foster mother's face contorted, and scrapes on the baby's head seeped blood.

Then she was flying too, toward the white Buick that was waiting, as it had been waiting for her all along, for weeks and weeks.

When Bruce Stout threw Ivy into the backseat and the car roared off, she wasn't even surprised. But she was scared. Very, very scared.

Chapter Forty-Three

A BRISK WIND blew through the open windows of Judge Calla-way's courtroom. Elsie was grateful for the breeze; it cooled the packed courtroom more effectively than the worn central air system in the courthouse would have. In the crisp days of October, the judge's fresh air prejudice made sense.

Because the courtroom faced west, the heavy traffic and chants of the death penalty protesters couldn't be heard. Elsie focused on Madeleine as she addressed the jury with her closing argument. Madeleine's posture was rigid, her voice quaking as she summarized the State's case for execution.

"The State of Missouri has given you great power, ladies and gentlemen of the jury. The power to see justice done."

Madeleine coughed into her closed fist, then went on. "A terrible crime occurred in this county. An act so vicious, so horrific, that it qualifies for the death penalty. Our criminal code in Missouri provides that if a murder is committed with depravity of mind, then the defendant can be put to death."

She paused, studying her typewritten outline. With an apologetic air, she said, "I know you heard some bad things about the victim, Jessie Dent. Things about the life she led. About using substances during pregnancy. About contracting AIDS. The things you learned about in court may have hardened your hearts to her."

"But ladies and gentlemen, no one deserves to die the way she did. No one in McCown County. No one on earth."

Play your card, Elsie thought; and as if Madeleine could read her mind, she did. "And what about the baby? What about the death he suffered? What about the way the defendant took his life before he ever drew breath?"

Then the screaming began. Screeching and piercing shrieks came through the open courtroom windows. The shrill cries were so deafening that it seemed they came from inside the room.

Madeleine dropped her notes. Sinking to her knees, she picked up the outline and pivoted as she stood upright, turning to the judge with a desperate expression.

The screaming went on; it seemed interminable. Then a babble of voices chimed in from outside the window, combining with high-pitched shrieks that could only come from a baby.

Judge Callaway turned to his bailiff. "Shut the windows," he said.

Emil sped to close the windows, tugging at the wooden frames to secure them. It muffled the noise but didn't silence it.

"Better shut the storms first," Judge Callaway said.

With an effort, Emil pushed the window sash back up, fumbled with the latches on the storm windows as the shrieks echoed in the courtroom. When he pulled down the window sash a second time, he turned to the judge for affirmation.

It was quieter. The judge nodded, and Emil sat back down.

Visibly shaken, Madeleine quickly wrapped up her argument,

asking for justice for the baby, the blameless infant, without further mention of the child's mother. When she sat down, Elsie could see her knees tremble.

Claire O'Hara stood and advanced on the jury. She had a single note card in her hand.

"Ladies and gentlemen, the prosecutor talks about justice. She's playing a game with you: a word game. What she seeks is vengeance."

She raised her hands, exhibiting her palms to the jurors, her fingers spread. The late afternoon sun caught on her ring and made it sparkle in the light.

"We've been straight with you, haven't we? A crime was committed. A woman died, a woman who was carrying a child. Who bears responsibility for that? My client. In part, my client does."

"But when we're talking execution, lethal injection, death penalty—let's look at the bigger picture. Who else played a part in Jessie Dent's untimely end, in her violent demise? I maintain that the Barton Police Department should claim part of the credit. Because they could have prevented it, don't you see? Not once; not twice; eight times, ladies and gentlemen, the local police turned their heads."

The wail of a distant siren could be heard from outside. Claire continued.

"And irony of ironies," Claire said, and paused to shake her head with a hollow laugh. "Who else failed the deceased, Jessie Dent? Who could have come to her defense, stepped in and saved her from her fate? Why, none other than the McCown County Prosecutor's right-hand man, Mr. Chuck Harris. And what did he do? What did Chief Assistant Prosecutor Chuck Harris do when he was directly confronted with my client's abuse of pregnant Jessie Dent? He ran. Ran like he had a yellow stripe down his back."

"Objection!" Parsons said, rising from his chair.

The sirens were louder; it was difficult to hear Judge Callaway speak as he said, "Overruled. This is argument."

To overcome the wailing noise coming into the courtroom from the street below, Claire O'Hara turned up the volume of her voice.

"It was your duty to return a verdict in this case, and you did; you have spoken; you found the defendant guilty. But you don't have to execute him. Because you know, ladies and gentlemen— you know that Larry Paul is not the only one at fault here."

Her voice carried over the sirens as she said, "But if you believe that he should die for what he has done—if you want him to suffer— you want vengeance, folks? Then, hear this: let him die of AIDS. If you truly believe that vengeance is what he deserves, let him die the horrible death that currently awaits him. The two shots in the arm that the State of Missouri will administer will be a cakewalk, compared to the death he's facing. If you really want vengeance on Larry Paul, then killing is too good for him. Give him life without parole—and let God take care of the death penalty."

Claire picked up her note card. She hadn't looked at it, Elsie marveled, not once during argument. And she walked to the counsel table with a resolute step.

The sirens still wailed. Madeleine took to the podium. As she launched into her final five minutes of rebuttal argument, Elsie could see the jurors nearest the window craning their necks to view the activity was causing all the commotion. More police cars must have clustered on the street below; the sirens wailed in chorus.

Madeleine struggled to raise her voice above the babble, but it was impossible. At the prosecution counsel table, Elsie could only make out snatches of Madeleine's rebuttal. Looking at the jury, Elsie supposed it didn't really matter that the argument was drowned out.

No one was listening, anyway.

Chapter Forty-Four

ASHLOCK WAS MARKING time in the courthouse rotunda when the uproar began. Footfalls rang on the marble floor as a man ran in from the street and tried to bypass security. "Help!" he cried, as a deputy seized him. "A woman has been attacked! You have to get an ambulance. She's on the sidewalk. The baby is bleeding."

Though Ashlock was two floors up, he could clearly see the scene at the security entrance through the open rotunda. He bounded down the stairs. Without stopping to consult the man who still struggled with security, Ashlock bolted outside, where the death penalty protesters had dropped their placards and knelt beside a woman who lay on the pavement, shrieking.

It was Holly Hickman, clutching her wailing infant. As Ashlock ran toward them on the sidewalk, he scoured the crowd for Ivy, but couldn't find her in the crowd of people clustered around the mother and baby.

He shouldered through the people who were ogling the scene. Squatting on his haunches, he said, "Mrs. Hickman, you know me; I'm Detective Ashlock. What happened?"

She turned frantic eyes to him, but didn't answer. Her screaming continued, in chorus with the cries of her son.

Ashlock looked up at the middle-aged hippies who loomed over him. "Who saw what happened?"

A man with a ball cap that depicted a "No" symbol over a hypodermic needle shook his head. "We were over in front of the courthouse, by the courthouse steps. We were marching. Well, kind of marching. And we heard the screams. So we came to help."

"But you didn't see the assault?"

"Not me."

His eyes scanned the crowd, but the faces exhibited concern, rather than insight. However, one woman loitering on the outskirts seemed skittish. She wasn't a protester; she was a local, a woman employed at the bail bondsman's office nearby.

He focused on her. "Starla? Starla McDonald. What did you see?"

She shook her head and pointed at her ear. "Sorry. Can't hear you, Detective." The cries coming from Holly and the baby were deafening.

He rose and stepped over to her, pulling her aside. "Starla, you work for the bail bonds office, right?"

She nodded.

"Right across the street there?" He pointed. The window in the storefront bore AAA BAIL BONDS in bold black letters. "Did you see something through the window?"

"No. I was taking a break. Over by the Dumpster." Her eyes shifted. "The boss wouldn't like it if he knew. I'm not supposed to step away from the phone."

"What did you see?"

"Old white car, kind of idling on the street. And a guy knocked that lady down. Don't know who. It happened real fast."

She pinched her lips together, then looked Ashlock in the eye. "Seemed like there was a kid. I saw a yellow dress. He pulled her in the car. I think. But I don't know the kid; maybe she belongs with the white car."

Ashlock pulled his phone from his pocket. Turning away from the noise, he punched in the numbers.

When he got an answer, he said. "Issue an Amber Alert. We've got a kidnapped child. Ivy Dent, six years old." He paused, nodding in response to the voice on the other line. "Yeah. Her foster mother and brother are here on the west side of the courthouse. We need an ambulance. And we need to find the Dent girl. Get every patrolman in the city force and anyone Sheriff Choate can spare from the county."

Another moment's silence, before he answered in a hushed tone. "Because I think whoever has her means to kill her."

He ended the call and turned back to Starla. "Describe the vehicle."

"Officer, I hate to get in the middle of this. My boss is going to be furious at me for leaving the office empty."

His jaw twitched. "There's a child missing, and if we want to find her alive, we're going to need you to give any facts you can recall. Tell me about the car."

"Old white Buick, you know. Pretty much a rust bucket." She hesitated.

"Did you see the license plate?"

"Not sure it had plates. Oh, Lord." She was breathing hard. Sirens could be heard down the street, drowning out Holly Hickman. "I hate to get involved in this. 'Cause I can't swear to it; I'm not, like, one hundred percent positive."

"What? Tell me."

She exhaled deeply. "Officer, seems like it could've been Nell Stout's car. We've bonded her boy out before; I've seen them at the office. But I couldn't swear to it on a Bible or nothing."

The first car that pulled up was Deputy Franks, in a black and white McCown County squad car. Before Franks pulled to the curb and brought the car to a complete stop, Ashlock pulled the passenger door open and jumped inside.

Chapter Forty-Five

IVY'S FOOT WAS trapped under Bruce Stout's butt, twisted at a painful angle. She kicked at him with her free leg. "Get off of me."

Nell spared a glance over her shoulder as she barreled down the city street. "Pin that child down and shut her up."

Bruce tried to grab the skinny leg that thrashed about his face and neck. "Damn. Settle down, or I'll punch your lights out."

She reared her leg back, bending it at the knee, and kicked him hard in the belly. Bruce made a soft *oof* sound, leaning forward to grab his gut, and easing off her twisted foot. She jerked her foot away from his weight and cradled it, rubbing the sore ankle.

"Damn it to hell, Bruce—quit fighting that little shit and look behind you. Is anyone tailing us?"

Bruce jerked around in the seat and looked through the dirty back windshield. "Don't think so. Can't rightly tell."

"Well? Yes or no?"

"No. Don't think so."

Ivy wedged herself tightly into the corner of the backseat, as far away from Bruce as she could get. She cut her eyes to the door, thinking she would slip her hand over and pop up the door lock; but it was missing, broken clean off.

Her heart rattled in her chest like a wild creature was trapped inside her rib cage. Bruce's neck was still craned to see out the back. She focused on Nell Stout, steering the car in the front seat; and saw that Nell's gray eyes were watching her in the rearview mirror.

Ivy knew that she shouldn't act afraid. If you let a mean dog know you were scared, it would lunge at you.

"I'm not supposed to be with you. You better let me out of here. My foster mother's gonna tell the police about you."

Nell let out a dry laugh, like the yip of an old cur. "I bet you tell the police all kind of things. You do way too much talking to the police. That's your problem."

Ivy's voice came out in a whine; she couldn't help it. "I didn't say nothing. I seen her in court and I kept my mouth shut. I said, I don't know nothing."

"Maybe today." Nell had turned onto side roads; the pavement was bumpy. It jolted Ivy in the backseat. "But you've been shooting off your mouth ever since your mama died. You ought to know better."

"Shoulda known better," Bruce echoed.

Nell settled back in her seat, stretching her arms against the steering wheel and locking her elbows. "Girl, you have become a liability."

Bruce leaned his face close to Ivy's. "A liability."

His breath was rank, smelling of stale beer and tobacco and rot. It had been a while since Ivy had a whiff of such a stink. Her foster parents were long on tooth-brushing.

She lifted her head and peered out the window. They had passed the outskirts of town, and were turning onto a farm road. Nell was driving with one hand, fumbling with a pack of cigarettes. When she got one into her mouth, she lit it with a black Bic lighter.

Some dogs couldn't be bluffed, but Ivy gave it one last try.

"Let me out here at the side of the road. Just drop me. I won't say nothing to nobody."

Nell didn't answer. She took a long drag on the cigarette and blew out the smoke.

Ivy dropped her head to her chest. She had no hope that her foster mother was in pursuit of Nell. She'd never had any confidence in Holly's ability to protect her; Ivy had learned from the cradle that no one could be counted on to keep trouble or danger away.

Bruce was grinning at her like a half-wit. He nudged Ivy's bare shoulder with a hamlike fist. "Better say your prayers."

If Ivy could have spared the energy to scoff at Bruce Stout's religious advice, she'd have done it. For all the sucking up she'd done to that preacher at Riverside Baptist, telling him what he wanted to hear and doing his bidding, he couldn't help her now. And she wasn't about to waste her time praying. God wouldn't help her, not against an adversary like Old Nell Stout. Not against Smokey. They were in cahoots with the devil himself.

Her eyes narrowed. Nothing had changed, not really, with her mother's death. Every day was a battle; destruction was always a possibility. The only person she could count on was herself.

When you couldn't fight off the enemy, you should play possum. It worked in the woods sometimes; she'd seen it with her own eyes. Ivy closed her eyes. Bonelessly, she slid down in the seat.

Chapter Forty-Six

AFTER CLOSING ARGUMENTS and the jury instructions, Elsie knew the jury would take another bathroom break. She took the marble stairway to the ground floor, pausing to look through the side exit to examine the activity outside.

An ambulance sat at the curb, red and blue lights flashing. It looked like EMTs were wheeling someone on a stretcher; but her view was blocked by the crowd of onlookers. She couldn't see who was injured. Elsie pressed her face to the glass. She didn't see signs of an automobile collision. Maybe someone had had a heart attack. But recalling the screams she'd heard through the courtroom window, she worried that there had been a violent ruckus of some kind.

Though she was tempted to step outside and investigate further, she had been waiting for a bathroom break with increasing urgency while listening to Judge Callaway read the jury instructions in a slow and ponderous voice. Elsie had sustained herself all day with Diet Coke, chugging a can at every recess. She turned her back on the exit and headed for the women's restroom, opening the door just as a toilet in the facility gave a violent flush. A filmy smoke cloud drifted up from inside the stall, and Elsie wondered whether the probate clerks had returned. She squatted to look under the stalls, to see whether there was one pair of feet inside or two.

The cherry red high heels positioned on either side of the porcelain bowl could only belong to Claire O'Hara. No woman in McCown County sported such high-end footwear.

She heard a whisper. Claire said, "Everything is cool. Quit worrying."

Elsie frowned. Sounded like Claire was declaring victory before a verdict was returned.

The voice sounded again, with a hushed hiss. "Goddamn it, honey, I handled it. She didn't spill. Don't do anything stupid." There was a brief pause, and Claire said, "Don't tell me you're turning her into sausage. Don't say that out loud."

Elsie had been holding her breath; but after hearing Claire whisper into her phone, something clicked in Elise's head. It gave her such a shock, it literally threw her off balance. She fell backwards and landed on her butt, with her legs sprawled on the cold tile of the bathroom floor.

The whispering stopped. Elsie heard Claire say in a sharp voice, "Is someone out there?"

Elsie didn't answer; she scrambled to the door as the lock rattled in the closed bathroom stall. Once outside the women's restroom, Elsie ran for the elevator; but the ancient brass arrow indicator showed that the elevator was headed to the third floor of the courthouse.

She scrambled up the stairs at a run, dodging news teams carrying camera equipment down to the parking lot. Once safely back inside her office, she grabbed the computer keyboard and got on CaseNet, the search engine which provided public record of all case files in Missouri.

She typed in Dean Mitchell, Junior, and waited for a hit. No criminal lawsuit appeared. Only civil matters, contract cases, mechanics liens.

Discouraged, she stared at the screen. Then she typed Larry Paul's name, and found an old drug charge, possession of a controlled substance with intent to distribute. Defendant's attorney: Claire O'Hara.

Had they known that? Did it mean anything? Her fingers pecked at the keys again, searching another name: Bruce Stout.

A handful of case names appeared: all entitled *State of Missouri v. Bruce Stout*; traffic offense, minor drug charges, one count of urinating in public. And each time, the defense attorney of record: Claire O'Hara.

She reached down and opened the door of her small office refrigerator. Taking out a cold silver can, she pressed it to her neck, where a pulse was beating hard and fast.

With one hand, she cleared the search and typed: Dean Mitchell, Senior. There it was: an old arson case, tried in Greene County; two counts of fraud, filed in Douglas County; a conspiracy case in Federal Court. All charges were ultimately dismissed, but for the arson, which had gone to jury trial. The jury found Old Smokey Not Guilty.

And his defense attorney, in each case: Claire O'Hara, Esquire. In the 1989 conspiracy case; the fraud in 2002; the arson trial in 1996.

The Mitchells were dirty, just as Ashlock suspected. And just as Elsie's mother always claimed.

"She's his bitch," Elsie whispered.

Her eyes were still glued to the computer screen when Emil Elmquist knocked on her door. "Question from the jury, Elsie. Judge wants you all in court."

She stared blindly at the old bailiff as a word took shape in her head: *sausage.*

"Oh, Jesus Christ," she gasped. "Jesus fucking Christ."

"You watch your mouth, young lady," Emil said, but she grabbed her purse and pulled out her car keys. As she pushed by the bailiff, he said, "You're heading the wrong way, Elsie. Judge wants you all in court."

She paused long enough to say, "I'm third fucking chair. They can handle it without me."

Emil followed her out into the second floor of the courthouse, shouting, "Where do you think you're going?"

She didn't bother to reply.

Chapter Forty-Seven

THE SIRENS OF the McCown County squad car blared as Deputy Franks tore down the road, almost drowning out the ringtone of Ashlock's cell phone. He checked the number and answered.

"No time to talk now, Elsie."

"Ash! Where are you? It's about Ivy!"

He braced himself against the door as Franks took a curve. "She's been abducted. We're on our way to Nell Stout's house."

"Ash, no—I heard Claire O'Hara on the phone. Ash, they're taking her to the packing plant."

His brow furrowed. "Smokey's?"

"Ash, I swear—I heard it. Something about making her into sausage. Shutting her up. What the hell else could it mean?"

He cut off the call, turned to Deputy Franks, and said, "Head for the highway. We need to get to Smokey's commissary."

Joe took a moment to look over, perturbed at the change. "But you said we was checking out Stout's house."

"Turn this fucking car around."

Franks shut his mouth and obeyed, making his way to the

highway and fairly flying to the farm roads, passing the pickup trucks that dodged to the side of the road at their approach.

"We ain't got no warrant," Franks said. When Ashlock didn't respond, Franks glanced over at him. Ashlock was gripping the dash on the passenger side, as if willing the car to go faster. Franks repeated, "We ain't got a search warrant."

Ashlock said, "We got exigent circumstances, Joe."

"What's that mean, exactly?"

"Just drive."

The old sedan climbed a hill at remarkable speed. As they crested the hill, the Smokey Dean's butcher shop and packing plant came into view. "There's Smokey's commissary," Ashlock said; but Franks was already pulling onto the curb, hitting the brake to turn in to a gravel drive.

"Park in front?"

The late afternoon sun shone into the windshield of the squad car. Ashlock pulled the visor down to block the glare. Squinting at the storefront, he said, "Sign says closed. Go around back."

The car squealed to a stop, sending a cloud of white gravel dust in its wake. Franks said, "No cars back here, Ashlock; no white Buick or nothing."

Ashlock jumped out of the car without offering a response to Franks. He reached the metal exit door; it was locked. He pounded on it with his fist. "Barton Police!" He continued to beat on the metal door; the sound echoed in the quiet countryside. A bevy of doves took flight in the distance. "McCown County Sheriff's Department! Police! Open up!"

He heard the crash bar click on the other side of the door. A man's head poked through, a pasty pockmarked face with greasy flaxen-white hair confined in a mesh hairnet.

"What the hell?" he said. "We're closed."

Franks ran up behind Ashlock, sending gravel into the spiky grass. Ashlock said, "We need to come inside." He did not enter, but he placed his booted foot in the narrow opening of the door.

"What for?"

"We need to come inside. It's police business." He flashed his badge and put his hand on his holster.

"Okay, okay. But the boss ain't here." The man opened the door and Ashlock and Franks stepped over the threshold. "I'm just the cleanup crew."

They walked inside, peering into the dim facility around the room, taking a quick inventory. "Who's here?"

"Nobody. Just me."

"Who are you?"

"Whitey. Whitey Phillips."

Ashlock checked his watch: it was four-thirty. "Not even five o'clock. What kind of business they running here, that doesn't stay open till five?"

Deputy Franks was nosing around the room, checking inside cabinets and under the counters. Franks rattled the knob of a door marked PRIVATE but it didn't open. Whitey Phillips watched Franks, his mouth jerking with a nervous twitch. "That there's the toilet, you got to have a key. Are you'uns the health department? County health inspector? Smokey didn't say we had an inspection coming up."

"We're not the health department." A buzzer sounded. "What's that?" Ashlock said. With a quick move, his hand moved to the Blackhawk holster on his belt and rested on the model 19 Glock it held.

Whitey began to walk backwards toward the swinging door that connected to the front of the building. "That's the front door."

"Thought you were closed."

Joe Franks was on his hands and knees, peering under the stainless steel table that adjoined the wall. "Yeah, that's right. Didn't you say you was shut down for the day?"

The connecting door flew open, and a tall, barrel-chested man wearing a white Stetson walked through, his cowboy boots ringing on the floor.

"What the fuck," he said. "It's the po-po."

Whitey ran to the man's side. "Smokey, they just barged in here like they owned the place." Whitey's voice had taken on the whine of a whipped dog.

Deputy Franks stood up, knocking the dirt from his knees, and extended his right hand. "Hey there, Smokey Junior. I'm Joe Franks. I was in the Elks club with your daddy."

Smokey looked at the hand without making any move to shake it. "Is that right? Well, let me tell you something: if my old man was alive, he'd be kicking your ass right about now. What the hell you doing on my private property? You got a warrant?"

Ashlock stared him down. "Your buddy here invited us in."

"I thought they was the health department. They ain't the health department."

Ashlock dropped his hold on the Glock and eased over to a stainless steel door. Hanging from the door handle was a padlock. Ashlock toyed with the padlock, flipping it with his hand. "What you got in here, Smokey?"

The big man took off his white cowboy hat and tossed it onto a metal table. He ran his hand over a thick head of hair. "That's the walk-in cooler. Nothing in there but dead meat. But I don't have to show it to you. Or answer your goddamn questions. Get out of here. You got no right."

Franks looked over at Ashlock, rubbing his nose reflectively. "What was them circumstances you was talking about, Ashlock?"

Ashlock didn't answer. He reached for the padlock and gave it a jerk. It remained secure.

"Funny you got your meat locked up. Doesn't seem efficient. Seems like you'd need to get at it, to do your meatpacking. This is a butcher shop."

"Keeps the employees from stealing. People will steal you blind." Smokey flashed a feral grin. "Learned that from my old man."

Ashlock turned his back on Smokey. Running his hands over the door of the metal cooler, as if checking it for size, he said, "What's your capacity in this thing? Does it hold the carcasses? You keep them hung up in there before you process them?"

"Got them hanging on hooks. But if you want something, you'll have to come in the front way, like a paying customer. And we're closed for business right now."

Ashlock shook his head. "That so?"

A lull in the conversation highlighted the mounting tension in the room. Franks looked from Smokey to Ashlock, holding his tongue. Finally, Whitey grabbed a push broom leaning against the wall by the restroom door marked PRIVATE.

"Guess I better get back to work," Whitey said, grasping the broom handle with both hands. No one replied.

In the silent room, a faint sound could be heard, like a woodpecker drilling on a metal pole.

It came from the walk-in cooler.

"Damn," Ashlock said, pulling his Glock from its holster. "One of those pigs in there isn't quite dead."

He shot the padlock; it exploded, flying from the handle in

metal fragments. Ashlock grasped the handle, and pulled open the door.

In the open doorway, they saw Ivy, shrouded in icy fog. She was surrounded by carcasses of cattle and pigs, which dangled from the ceiling of the cooler.

In her fist, she held a bloody hook, poised over her head to strike. Her face was savage, her teeth gritted like an Amazon warrior.

When she saw Ashlock, her arms fell, and she dropped the hook to the floor. "Thank you Jesus," she whispered through blue lips.

Ashlock stooped down and picked the girl up. Her bare arms were like ice as she clutched them around his neck. Her body began to shake; he holstered his gun to tighten his grip on Ivy so that he wouldn't drop her.

When he turned and stepped outside the cooler, he heard Smokey call out, "Come on out, Nell."

The door marked with the PRIVATE sign opened and Nell emerged from the employee toilet; a porcelain stool was visible behind her. Nell's eyes locked on the figure of Ashlock and Ivy with a squint. She had a Smith and Wesson .357 revolver in her right hand and a shotgun held loosely under her left armpit. She jammed the revolver into the back of dumbfounded Joe Franks as Smokey relieved her of the shotgun.

Smokey cocked the shotgun and trained it on Ashlock. Ashlock swiftly dropped Ivy to her feet and pushed her behind him, his free hand reaching for his holster.

"Don't move a hair, man. You pull that gun and you're all dead."

Whitey wailed, "I ain't burying no cop."

"Shut the fuck up."

"Smokey, this ain't what you done told me. I'm not digging no cop grave."

"Whitey, you're asking for an ass-kicking. Nell, where's Bruce?"

A look of disgust crossed her face. "Took the car to get a case of Natty Light. Said it was gonna be a long night." As she spoke, she reached into Joe Frank's holster and relieved him of his gun, tossing it across the floor in Whitey's direction.

The buzzer from the front door rang. "Ash!" a voice called.

Smokey pulled a face of disbelief. "Shit."

The swinging door flew open with a bang, and Elsie appeared in the space. Her eyes widened as she took in the scene. "Oh my fucking God," she whispered.

"Elsie fucking Arnold," Smokey said. "Shit," he repeated. He jerked his head in Ashlock's direction. "Go stand over there by your boyfriend."

But Elsie remained frozen. "Oh my God," she whispered again. A large stainless steel sink stood beside the door; she clutched it for support.

With exaggerated patience, Smokey said, "Get your ass over there by your boyfriend before I blow a hole in him. You want me to blow a hole in him?"

Elsie's right hand flew to her throat, reflexively rubbing the scar around her neck. "You used to hold my head under at the swimming pool. You were always a worthless piece of shit," she said.

"And you were a loudmouthed bitch. Still are. Did you hear what I told you? Go over by your buddy." He jerked his head at Elsie, still keeping the shotgun pointed at Ashlock's chest.

She edged along the sink, facing the circle of players in the room, taking tentative, careful sidesteps along the floor. Glancing into the sink, she saw a dozen implements soaking in a couple of inches of soapy water.

She didn't take time to consider. On impulse, Elsie reached

into the sink and seized a dirty metal meat hammer, then swung at Dean Mitchell and knocked him upside the head.

Smokey Dean reeled, screaming, clutching at his head. Nell started to move toward Smokey, then turned back, hastily raising her revolver over Joe Franks's shoulder, and firing at Ashlock. Nell's shot went wide. She didn't get a second chance. Ashlock returned fire, hitting Nell in the right shoulder. The force of the bullet flung her back into the wall, and she dropped to the floor.

Franks jumped on Smokey as he reeled from the blow to his head, and wrested the shotgun away. Whitey dropped his broom. "Don't shoot," he said, raising his hands in the air. "I'm just the cleanup!"

The adrenaline that had supplied Elsie's strength deserted her; she dropped to her knees. Ivy edged along the wall and made her way over toward the sink. When she reached Elsie, she patted her on the shoulder with a small, cold hand.

"You done good," Ivy said.

Chapter Forty-Eight

THE COURTHOUSE WAS dark when Elsie walked into her office that night. She dropped her suit jacket onto the floor and kicked off her shoes. Collapsing into her chair, she leaned back, propped her feet on the air-conditioning unit and closed her eyes.

Her head felt like it might split in two, and her heart rate was ragged, but she repeated a mantra in her head: *she's safe. Safe. We're all safe.*

She heard footsteps pause in the hallway, and opened one eye to see who it was. Breeon stood in the doorway, watching her with a rueful expression.

"Hey, girl," Bree said.

"Hey, you. Come on in here." With a weary grunt, Elsie dropped her bare feet to the floor.

Breeon walked in and sat in the chair facing the desk. "Heard you had quite an afternoon."

Elsie gave her a wry grin. "I lead an exciting life."

"You do, little sis. You do indeed."

Both women sat in silence for a long moment; but the silence was a comfortable one, without the strain of the past weeks. Elsie broke it.

"I've gotta unzip my skirt." Reaching behind her, she removed the safety pin that substituted for a button and pulled the zipper down. "Aaah," she said, breathing out with gratitude.

"I know you've been tied up, running to that child's rescue and bringing down the bad guys. But did you hear about the verdict? Larry Paul?"

"I did. Chuck sent a text. When I was at the PD giving my statement."

She waited for Bree to broach the topic, to face the bone of contention that had pushed them apart. But Bree switched topics; she said, "Is the little girl going to be okay? Ivy?"

A wave of weariness washed over Elsie, mixed with a sweet sensation of relief. Elsie crossed her arms on her desk, resting her head on them. "She's with Tina Peroni. They took her to the hospital, just to check her out. Tina called and said she's okay; and the Hickmans are fine, just mostly flipped out by the assault. But they want to keep her, keep her in their family. And Ivy wants to stay with them."

"Chuck and I just got the charges filed on Nell and Dean Mitchell. Not that they'd be going anywhere, cuffed to a hospital bed. And they picked up Nell's son. He was hightailing it out of the county, drinking beer while he drove and chucking the cans out the window."

"Not the sharpest tool in the shed. Is he talking?"

Bree shook her head. "Nobody's talking. Not Mitchell or Nell or Bruce. The Feds searched Claire's office. Guess who had about two hundred grand in cash, tucked away in her coat closet?"

It was no wonder she could afford those shoes, Elsie thought. And the shiny bangles. "RICO?"

The Racketeer Influenced and Corrupt Organizations Act made it a federal crime to use income made from organized crime as part of a legitimate business. If Claire was running drug money through her law practice, she was in trouble.

"Oh, girl; that money's gotta be dirty. What honest citizen has that kind of cash?"

Elsie nodded, thinking she was glad that Claire O'Hara would be the US Attorney's problem. Money laundering was a federal crime. But the charges arising from today's crisis—kidnapping, witness tampering, attempted murder—were crimes under Missouri's criminal code. The McCown County Prosecutor's Office would be a busy place in the coming months.

"Did Ivy talk about it yet? Does she understand what happened?"

"More than you can believe. She knew they were watching her. Because she had a general idea of what her mother and Larry were involved in: that they worked for Smokey in the drug trade, as well as the food business. And Nell was the cook. Barbeque and meth."

"Poor baby. Poor baby girl."

Elsie nodded. "If that kid gets half a chance, I think she's gonna overcome all this shit. That girl is incredible. She has, what's the word? An indomitable spirit. Like the unsinkable Molly Brown. You know?" She picked up the safety pin on her desk. "If I'm going to wear this suit again, I have got to get a bigger pin."

"Maybe you need a new suit."

Elsie pulled a face. "Not in the budget, Bree."

Bree donned her maternal face. "If you didn't blow all your spare cash at the Baldknobbers, you could save a buck."

Elsie nodded in agreement, frowning. "I think I'll give up drinking."

Bree's brow lifted in surprise. "Really."

Elsie scoffed. "No, not really." She paused, then said, "Maybe I'll give up gin."

Bree shifted in her chair. "Well, shit." She hesitated, then rose and walked over to Elsie's refrigerator. "Wish I'd known. I got you a present. Kind of a 'let's make up' thing."

When Bree opened the refrigerator door, Elsie saw four miniature green bottles of Tanqueray and two small bottles of Schweppes tonic water.

She cocked her head, taking in the sight. "I changed my mind," Elsie said. "You got cups?"

Breeon couldn't hide a knowing grin as she pulled two Styrofoam cups from her purse.

"You stole those from the coffee shop."

"I didn't steal. He gave them to me."

"Well, all right, then. That's not diet tonic water, is it? I hate diet tonic water."

"I know what you like, hon."

Bree made the cocktails with brisk efficiency, and the women tipped them together to toast.

"Aaaahh," Elsie said with an appreciative moan. She picked up the bottle and spoke to the label pasted onto the green glass. "I'll never leave you again."

Breeon took a meditative sip. "I've been doing some thinking. You know, girl, we don't have to agree on everything." She gazed at Elsie with regret. "I shouldn't have turfed you over the death penalty. Our friendship is important. To me, anyway."

Elsie chugged her Styrofoam cup and unscrewed the green bottle to pour another. In a low voice, she said, "Here's a dirty little secret. When I read that text and heard the jury gave Larry Paul life imprisonment, it was like a boulder rolled off my back."

Breeon nodded.

Elsie gave a humorless laugh. "Maybe I can sleep through the night now. You know, Bree, it's one thing to think philosophically, or hypothetically, that a man should die for his sins. But being a person who personally bears responsibility for his execution . . ." Her voice trailed off.

"I get it. Believe me." Breeon poured another dose of gin into her cup. Lowering her voice with mock seriousness, she said, "I suppose you know we're violating state law by drinking spirits in the courthouse?"

"Aw, chill your tits."

Breeon squawked in reply; and they laughed together.

Elsie rose from her chair. "I probably ought to lock us in here. You never know who'll be nosing around."

As if conjured by the suggestion, Madeleine appeared in the open doorway. Elsie froze, cup in hand. Madeleine looked at the desk, now littered with bottles bearing labels of Tanqueray and Schweppes.

She and Elsie locked eyes. Madeleine's appearance was still bandbox fresh: her bobbed hair smooth, makeup pristine, clothes unrumpled.

Elsie waited for the hammer to fall. And not just for drinking in the courthouse. Elsie had run out on the trial, in which she represented the State; she missed the verdict. Waiting for the volcano to erupt, she held her breath.

After a protracted pause, Madeleine let out a long sigh. "I'll see you ladies tomorrow. Have a nice evening." And she pulled the door shut with a click.

Elsie listened to Madeleine's footsteps as they retreated down the hallway. Turning to Bree, she widened her eyes in amazement.

Breeon smiled. "The times are a-changing." Lifting her cup, she said, "Here's to you, kid."

Elsie tapped her white cup against Bree's, splashing the liquid onto Bree's pants. "Here's to us, girlfriend."

Acknowledgments

BRINGING *THE WAGES of Sin* to the page was a joy, and I had fantastic help along the way. Many thanks to the team at Harper-Collins/Witness Impulse: Dan Mallory, Nicole Fischer, Shawn Nicholls, Maria Silva, and Nancy Fischer. And words can't express my high regard for Trish Daly, who helped bring Elsie to readers and edited my first three books.

I'm beyond fortunate to be represented by Jill Marr of the Sandra Dijkstra Literary Agency. Thanks, too, to Andrea Cavallaro of SDLA and Kevin Cleary of Pooka Entertainment for their help this year.

Closer to home, I am most grateful to John Appelquist and Susan Appelquist, for legal expertise; to Dr. Manuel Salinas, for providing answers to medical questions; To Brandi Bartel of The Victim Center, for sharing her wealth of knowledge; to Detective David Asher, for his excellent assistance; and to Daphne Meine, for serving as my editorial assistant and making sense of my hand-scrawled manuscript.

As always, love that Missouri State U; thanks to Dean Bryant and to my friend Kim Callahan for their support. To my LAW students and my advisees in Alpha Kappa Psi, who make it a pleasure to come into Glass Hall: I heart you all. To Lance Rycraft, for his help in the launch of Book 2: many thanks!

The best for last: to my wonderful husband Randy and my marvelous children, Ben and Martha: I thank you; I love you; you're the light of my life.

About the Author

NANCY ALLEN practiced law for 15 years, serving as Assistant Missouri Attorney General and as Assistant Prosecutor in her native Ozarks (the second woman in southwest Missouri to serve in that capacity). During her years in prosecution, she tried over 30 jury trials, including murder and sexual offenses, and is now a law professor at Missouri State University. *The Wages of Sin* is her third novel.

@TheNancyAllen
www.nancyallenauthor.com
www.witnessimpulse.com

Discover great authors, exclusive offers, and more at hc.com.